CLASSIC MISTAKE

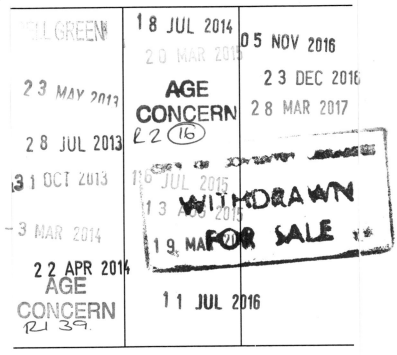

CLASSIC MISTAKE

A Case for Jack Colby, the Car Detective

Amy Myers

This first world edition published 2013
in Great Britain and in the USA by
SEVERN HOUSE PUBLISHERS LTD of
19 Cedar Road, Sutton, Surrey, England, SM2 5DA.

British Library Cataloguing in Publication Data

Myers, Amy, 1938-
  Classic mistake. – (A Jack Colby mystery ; 4)
  1. Colby, Jack (Fictitious character)–Fiction.
  2. Murder–Investigation–Fiction. 3. Automobile theft
  investigation–Fiction. 4. Detective and mystery stories.
  I. Title II. Series
  823.9'14-dc23

ISBN-13: 978-0-7278-8265-3 (cased)

All Severn House titles are printed on acid-free paper.

Severn House Publishers support the Forest Stewardship Council [FSC], the
leading international forest certification organisation. All our titles that are printed
on Greenpeace-approved FSC-certified paper carry the FSC logo.

MIX
Paper from
responsible sources
FSC
www.fsc.org   FSC® C018575

Typeset by Palimpsest Book
Falkirk, Stirlingshire, Scotlan
Printed and bound in Great B
MPG Books Ltd., Bodmin, C

*To Tom and Marie O'Day
with gratitude*

AUTHOR'S NOTE

Frogs Hill farm, where Jack Colby lives and works, is set near Pluckley in Kent, and most of the villages and towns referred to in this novel are real locations. Some, however, are not, including Woodlea Hill in Eastry, for which I have expanded the distance between Eastry and Northbourne and have added my own fictitious contribution to their history. Some other locations, including Piper's Green, which is Jack Colby's nearest village (and pub), Burchett Forstal, Tickenden and Boyfield are also fictitious.

ONE

Some days begin with a nightmare and just get worse. This time a phone call was all it took. It came at a quarter to nine in the morning, a time when Frogs Hill Classic Car Restorations is normally peacefully engaged in its exciting tasks for the day – such as overhauling a Jensen's dynamo. Not for me, not this Tuesday.

'Ja . . . a . . . ck.' A wail that made my goose pimples leap into instant action. I knew that voice all too well, albeit I had not heard it for a blessedly long period of silence. It had been some years since my Spanish werewolf, otherwise known as my ex-wife Eva, had last tornadoed her way through my life.

Tread carefully, I warned myself. 'What's wrong?'

'*Carlos*, he is wrong.'

'He's left you?' My sympathies were with Carlos. I could guess what he had been through.

'He is dead. Shot. Murdered!'

That shook me. For a moment I thought I'd misunderstood, but fond of exaggeration though she was, it must be serious if she was telephoning from South America. Her husband Carlos was Mexican, and I had an immediate – and no doubt stereotyped – image of vengeance in seedy nightspots. That, of course, could be true of anywhere now, including England's once green and pleasant land, but somehow Carlos and crime seemed to be a natural fit.

'I'm sorry, Eva,' I said sincerely. 'Have you someone you can call on to help you?'

'Y . . . o . . . u, Jack.'

'Me?' Extreme caution needed now. 'I can't do much from here.' Frogs Hill is in the midst of the Kentish countryside and a long way from Carlos-land.

'You come!'

'To *Mexico*?' She had to be joking.

'Not Mexico. You come to Maidstone. We here. Carlos killed here.'

The receiver felt clammy in my hand. Some joker, somewhere, had shot a thunderbolt into my life and poisoned it for good measure. Mexico was safely across a very wide ocean. Maidstone, capital of Kent, England, was a mere fifteen miles or so from where I was standing. When, over twenty years ago and after only four years of marriage, Eva had run off with her Mexican bandleader lover, it would have been a matter for celebration if it hadn't been for the fact that she had snatched Cara, our then toddler daughter, to take with her. I returned to an empty house with no forwarding address provided. Cara reappeared in my life years later as a student and then settled in England. Thankfully, Eva had only disrupted this picture for one or two brief visits. *So far . . .*

'*Why* was Carlos shot?' I asked Eva, perhaps a trifle tersely.

A pause. 'You detective, Jack. You find out.'

'That's the police's job,' I pointed out. 'Whatever you might have heard, I'm only a car detective, not from the Serious Crime Directorate.' It was true I'd been involved in one or two of its cases, but that was beside the point.

'Then I tell police about you, Jack.' The sweetness in her voice concealed the venom that I remembered all too well from past experience. What fairy-tale was she about to concoct now? That I was still a jealous husband bent on revenge? That I was a wife-beater? That I was a child molester? She was quite capable of accusing me of any of these, especially if, it occurred to me, she had shot Carlos herself. She was handy with a pistol, and in one memorable episode in our marriage I'd found myself facing it. Luckily, the ensuing shot missed.

I'd no choice. I had to find out what was happening – *now.* 'Where are you? Are the police there?'

'I go with policewoman to towpath. You come there.'

'Whereabouts? In the town itself? Halfway to Allington Lock? Or in the Teston direction?' The River Medway runs through Maidstone down to the sea; the upriver direction heads towards Tonbridge.

'Yes,' she said and switched off. It was a mobile, and when I rang back it was on voicemail.

Len Vickers and Zoe Grant, my two stalwart staff, were blithely working in the Pits when I stumbled in, shaken by the shock. The Pits is the name we give the converted barn where the restoration of classic cars takes place. It cares for Alvises to Zodiacs and from tune-ups to chassis-up rebuilds, and no classic goes uncherished. Len is nominally in charge, although Zoe tends not to see it that way. She's getting on for forty years younger than Len and has learned her skills from him so successfully that there's a tacit understanding between them as to how they work together. Who am I to probe into the mechanics of this? It works – I merely pay them and admire their handiwork.

They've only met Eva once, but that had been enough. Eva had blessed Frogs Hill with the warmth of her presence one afternoon when I was out. I returned to the farmhouse to find a white-faced Len even more bereft of words than usual while Eva gave him instructions on how to tune a Talbot's ignition, a subject about which she knows nothing. There had been no sign of Zoe. I discovered her later in the Glory Boot, the collection of automobilia stored in an extension to the farmhouse by my late father. Zoe had locked the door from the inside and was only persuaded to let me in when I promised on my word of honour that I was alone and that the gorgon had left Frogs Hill for ever.

Fortunately for my parents' sanity, Eva had rarely accompanied me to Frogs Hill during our brief marriage, which we'd spent either travelling for my job in the oil business or, after Cara's arrival, in an ultra-modern house near Chartham, a few miles from Canterbury – Eva's choice. 'You pay for house, I run it,' she'd pointed out. Unfortunately, she hadn't.

It was somewhere around that area that Eva had met Carlos. He'd been the leader of a locally formed Mexican mariachi band, which travelled around the south of England winning a precarious living from playing at weddings and other events, from pub evenings to football matches. Carlos must have been over fifty by now, I realized, although I still naturally thought of him as the thirtyish suave gigolo type he was at the time he'd run off with my wife and daughter.

This fateful Tuesday morning in May, Len and Zoe were admiring the subtle simplicity of a maroon Alvis TD21 before launching themselves into the glorious task of its restoration. I longed to be able to enter into an enjoyable discussion on what needed doing. Instead I had to break my appalling news.

'She's back.'

Zoe's head popped up immediately for once. 'Louise?' she asked. One look at my face must have told her that I wasn't referring to my lost love, who was now capturing the headlines on the West End stage as well as international screen.

'No such luck. It's Eva, and it's bad,' I told them. 'She's in Maidstone. Her husband's been murdered.'

Len lay down his torque wrench, a sign of how serious this was not just for me but for all of us.

'By her?' Zoe wasn't being flippant.

'Not known. She wants me there, anyway. It happened on the towpath opposite Allington Lock.' After the call from Eva, I had rung my contact in Maidstone police to get what limited information he had as yet. Allington Lock is about two miles downriver from Maidstone and a lovely spot – usually. The Malta Inn is set on one side of the river and the lock on the other side. Shortly before one reaches either of them, the stunning Allington castle looks down upon the river. Originally built in the thirteenth century, the castle has been adapted over the centuries and seen poets, knights and rebels pass through it, notably in Tudor times.

'What about Cara? How's she's taking it?'

Zoe has a lot of time for my daughter – as do I and everyone else who meets her. True, she has a calm infuriating assurance that she knows best, but somehow in Cara that's not off-putting. It has a charm about it, probably because she really does care about you and wants you to have the best advice possible. I suspect that this assurance hides a vulnerability that so far has not manifested itself, hence my caution in this current emergency.

'I'll size the situation up first. No point calling her before I know what's happening.'

'Take care, Jack.' Len looked worried. 'This could mean trouble.'

There was no need to reply. I was all too aware of that. Life was not looking good.

As I jumped into my Alfa, I reflected on what had been to the best of my recollection the only occasion I had ever met Carlos Sergio Vicente Mendez (to give him his full and formal name). Eva had been out somewhere that evening, and I was baby-sitting a far from well three-year-old Cara under the impression that her mother was at a flamenco evening class. Life with me, Eva complained, was not exciting. She was entitled to excitement. I was watching anxiously for her return, when I saw an old but still flashy Mercedes Benz saloon draw up and its occupants dismount. Eva then engaged in a passionate embrace with its driver. I was still delivering my point of view even as Carlos bravely jumped into his car, slammed the door and reversed to get away from me. It was a week later that I came home to an empty house.

Now Carlos was dead and Eva was my problem. I parked by the incident vans in the side lane leading to the towpath opposite Allington Lock, intending to walk down to the river. It was hardly surprising to find my way barred by police cordon tape, and the PC guarding the entrance showed no inclination to let me in. Instead I was directed back to the vans where, sure enough, I could hear Eva's all too familiar voice in full throttle. Outside the van DCI Brandon was conferring with a couple of white-suited SOCOs. Brandon was stationed locally in Charing but was part of the Kent and Essex Serious Crime Directorate. He's a cool customer. He doesn't throw his weight around but makes his presence felt, and so it's easy to underestimate him. He's no great chum of mine, although we have reached a working arrange-ment for the times when our paths cross. This usually occurs through my freelance work for the Kent Car Crime Unit under Dave Jennings, during which, on occasion, I clash with the SCD.

Brandon glanced up briefly. 'I may need you later, Jack. Are you around at Frogs Hill all day?'

At least I was 'Jack' now. 'Yes.' No point in any other answer.

'I presume you're here to see your wife.'

'Ex wife,' I pointed out.

'Of course.' His expression was as impassive as police faces often are. Sometimes I think they're handed out with the uniform. At that moment the van door was flung open and Eva herself was framed dramatically in the doorway. I took a deep breath and walked over to her.

When I first met Eva she was twenty-one, very, very beautiful, passionate and sexy. She was still all of these, save for the twenty-one. The decades had filled her out, and matured but not lessened her startling looks. Her dark hair, her complexion, her figure all commanded attention, and even from where I was standing at the foot of the van steps she exuded a confidence that life had received special instructions to look after her.

It was at least five years since I had last seen her, and today, naturally enough, she was white and drawn. I felt contrite at my unloving thoughts about her. She still seemed in command of her formidable presence, however. She was clad in black, with a black shawl and coat over a long skirt. Fashion was irrelevant for Eva as whatever she wore suited her style. Even today that had not deserted her. I realized that Brandon had followed me over, and I was glad of his presence.

Me? Scared of Eva? Yes.

She came gracefully down the steps and threw herself into my arms, which somewhat surprised the young female PC behind her. No doubt she had just heard Eva give an entirely different account of our relationship.

'You have come, Jack,' she sobbed. 'I feared you would not – knowing how badly you still feel about my poor darling Carlos.'

So that was the game we were playing. Two could play this one, however. 'I met him once for five minutes,' I said mildly – and loudly, 'twenty years ago.'

'And yet –' throaty voice now employed – 'you have not

forgotten. Not him, not me. It is growing always in your mind. I know that.'

Deflect the blows quickly. 'Have you called Cara? She's our daughter,' I added for Brandon's benefit, as he was taking a great interest in the proceedings.

My question took Eva aback, but she rallied. 'I could not bear to hurt her by telling her that her beloved stepfather lies dead. How could I sadden my precious child?'

'I'll do it,' I told her.

'It is a mother's job.'

OK. Play her game. 'You're in no state to do it, Eva,' I said gently. 'I'll call her from home.' I felt the body in my arms tense. I'd made a mistake, but it was too late. 'Where are you staying?' I asked warily.

'The Penenden Palace Hotel. But I know you will wish me to come to your home . . .'

I froze. 'No, Eva. You would be sad there. You will want to be close to the investigation. To find out how this happened to your dear husband. You can help the police by staying here.'

This high-flown conversational style was hard to keep up, especially as for one insidious moment the sexual attraction that years ago had bound us as unlikely partners returned, even in these ghastly circumstances. I fought it away as she disentangled herself from my arms and shot a random arrow.

'But you will not desert me, Jack. Not like last time.'

Eh? When was that? I wondered. 'I'll help the police all I can. Though I doubt they will need it.' I was aware of Brandon's cynical eye upon me. I meant it though. I would help – anything to get this solved quickly. 'Tell me what happened. Why were you and Carlos here in Maidstone?'

She replied just a little too quickly. 'For business – for my darling Carlos. He work with his music in the north of England for six months but then he say we must come here. It is recession. He needs money.'

Don't we all, I thought, and I wondered just how Carlos had planned to get it.

'I say no, Carlos,' Eva continued. 'I do not like to be near where once we were so happy, Jack.'

'You walked out rather quickly, Eva.' Mistake, mistake. That's what she'd been waiting for.

'Love, Jack. *Love*. I loved my darling Carlos, and now he is *dead*. Who could have done this? Only someone who was envious of me, who loved me and wished to hurt me. Who, Jack?' A soulful look at Brandon. I thought I saw the glimmer of a grin on his usually deadpan face.

Keep cool, I told myself. 'When did the murder happen?' I asked Brandon, but it was Eva who replied.

'This gentleman –' a little coo for Brandon – 'says in the night.'

'Early days,' 'this gentleman' replied. 'But it looks like well before midnight. He was found early this morning by a dog-walker.'

'Were you there, Eva?'

'Me?' She looked shocked. 'It was a business matter, Jack. I was at the hotel waiting for poor Carlos to come back to me, but he did not.'

'Business on a towpath?' I queried. 'At night?'

'Or possibly on a boat,' Brandon said laconically. 'There are no signs that the body was moved, but we won't know that for sure until—'

He broke off, and I quickly said: 'When did you notice he was missing from your hotel room, Eva?'

That wide mouth gaped. 'Oh, *Jack*!' Tears now, and a glance at Brandon. 'I did – I didn't. I couldn't—' A furious look. 'We had separate rooms,' she said sulkily. 'For business, you understand. Carlos so kind, he not want to disturb me. Not until the police ring hotel did I find out this morning.'

Tears overcame her now, and the policewoman moved in to take her back to the van. I was alone with my favourite cop.

'How did Mendez get here?' I asked Brandon. 'Any car around?'

'Your wife – *ex*-wife – told us he went off from the hotel in their old Ford Granada estate and we found it parked just over there.' He pointed to the line of cars where I'd just left the Alfa. Odd that Carlos hadn't gone into the large pub car park, the entrance to which he must have passed.

'Had he been robbed?' I asked.

'No. Full identification on him, including the hotel welcome card. That's how we contacted Mrs Mendez.'

Not robbed – that was a bad sign. It removed casual theft as a motive for Carlos's death. 'Any witnesses?'

'Nothing so far.' Brandon paused. 'Want to see him? I'm just about to have him moved out.'

I'm not partial to corpses, but I steeled myself and followed him down the lane to the riverside, having been hastily kitted out with scene suit and shoes. Coming from Brandon, the invitation could be seen as a compliment, although I suspected a test here. I was uncomfortably close to having a motive for wanting Carlos dead, and my reactions would be noted.

Brandon turned on to the towpath and led me away from the pub along a narrow stretch on the far side of the bridge. The bridge only crosses the river as far as a halfway island, from which pedestrians then take the lock bridge to the far river bank and the lock controls; so the island, although lit, was not likely to have been swarming with people at the time Carlos was killed. Nevertheless it was hard to see a 'business meeting' taking place on the towpath that Brandon and I were now walking along; it was hemmed in between the river and a row of straggling bushes and trees. For a murder, however, it must have held possibilities. It would be too late and too gloomy for there to be casual walkers along here, and even if there were light enough to be observed from the central island or the far river bank I knew that the lock-keeper was only on duty in person until seven p.m. Thereafter he was on call, and although he probably lived nearby he would not be aware of what was going on on this side of the river. The same would apply to the Malta Inn which was too far back beyond the bridge. Nothing faced the towpath at this point but the walled central island, but even so, I thought it was a curious choice for a planned murder.

Carlos lay to one side of this narrow towpath, almost hidden by shrubbery. I forced myself to look down at the pitiful remains of the man who had saved me from Eva, although I admit I didn't see it in that light at the time. I was flaming with anger that evening, not at him, true, but at Eva, and the cocky little runaway twerp had got up my nose. My fury only came a week later when I found Cara missing, although when I calmed down I had to admit Carlos must have some saving graces. It was unlikely that a 'cocky little twerp' would have landed himself with a child to support when what he really wanted was only the wife. Now a casually dressed balding middle-aged man, in linen trousers, T-shirt and jacket, lay on one side, spatters of congealed blood on the grass around him and all too obvious on his cream-coloured coat. I made myself take a brief glance at what remained of his head and face – which registered, or so I imagined, surprise at life's unfairness – and I turned away.

'Pistol?' I said abruptly to Brandon, for the sake of saying something.

'Not yet found. Does your ex-wife have a gun?'

I wasn't prepared for that. 'I don't know, and I doubt it. Not here.'

He pounced on that. 'So she can use one.'

I didn't answer, but he nodded as though I had.

I drove away, my mind whirling and a sick feeling in my stomach. There was something very odd here and I was all too glad that the case was on Brandon's desk. Eva was doing herself no favours, whatever she might imagine. Was she really at the hotel at the time of Carlos's death, I wondered.

Driving through the lanes back to Frogs Hill gave me a breathing space. Spring was here now in full force. Trees, birds, crops were all coming to life in the eternal pattern that had little to do with the urban nightmares that man has concocted for himself. Through the open windows of my Alfa the smells of May were strong and a million miles away from violent death.

As I arrived at the farm, it looked a paradise of calm and order, and I needed both. As I closed the front door behind me, the invidious thought came right back: where was Eva at the time of his death? And with that thought came others. The funeral – that would have to be arranged. Were Carlos's parents alive? Quite possibly. Such stray thoughts continued to rush through my head, perhaps because I had no clue on the real question: should I begin to look for the truth?

Thinking of Carlos's parents took me back to the day I married Eva, where I had met them, but that reminded me of our wedding night, and that sexual memory stirred me again. One outward sign of that, however, and Eva would move in for the kill. Perhaps it was the very inappropriateness of that phrase that steadied me. Cara, not Eva, was my responsibility now, and I rang her as soon as I was inside the door. I was aware that both Len and Zoe were at the door of the Pits expecting to hear what had happened, but I'd report to them later.

Cara is in her mid twenties now. She'd had a job with a magazine based in London, but had thrown it up to help run a smallholding in Suffolk with a nice guy called Harry, who like her seemed very sure of his path in life, even though their business could hardly be without its problems in this day of supermarket tyranny. Nevertheless, it suited them both, and Cara seemed happy. I've never pried into her relationship with Eva, but it couldn't be that close because she saw her mother only slightly more often than I did. There must be a bond there, however, and I usually hesitate to impinge upon it. Today I had to do so. What was the real reason Eva had not rung Cara herself? That was not only odd, but possibly ominous.

Cara took the news on the chin – or appeared to do so. 'Not that surprised,' she said. 'Carlos wasn't always too careful about his business associates.'

'Were you fond of him, Cara?'

'He was OK if you didn't rely on him or stand in his way. Kind, in an offhand way, but slippery. You know the sort, Jack.'

By the time Cara and I had got reacquainted, when I came back to Frogs Hill from foreign parts and the oil business, she was in her late teens and a student in London, and she was naturally wary of me. I was 'Jack' not Dad – and, more oddly, her mother was 'Eva'. This might have been Cara's way of distancing herself after a lack of training in relationships, or perhaps she'd had too many bad ones, so I try to take life onwards, not probe into her past. It seems to work and we get on well, although I tread with care.

'I'll come down right away,' she told me briskly. 'I take it she's trying to pin this on you?'

'Got it in one, I suspect.'

'Leave it to me.'

'Don't let her mess up—'

'My life?' Cara cut in. 'No way.'

Thankfully, Eva comes from a large family in Spain who are all too willing to close ranks when required. I was an only child and during our marriage had been somewhat over-whelmed at the constant stream of family members who stayed with us for endless paellas and monopolized the phone before the days of Skype and Facebook. It was all very jolly – until things turned sour and from having been my in-laws' best mate I became public enemy number one.

I sank down in the farmhouse after the call. Frogs Hill is indeed a refuge. It is set on the Greensand Ridge looking down towards the Weald and is about two miles (via winding single track lanes) from Pipers Green, our nearest village, and five from Pluckley, reputed to be Kent's most haunted village. In addition to my Alfa, I have two classic cars, my Gordon-Keeble and my Lagonda, which together with the Pits keep me sane at the worst of times. There is a solidity about classic cars that helps their owners withstand the unexpected shocks of life. Essentially, they are there for you, like the best of families. Like pets you feed them and keep them in good condition and you will get your reward. In times of trouble they bring comfort. I needed that now.

However quickly the police found Carlos's killer, I was going to be affected. There would be Eva's future to settle, the trial, the funeral – I blenched at the implications. Even if Eva's family and Cara took over some of the nightmare, I could see that I was going to be right in the middle of it. To take my mind off it, I decided to embark on a complete polish of the Gordon-Keeble. Dad had bought it for its rarity; I cling to it for the sense of endurance it gives me. Its fluid lines and its sheer understated elegance are a panacea for the worst of problems. At times such as this, it soothes the spirit.

*   *   *

Brandon arrived that afternoon, by which time I had managed to convince myself that he wouldn't be coming. After all, some killers are found very quickly and I could contribute nothing myself to their case. That at least was true, but Brandon might not see it that way. I was talking to Len when we heard the car draw up, and I saw the look on Len's face.

'Here we go,' I said to him in resignation and then went to greet my 'guest'. At least he didn't have a sidekick with him, which might mean this was not going to be too formal.

'How's it going?' I said to Brandon as he climbed out of the car and followed me into the farmhouse living room.

As before, he replied, 'Early days.'

Not good, that. It implied I was a witness, not just a side issue. Whether approvingly or disapprovingly, Brandon looked around him at the comfortable but ancient armchairs and sofa and my choice of pictures, ranging from a nude to a photo of Louise and an original painting of a Karmann Ghia by my famous chum Giovanni. 'Did you know Carlos Mendez was coming to Maidstone?' he added casually.

'No. Nor Eva. Bit of a shock to hear from her this morning.'

'She came two days later than he did,' Brandon corrected me. 'Because, she claims, he was down here to look up members of his former band and make new contacts.'

I spoke without thinking. 'That rules me out.'

No comment from Brandon. 'Did you know he and your ex-wife were in England?'

'Not till she rang. We're not in touch.'

'Is your daughter?'

'You'll have to ask her. She's not that close to her mother.'

'Or her stepfather?'

'Ask her,' I repeated. 'She's on her way here.'

'I understand your wife met Mendez when she was living with you here.'

'Not *here*. We were living near Chartham when she scarpered with him. That was in 1991, and I gathered he'd been based in Kent for several years. I haven't seen Carlos since that time, though Eva blew in occasionally.'

'She must have been quite a stunner.' An unexpectedly human comment from Brandon.

'She often stunned me. Sometimes with a frying pan.'

Brandon grinned at the weak joke. It was a brief lull but then it was back to business. 'Did you know his band was based round here? It was called Carlos and the Charros.'

'I knew he had a band, but not the name. I was busy baby-sitting while she was following the drums.'

'It disbanded after Carlos left with your wife. Did you know any of them? Carlos plus four others and a singer, I gather.'

'As I said, I didn't know Carlos or his band.'

'Your wife claims otherwise.' He said it so lightly that I didn't instantly get the message. Then I realized he was looking at me so intently that there had to be some reason.

I groaned. 'OK. Tell me the worst. What else did she say?'

'That you could not be blamed for feeling the way you did about Carlos.'

I closed my eyes and counted to ten. 'And what way was that?' I enquired.

'You tell me, Jack.'

At least he was still calling me Jack, so there was hope yet. 'Answer: my only feeling was that I was sorry for the poor sap.' Plus – though I wasn't fool enough to tell Brandon this – a mild antipathy, after the one brief encounter I had with him.

'He was married to her for a good many years. No need for sorrow on your part. Marriage to her seemed to suit him.'

'Eva has a lot of rich relations – that could have suited him very well.'

An eyebrow shot up. 'Sure you don't feel resentment? They brought up your daughter after all.'

I ignored the reference to Cara. 'I've never pretended to be overfond of Eva but have always thought Carlos was the relatively innocent party.'

'Generous, Jack.' There was no inflection in Brandon's voice to tell me whether he believed me or not. Nor was there when he added: 'Not planning to leave town, are you?'

I wasn't, but I felt the nightmare closing in with a vengeance. Rumbles of approaching storms were not going to vanish. I watched him drive away and wished I could do the same, at least emotionally. I couldn't, however. I realized that Brandon probably didn't think I had anything to do with this murder, but that he couldn't discount it. He had to go through the motions, and he would. What that meant was that I would have to look after my own interests as well as Eva's by trying to find out who did kill Carlos.

Emotionally, however, I was in no state to do so. Seeing Eva again normally shakes me up for a while, not because I still harboured loving feelings for her (despite the day's earlier sexual blip), but because of the knowledge that I had been so stupid in my youth. Only Cara remains the golden linchpin for those days. I'd never *resented* missing so much of her life, just regretted it. In the oil business you accept life as it's thrown at you. Now it had thrown it in plenty, and I had to put that to rights or the glory that was Frogs Hill would be tarnished.

And then fate tossed me a lifebelt – although it hardly seemed like that at the time.

I watched in amazement as, in a cloud of smoke, a noisy, battered and ill-kept Volvo 144 drove into the Frogs Hill fore-court, swung round, and drew up with a cough and a splutter. Its driver emerged and marched towards me.

Daisy had entered my life.

TWO

A cloud of golden hair, blue eyes blazing in indignation (obvious even from where I was standing), an English rose complexion, perfect figure, twenty years old at the most and apparently oblivious to all her attributes. True beauty doesn't have to be sexy, just admired. I took all this in in an instant, and mentally put it aside while I wondered what caused the indignation – and, indeed, the visit. I could not recall any cars under restoration in the Pits that would have a Venus such as this as owner. She wasn't dressed for effect, that was for sure: black tights, long blue dress and an old green anorak thrown over them. Rain was threatening, although this apparition walked with sunshine around her.

I had never seen her before and yet I seemed to be far from the top of her list of favourite people. I remained where I was outside the farmhouse front door, unable to move with shock. She marched up, planted herself in front of me and, yes, folded her arms grimly under her perfectly-sized (from what I could see) bosom.

'Mr Colby?'

Usually, a stranger's voice shatters any dreams that appearance might have inspired. Not with this young lady – except that the 'Mr' she employed would suggest I was way out of her range for anything closer than a business relationship. Her voice was low, musical, and on a different mission might have been honey-filled. I didn't know what her mission was, but her angry eyes did not instantly suggest honey.

'They told me you do the Morris Minors.'

I must have gaped at this unexpected pronouncement of hers because she patiently repeated it, to which I managed to reply: 'We restore any classics. Morris Minors are—'

This brought forth a far from patient: 'You *find* them, don't you?'

'You want to buy one?'

Heavy silence now, and I thought she was about to turn on her dainty heel and walk out. If so, she changed her mind. 'They told me you were some sort of cop. Are you or aren't you?'

I pulled myself together from wherever my fancy might have been planning to take me. 'In a way. I work for the Kent Police Car Crime Unit.'

'I know,' she said crossly. 'I called them to find out what they were doing about Melody because nothing was happening. They said you would be dealing with her.'

I was lost. 'Who's Melody?'

'My Morris Minor.' Her voice now held a note of kindliness, as if speaking to a very ancient person. 'I'm Daisy Croft.'

I was still lost. Dave commissions me job by job, but none had been forthcoming recently – a fact of which my bank balance was well aware. He and the jobs he gives me are a major factor in Frogs Hill's survival under my ownership. The classic car restoration side of things is patchy from the economic viewpoint, dependent not only on the flow of cars coming in but on the flow going out. As Len and Zoe pride themselves more on workmanship than deadlines, the latter can be a very slow process.

'Your car's been stolen?' All right, that was a fatuous question too, but it was all I could cope with.

'Last week. Outside the bakery. I left her there the night before because I only live down the road, so sometimes I walk. This old heap's my boyfriend's dad's.' She waved a disparaging hand at the Volvo.

'And where is the bakery?' My turn to be very, very patient.

'Burchett Forstal. I work there.'

I wasn't that surprised Dave hadn't contacted me on this case. A Morris Minor is an odd car to steal. It was the first car built after the war to be accessible to everybody, and everybody duly loved it. It was Britain's answer to the Volkswagen Beetle, although it never spread its fame worldwide, as did its rival. Production of the 'poached egg', as Lord Nuffield, founder of the Morris Motors company, pejoratively called it from its softly curvy shape, stopped in 1971, but the Morris Minor was so reliable it still defies oblivion in large numbers.

My guess was that Dave's team had probably put the theft down to joyriders, which meant Melody would show up sooner or later, but after a week that scenario was beginning to have a question mark over it. Burchett Forstal is a hamlet roughly ten miles away from Pluckley and Piper's Green. It's in the Charing–Challock area, and it's chiefly known to non-residents as the most unfindable destination in the long list of Kentish hidden villages. A pretty spot though.

I realized I'd been silent too long.

'Well?' Daisy asked. 'Are you going to find Melody or not?'

'I wish I could. But I have to wait until I'm asked to investigate.'

'*I'm* asking you.'

Faced with this implacable goddess, I surrendered. Who wouldn't? 'I'll find out what's happening.'

This wasn't enough. 'I mean,' Daisy said earnestly, 'I'll pay you and all that. Private-like.'

Difficult. 'The problem is that it's a police job as you've already reported it. I can't barge in.'

As I hope I've made clear, Morris Minors are very special cars. They aren't motor cars so much as symbols of a way of life, which puts them in a somewhat different category. Classic car-lovers usually fall into two main groups: those who remember a classic fondly from their youth, and those who admire beautiful objects from the past whether or not they have personal resonance for them. The Minor is almost in a class of its own, however. It rings bells from the past with those who owned them or grew up with them, whether in the fifties, sixties, seventies or even eighties. Whether new or second-hand, the bells ring so loudly that it has inspired a sort of folk memory down the generations, and today it flourishes in clubs and get-togethers. It's nice and curvy to look at, has good engineering, and has entered the twenty-first century 'trailing clouds of glory', to quote Wordsworth's poem. It becomes the centre of attention at picnics galore and carefree days out.

I saw Miss Sunshine's face fall at my refusal to be drawn, so I added hastily, 'Tell me about Daisy – no, Melody. Sorry,' I corrected myself as she dissolved into giggles. 'Wrong way round. A Morris Minor isn't usually a first choice as a vehicle for someone your age.'

'Melody belonged to my gran,' she explained. 'We lived with her, Mum, Dad and me, for a few years when I was still a kid. Mum and Dad were working, so Gran and I went on all these picnics and explored everywhere. She's great is Gran. She's pinky-coloured.' More giggles. 'Melody I mean, not Gran. Melody isn't just a car.' She searched for words. 'She's like part of us, see?'

'I do.' Pinky-coloured, I thought, was probably Daisy's name for the glorious Rose Taupe Morris Minor pinky-grey. 'Is it split screen?' I asked. 'What year?'

Daisy looked blank.

'The windscreen,' I explained. My turn to be patient. 'Does it have a strip down the middle? And is it a convertible?'

'Oh. No, it doesn't. And it's got a proper roof. Don't know when Gran bought it.'

'A Traveller?' Another blank look from Daisy so I amplified this: 'An estate car?'

'No.' Indignation now. 'She's a real *car.*'

Not a convertible, not a Traveller and had to be 1956 onward. It was obviously a Minor 1000. I was getting somewhere, I supposed. 'How many doors, and what time of day did it disappear?'

'Two, and she must have gone in the night,' Daisy told me solemnly, and I could swear there were tears in her eyes. 'I get to work at seven thirty for the first bread and rolls and stuff and found her gone. Last Wednesday it was.'

'Any witnesses?' I asked solemnly, knowing this question would be expected of me.

'No. Come over and see the scene of the crime.' Daisy was cheering up now I was taking her seriously, or at least appearing to do so. 'Come on then,' she added, when I made no move. 'Let's go.' And when I still didn't budge: 'Look, do you want this job or not?'

I looked at Daisy, and I remembered the hornet's nest busily building up with Eva. It could be a good excuse to dodge visits. 'Yes, but two conditions: first it'll have to be tomorrow morning, and second I have to clear it with the police.'

'Why?' she asked suspiciously.

'Don't you have to ask the boss before you march out on a working day?'

'Yeah,' she conceded.

I watched her reluctantly climb back into the Volvo, clearly thinking she was being short changed. She wasn't. Give me a choice between Daisy's Melody and sticking my neck out with Eva's affairs and there'd be no contest. But there was no choice. For all sorts of reasons, Eva had to be top of my agenda.

Dave was only too willing to agree when I rang him the next morning about Melody – with one small exception. The Budget. Fine if I found the car. A small fee would then materialize. Any complications, however, and it would appear I should have left it to the team. 'All clear?' Dave asked me jovially.

I said it was, then prepared for my trip to Burchett Forstal, which began to seem a picnic compared with the death of Carlos Mendez. I was just pondering whether to take the Gordon-Keeble or the Lagonda, when the decision had to be abruptly postponed. My mobile rang, and it was Eva.

'Darling, I come to see you,' she announced. 'I take taxi. You pay him.'

Panic made me undiplomatic. 'You can't.' The brief silence that greeted this gave me a chance to think. 'Cara's on her way, and the police will need you close at hand to help them with their enquiries.' This sounded uncomfortably formal, so I rounded it off with, 'Anyway, I have an appointment this morning.'

'A woman?' she screeched. 'But I am your *wife*.'

Oh, how that brought back the old days. No point in reminding her she wasn't my wife and that I was a car detective with several jobs to do. So . . .

'Yes,' I said. 'A woman. She's been kidnapped. Her name's Melody.'

After assuring Eva I hadn't forsaken her and that I would contact her very shortly, I set off for Burchett Forstal with a pleasant, if temporary, sense of release. In my agitation I had initially found myself fastening the seat-belt in the Alfa and not one of my two beloved classics, but had decided to take the extra time and replace it with the Lagonda, which I guessed would be a hit with Daisy. Even so, it was Eva who was occupying my mind as I drove my beauty down the Frogs Hill Lane. Tackle the dirty fuel line first, son, my father would always advise. Polish your bonnet later. I'd take his advice. Turning off into the maze of lanes leading to Burchett Forstal, I began to calm down and think rationally about Carlos's death.

His murder, it seemed clear to me, was no random attack but something to do with the 'business' he had expected to transact in Kent. After Daisy had left me the previous evening, I had tackled the Internet to see what it could produce on Carlos. I had a feeling that good though Brandon was at his job, I was going to need all the background information I could get. I can't say I hit pay dirt in my search but it was interesting. Carlos's father Vicente had run a band in England in the 1970s, which is presumably how Carlos had learned his trade. The last mention of Vicente's band was in 1981 – though that didn't necessarily mean it wasn't still active, either in the UK or South America. The only mention of Carlos and the Charros was in 1988 at a gig in Brighton. These were pre-Internet days, and records of them on the net would be scanty.

Burchett Forstal is deemed a hamlet, not a village, because it doesn't boast its own church, but it does have a farm shop and bakery. In Kentish dialect a forstal is open land bordered by farm buildings, and Burchett was a prime example. Its one through-street passes a stretch of grass rising up to the farm shop and a granary barn, flanked by terraced cottages. Daisy lived in one of these a little further along the street. I'd already passed the bakery. I couldn't miss it. Burchett Bakery announced itself with flags, signposts and a parking area. Understandable, I thought. A bakery for a community this size needs to draw custom from a wide area.

Driving the Lagonda was a treat, and as I parked in front of Daisy's home I was conscious that my arrival had been noted. The cottage, in which she probably lived with her parents, had been built in the days well before people thought of better things to do with their gardens than growing fruit and flowers (such as parking cars). The front garden was a wonderful mix of spring flowers, trees coming into leaf and rows of vegetables – in short, a traditional country garden.

As I drew up, Daisy emerged like a ray of sunshine. She'd asked me to come when she had an hour's break from the early morning shift, and she screamed with delight when she saw the Lagonda. This is a 1938 V12 drophead in all its glory, and it came into my life with treasured memories.*

'Hey,' she cried, 'this is a real picnic car, just like Melody. Let's go, Jack.'

'Picnicking? I'm here on business, miss,' I told her gravely.

She promptly saluted me. 'OK, Gumshoe. Let's get going.' No walking for her today. She jumped enthusiastically into the Lagonda and squealed yet more delight. Her high spirits deflated as we reached the scene of the crime. 'It was there,' she said dolefully as we reached the bakery.

I glanced around. The bakery had a second storey, and across the road were two cottages set well back. 'Did anyone hear anything?' I coached myself into remembering that the seriousness of a crime from the victim's viewpoint is totally different to that of the law's.

'No. Dad reckons it was a two-man job and they pushed it along there.' She pointed to where the hamlet petered out into open countryside – not far, and so her dad could be right.

'It would have been driven away, though. No gang would risk bringing a low loader here.'

Daisy regarded this as a marvel of detection. 'I never thought of that.'

'We sleuths have keen minds. I take it you didn't leave it unlocked or a key in the ignition?'

End of admiration from Daisy. 'You must think I'm nuts,' she said scornfully. 'No way.'

The bakery, from its display, catered for everyone, producing a range from Chelsea buns and doughnuts to quiches and

---

* See *Classic in the Barn*

interesting looking pies to tempt the palate. Two delivery vans were parked outside, which suggested there was a lunchtime delivery service.

'Is there a pub near here?' I asked, thinking that might be a rendezvous for joyriders.

'Closed down.'

A familiar fate for small country pubs. '*Anywhere* near?'

'Justie's dad's at Tickenden.'

I took it that 'Justie' was her own pet name for him. 'Justin's your boyfriend?' Bad lot? I wondered.

'He's like – well – hopeful. Can't make my mind up.' She grinned conspiratorially at me, and I felt privileged – in a fatherly way. This was a game I was long out of. 'His dad owns the May Tree Inn.'

'I've been there once or twice.' It's famous now for being a pretty country pub with good food. I'd been there in my youth, before marriage and I had disagreed with each other, and again quite recently. In a previous existence in the late 70s the pub was chiefly famous for something completely different – as a well-hidden dive for career criminals, a role that culminated in the May Tree Shoot-Out. A priceless collection of early English gold brooches, and cups etc, had been hijacked while in transit from its stately-home owners to be sold on the continent. The villains retreated to the May Tree, where they proceeded to have a serious falling out. The then manager of the May Tree had disappeared into one of her Majesty's prisons for umpteen years. The pub had abruptly been sold by the brewery and had forged a new life for itself.

'I think I met the owner,' I continued. 'Gentle giant of a chap.'

'Yeah. George is OK, so's Justie – but a bit, well you know . . .' She grinned sheepishly. '*Too* gentle.'

'No such thing,' I said sadly. 'You'll learn.'

She shrugged. 'Got to see the world first, haven't I?'

'And what would constitute the world for you?'

'Africa, China, Aussie, maybe America. That sort of place.'

I held my peace. Places are inhabited by people much the same as those she met in Burchett Forstal – good, bad, dull,

interesting, gentle, fierce – but who was I to knock her
dreams? I'd seen my 'world' in the oil business, and thankfully I was now back at Frogs Hill, determined never to move
again.

'Justie's got some evidence,' she told me.

'About Melody?'

'Yeah. Reckons he can get her back for me. But he hasn't
done it, has he?'

'Why not?'

'Says there are complications and he can't split on a mate.
I told him, stuff that. Just get Melody back quick. That's
why I came to hire you.'

I let this pass. 'I'll stand you lunch at the May Tree,' I
offered. It would be pleasant and would also, I thought guiltily,
postpone Eva's problem for another hour or two. I doubted if
it would lead to Melody's recovery though. 'Is Justin the
barman?'

'No. He works in Canterbury at a supermarket, but the
barmaid's off on maternity leave so he's filling in for her.'

Tickenden was only a couple of miles away, and if we'd
been crows even less. As it was, the winding lanes were a
delight in the Lagonda of which Daisy continued to show her
appreciation with little whoops of pleasure. She insisted on
having the top down even though it was spitting with rain.
'Bet the Queen doesn't have one of these cars,' she said
proudly, lifting her head back to the breeze and her face to
the spots of rain.

'Bet the Queen would like one,' I replied happily.

The May Tree looked as innocent of crime now as
Buckingham Palace. I could see its wooden tables outside,
and a village green with a chestnut tree in full bloom. History
alone knows what happened to the hawthorn that lent the pub
its informal name. The idea of a shoot-out here now was
incongruous; it was more like the idyllic Potwell Inn where
H. G. Wells's Mr Polly found his Shangri-La. Then I remembered that Mr Polly had had to fight for his paradise with the
formidable Uncle Jim, who chased him with broken bottles
all too vigorously. I comforted myself that Mr Polly had won
by guile in the end, and in any case George Taylor, the licensee

here, proved no such formidable opponent. Tall, well built and slow, the grin on his face reassured you that you were his favourite customer.

'I'll call Justin, Daisy,' he told her amiably.

'This is Mr Jack Colby,' Daisy announced importantly. 'He's going to find Melody for me.'

George shot me a conspiratorial look of despair and disappeared to find his son. Justin, when he appeared, was not yet his father's son where confidence and amiability were concerned. In his early twenties, he had a look of defiance in his eyes as he greeted me before turning them on Daisy in adoration.

'Told you *I'd* handle Melody,' he muttered sulkily when she did not return this sign of devotion.

'Yeah, but you haven't, have you?'

'Suppose we all have a drink?' I intervened hastily.

'I'm on duty,' he said obstinately, but his father took a firm hand.

'You go, son. I'll handle the bar.'

We ordered sandwiches and salad and adjourned to a table by the window. As Justin looked increasingly uncomfortable, I decided to take this head on. 'Daisy tells me you have some information about Melody.'

He hesitated, despite my non-confrontational tone. The view outside the window was clearly fascinating him. 'Think I saw her round here, but didn't want to say nothing till I'd checked it out.'

'And have you?'

'Yeah. Well, sort of . . . . I reckon it's in a barn.'

'Where?' Daisy was taking no prisoners. 'Why haven't you told me?'

'Don't know where. Somewhere.' Justin had a hunted look.

'Why not tell me? Why not tell the police?' she persisted.

'Wasn't sure, was I?' Justin grew even more defensive.

'Does this barn belong to a friend of yours?' I asked to help him out, wondering what on earth I was doing here when I should be chasing up every clue I could to Carlos's murder.

Justin finally cracked. 'Look, straight in your face, OK? I

should have told you before, Daisy. I reckon I know where it is, but I don't know nothing definite. But I'll get it back for you. I will, I promise.'

I could see the hurt of anxious youth in his face, but even without that I felt there was something I wasn't quite getting here.

Most girls would have shot back some cynical remark but not Daisy. She knew when to stop. 'I know you'll do your best, Justie.'

He looked at her with such adoration that my heart bled for him. Remembering that Daisy had to 'see places' before she would appreciate Justin, I only hoped he would wait long enough.

I wasn't sure that I appreciated him too much myself at the moment, though, so I moved things along by making it clear that I'd had enough. 'I'll drive you back, Daisy,' I said pointedly. 'It's a police job.'

'Melody?' Justin asked nervously.

'No. A murder case.'

'That one in Maidstone?' Justin asked to my surprise. 'Dad says the word's going round it's Carlos Mendez.'

Why should the word 'go round', I wondered. The police hadn't released the name, so far as I knew, but why should it be of such particular interest? Even if George Taylor knew Carlos, Carlos was apparently in Maidstone only for a brief visit. I glanced over to see the Gentle Giant George carefully polishing glasses. *Too* carefully, so I strolled over to him. 'Did you know Mendez?' I asked.

'Met him years back when I first got to know this place. I wasn't running the pub then. He wasn't too popular round these parts.'

'Not with me, certainly. He ran off with my wife.'

That caught his attention and maybe loosened his tongue. 'He started up a Mexican band with local lads in the late eighties – based here at the May Tree they were. Owner encouraged him. Mendez filled the lads' heads with dreams of glory, dressed them up in white suits, built up their reputation, then left them in the lurch when he walked out on them. Band split up – the Brits were no use without the Mexican himself.'

'Who was the owner of the May Tree then?' It was news
to me that Carlos was connected with the May Tree. My
youthful visits here had preceded Carlos's arrival, and it made
me irrationally uneasy at the thought that it was in this very
pub that Eva and Carlos had met and presumably cemented
their relationship.

'A chap called James Fever bought it when the brewery
sold it after the shoot-out,' George told me. 'I bought it from
him in the 1990s when he retired. He died a few years back.'

'So quite a few people would have been interested in the
news that Carlos was back in town. Apparently, Carlos was
thinking of contacting them.'

George did not reply. The subject, he indicated, was closed.

For me too. Daisy came marching up as I paid the bill.
'What are you going to do about Melody? Leave it to my
Justie to sort out?'

I considered this. I'd love to do just that so that Justin would
get the brownie points, but Daisy was in a fighting mood. I
had no choice. I had to be tough on the lad.

'Show us the barn where you think Melody's hidden,' I told
Justin firmly. 'It's time to get this settled.'

I thought he was going either to refuse or punch me, but
without great enthusiasm he led us along a lane that shortly
turned into a track, which, judging by the tyre marks, had
been used for more than cows. Certainly tractors, and possibly
a Morris Minor. When we reached Huggett's barn, as Justin
eventually named it, it did not even possess a lock. The door
was swinging open in the wind, and Justin seemed to be
swivelling between nervousness and belligerence.

As well he might. The barn was empty.

In the silence that followed I noted two things: the first was
that Justin looked anguished, presumably because he thought
he'd been wrong about the barn; the second was that there
was a number plate lying on the ground. I went over to pick
it up.

'Melody's,' Daisy breathed as she snatched it from me.
'Justie, where is she?'

'I don't know.' His terror at her threatening tone was so
great that even Daisy held back.

She turned on me instead. 'What are *you* going to do about this?'

'Start again, but not today.'

'Aren't you going to fingerprint this plate or something? Or get some DNA off it?' she said indignantly as I turned away.

I had a vision of what Dave would say if I marched in with a number plate and demanded instant forensic attention. I also noted Justin was near to tears.

'I'll get the team on it,' I told her.

'Promise?' She eyed me narrowly.

I came clean. 'No, but I'll do my best, Daisy.'

'OK,' she said, more peaceably than I had expected. 'And, Jack, you should meet my Gran.'

'You think she has pinched Melody back?' I joked.

'No. That other case of yours. She knew the May Tree Inn way back. She knew all about Carlos and the Charros.'

THREE

I parted from Daisy with some reluctance, because Melody had been a pleasant diversion from the sword of Damocles poised above me in the form of Eva. Unfortunately, it now seemed there was a tenuous point of contact between Melody and Carlos – the May Tree – and certainly I was curious to meet the famous Gran. I had been impressed by Daisy's attachment to Melody, which was a tribute both to the Morris Minor and her Gran. I'd told Daisy I was eager to meet the lady, but first I needed to catch up with events elsewhere. It was only just over twenty-four hours since I had become involved in Carlos's death, but in that time anything could have happened – not least to Eva.

The nearer the Lagonda brought me to Frogs Hill the more Damocles's sword began to wobble over my head. I didn't have long to wait until the action began again, although it was heralded pleasantly enough. As I drove along the lane I could see someone perched on the wall above the high bank, and I pulled into the Frogs Hill forecourt in a much happier frame of mind. There she was, my Cara.

I had not seen her for a while, not through any lack of a wish to do so, but because she was busy putting down new roots in Suffolk. Even though she had told me she would be galloping to the rescue, seeing her here, rather than in Eva's company, was a surprise to be welcomed. She looked at ease as she patiently waited for me to park the Lagonda. With her mass of curly dark hair and broad forehead, she looked at first glance like a younger edition of Eva, although where passion and anger beset her mother, Cara had assurance, and where Eva had stormy rages, Cara had control. Won at a price, I imagined, as a means of survival as a child. There was a detachment about her that always suggested to me that Cara did not give her trust easily. Does she trust me? I don't know, but she accepts me, as I do her foibles, and that is enough.

She smiled at me, and the detachment vanished. This was a lady bent on saving the situation *her* way. 'Gotcha,' she remarked, standing up to greet me.

'Did you fly here on self-propelled wings, sweetheart?' I looked round for a car but saw none.

'I told Eva she could have the Fiat to do some shopping to take her mind off things.' What else, I thought, when one's husband has just been murdered? Although I did concede that Cara had as so often hit the right nail on the head for the right time. 'I asked Len to pick me up from Charing station,' she continued.

That was a tribute indeed. Asked? Len did not ordinarily tear himself away from his beloved Pits, asked or not. 'Are you staying here? Spare bed always made up.'

'With Eva in full throttle? It's my public duty to stay at the hotel with her.'

'A medal for gallantry.'

She grimaced. 'Gallantry called for from you too, Jack. I want your help.'

'Willingly given,' I replied, 'with the proviso that the police think I'm suspect number one for Carlos's murder.'

'No. Eva seems to have reserved that spot for herself. I went straight to the hotel and she had just returned from police HQ. High drama. She claims I'm the only person she can rely on.'

'Funny. Yesterday she said that was me. Seriously, Cara, what was the story that came over to you?'

Unusually, Cara hesitated. 'You first.'

I obeyed. 'She told me she and Carlo had come down because he needed money and proposed to get it through some kind of business deal, perhaps to do with his former band members. He went out for the evening, and as they had separate rooms it was not until the police called yesterday morning that she knew he had not returned.'

'Ah. Did she tell you they were splitting up?'

'No. He was her "dearest Carlos".' This was far from good news.

'Did she tell you her "dearest Carlos" came down *before* her on what he thought was a lone mission, and that having insisted on knowing where he was staying she rushed down by train in pursuit?'

'No.' We were off again. This was the Eva I remembered so well. Depending on what she thought would fit the occasion, there was a different story every five minutes. Take your pick which one was true.

'She discovered, she *says*, that although he was skint he was planning to move in with some other woman. Carlos's band had not done too well in the north of England and he had indeed said he was coming here to get some big-time cash for them both. She presumed that both meant her, but she found out that it didn't. He had a floozie. So when Carlos announced he had to make this trip, Eva was sure he was bringing this other woman. So she followed him down here and found to her surprise that, with or without the floozie, he actually *was* staying at the hotel he had claimed to be honouring with his presence.'

'How does a business rendezvous at Allington Lock tie up with illicit liaisons? Or doesn't it? Do you believe her?'

'No. According to her, she stayed in the hotel although she knew Carlos had this meeting. The mother I know would be chasing him with a hatchet down that towpath if she thought another woman was with her beloved.'

'Or not so beloved, according to you.'

'It varies, Jack. She also told me Carlos was thrilled when she arrived at the hotel. The other woman wasn't in evidence, though she maintains this was merely because Carlos had secretly hidden her away. He was full of the big deal he was about to make.'

'Tell me the worst,' I groaned. 'Do you think she told the police about this other woman?' Eva was essentially naive. It would be typical of her to tell them about this probably non-existent woman, thus giving herself a motive for murder.

'If it was a business deal not an assignation for Carlos,' I continued, 'she'd have no motive for killing him. Not before he caught the golden goose, anyway.' Eva had never been one for missing an opportunity such as that. Her wealthy relations had done very well out of similar opportunities in their own country.

'I agree, and if she told the police about this floozie, that's scary. It's possible . . .'

I helped her out. 'That she did discover he was with his current flame and not a billionaire. And that, even worse, she wasn't waiting in the hotel for him.'

'Yes,' Cara said bluntly.

'No gun was found by the body, so the police wouldn't have much to go on,' I pointed out. 'Carlos was shot, and though Eva can wield a gun, it isn't like her to pack one on a trip like this one.'

'Even if she planned to kill him?'

I struggled with this one. 'She isn't one to carry out her own dirty work either.'

Cara nodded. 'She could have conspired with someone.'

'Who would—' I did a double take. '*Me*?'

Cara grinned. 'You're not always in the limelight, Jack. Quite apart from Spanish relatives, Eva has always had plenty of men around. I expect she did during your marriage. If I hadn't inherited your ugly face I might even wonder about my parentage.'

That took me aback. It implied she had done just that. I looked at my beloved daughter and could see myself in her. 'No way, Cara. You're mine.'

I winced when I remembered what a fool I had been twenty years ago, however. I'd had so many stars in my eyes that I couldn't see the meteors about to crash on my patch of earth. I don't know whether Eva was physically unfaithful to me throughout our marriage, but in the last year I had suspected that was the case. Plenty of men, all spellbound by her fiery southern beauty, as once I had been. I doubt whether any of them had forgotten her; she had the habit of blowing in and out of people's lives whenever she fancied, whether as a breath of warm air or a blast from the frozen north. Either way, she was unforgettable.

'Your point's taken, though,' I continued. 'I tend to discount the conspiracy theory though, especially with past chums. Carlos filled all her dreams at that time, and I doubt if any of her other conquests would resurrect themselves all these years later.'

'She could have brought a lover with her,' Cara said dispassionately.

From her face she was longing for me to shoot this down, which I could with ease. 'Why on earth would any lover want to assist in murder if she and Carlos were splitting up anyway? No, this business deal is much more likely – thank heavens.' I'd no wish to go chasing Eva's lovers.

Cara cheered up. 'Eva told me she and Carlos knew a man called James Fever, who owned the pub Carlos performed at before he did a runner. Would he be a candidate?'

'Hardly. He's no longer alive. He took over from the earlier manager, Tony Wilson, who served fifteen years for murder. I must have met Fever. In fact, in my righteous fury I think I went over to tackle him when Eva hopped it, because I thought he'd encouraged it. As far as I recall, he put me right and gave me a free pint to calm me down.'

'Nevertheless,' Cara said firmly, 'whether Eva did or not have old friends to call on round here, she told me that Carlos most certainly did, so we must follow that up. *You* can help out there.'

'OK by me.' That was sorted then. Cara was on the warpath.

Then she became my Cara again. 'Jack, do you really think Eva could have had something to do with Carlos's death?'

No point in beating about the bush, and we were in this together. 'She's capable and stupid enough to have let rip, but whether she did or not – well, who knows? If she did bring a pistol with her . . . I'll find out what's happening on the police investigation,' I finished hastily, seeing her face fall. Then I stepped awkwardly out of my comfort zone – and probably hers. 'And you, daughter mine, are you happy in Suffolk?'

'Yes, and for ever after.' She laughed, which for once made me struggle with resentment at having missed so many years of her life. For what? Had they ill-treated her, ignored her, cosseted her? As Cara never talked about it, I wasn't foolish enough to cross-examine her further. But I had my doubts, and that laugh had sounded just a trifle forced.

'Just a phrase,' she added airily. 'I'm not a great hand at being Mother Earth though, so Harry shoulders most of that. I work part-time for a local publisher, which suits me fine, and then help Harry out the rest of the week. We're running a farm shop now.'

'Don't miss the bright lights of London?'

'No way.'

'What if Eva . . .?' No, that was a step too far. Cara had retreated into Miss Self-Assurance again, and I didn't want to throw her off with a nightmare that might never happen. I need not have worried.

'Wants to move in with Harry and me?' she picked up. 'I'll refuse, don't worry.' She looked closely at me. 'And you need not worry about her moving in with you again either. She's determined to return to The Family.'

My turn to laugh partly in relief. The Family was a joke between us, and I had no doubt it would close its protective arms around Eva in due course, but it was good to hear this reaffirmed. Then I sobered up. 'Suppose she really did kill Carlos and it's me who finds the evidence?'

She came over to me and kissed me in a motherly sort of way. 'We'll sort this together, Jack. And now,' she added, 'drive me back to the station, will you? I fancy a lift in that Gordon-Keeble of yours.'

'Good taste,' I said approvingly. As Dad had bought it from its first owner in the late 1960s, I had known it all my life. It felt a family car therefore, and it was only fitting that its rare outing (due to an accident that had left it fragile) should be for Cara's benefit – even if she had ordered her 'taxi' in her best schoolteacher tones.

All went quiet for a day or two, which was both a relief and a worrying sign. Silence is not always golden: sometimes it's creepy. I tried to contact Brandon in vain; he replied with a put-off message that told me nothing. Cara had told me she would let me know immediately of any developments her end and undertook to investigate the story of the floozie, while my best – my only – course of action was to pursue the contacts that Carlos had had here in his previous life.

He had last come here (as far as my current information went) in the late 1980s for some years and had left when he ran off with Eva in 1991. Carlos and the Charros had been formed locally and presumably from local musicians, but where were they now? He was unlikely to have made any new contacts in Kent during his absence, so as Eva had said he was contacting former band members, I should do the same (even though this might have been one of her inventions). I'd forget about other lines of enquiry. Not that I could think of any, in fact.

Further Internet research on the Charros brought painfully meagre results, as did local newspaper archives. A few fuzzy photos and a few more places where they had held gigs. I was getting nowhere.

I heard nothing from Daisy for a day or two, for which I was grateful, although on that score I had one not very helpful nugget to follow up which had been thrown at me by Dave. Otherwise progress on Melody had been non-existent. That was odd in itself as her colour alone would help her stand out. I had taken the number plate in to Dave and been duly laughed all the way out again. He told me there had been no reports of any abandoned Minors, let alone pinky-grey ones, only this nugget of a sighting. Not a situation to get excited about: a thought that failed to cheer.

Just as I was nerving myself up to set off on Saturday morning on a carefully planned casual call on Eva, Zoe came over to the farmhouse. By grace and favour she and Len sometimes devote Saturday mornings to jobs that particularly interest them. Zoe wanted to know whether I was aware that Len was chatting about Morris Minors with a gorgeous blonde and could I please do something about it as she needed to consult him about a warped cylinder head and gorgeous blondes were my province not hers.

I groaned and accompanied Zoe to the Pits, where Daisy greeted me with her usual sunny smile and my clouds lifted a little. 'No firm news yet,' I said brightly, 'but lines to follow up.' I tried to give the impression that I had been working non-stop on Melody.

She looked somewhat bleak at this as she interrupted: 'Gran might help.'

'I thought you didn't want her to know Melody is missing?'

'No, but I had to tell her. She was incandescent, but she's—'

But then another gorgeous blonde arrived – although perhaps the hair had had a little help in this case. Gran was here in person.

I'd had a vague stereotyped image of a decrepit white-haired old lady forced to give up her beloved Morris Minor because she wasn't safe to drive any longer and had had to move into sheltered accommodation through declining health. What roared into the Frogs Hill forecourt was a stylish slim lady in a huge classic red Thunderbird convertible, which when it first came out was Ford's answer to the Chevrolet Corvette. This Thunderbird, however, was a two-door 1958 model, bigger and fatter than the original and made for large empty roads, of which America had plenty and the UK most certainly did not.

It churned up the gravel and drew up with a flourish. Out stepped Gran, looking in her forties, rather than the sixty-or even seventy-year-old she must be. She was clad in tight jeans, an elegant jacket, and a sporty hat and was clutching designer sunglasses.

'So there you are, darling,' she said briskly to Daisy, after a friendly wave to the rest of us and a disdainful look at the battered Volvo. 'What's the news about Melody?'

'Jack's a firm line on her,' Daisy lied unblushingly. 'He's a car detective. I've borrowed Justie's dad's wheels.'

Gran marched round the offending object. 'Justin's father, Daisy, has no style. One should always drive cars with which one feels an affinity, don't you agree, Mr Colby?'

I did. I wouldn't claim that owners grow to look like their cars, but they certainly acquire a relationship with them that goes beyond paying the maintenance bills. Gran then advanced towards me and, still stunned at this apparition, I shook her hand.

'Tell me what this lead is on Melody,' she demanded.

'Not a strong one.' I borrowed Brandon's get-out. 'Early days.'

She regarded me scornfully. 'To find a *Rose Taupe* Morris Minor?'

'Yes.'

She looked at me keenly and nodded. 'Don't leave it too long. Subject closed.'

Now, I thought, for the scarlet beauty. 'Is this Thunderbird yours?'

'It is. Rest assured I gave up car theft years ago.'

My admiration grew. She wasn't in her forties, she might be in her seventies, but I liked *her* style. 'Had it long?'

'Two years. I thought, why not? I've always wanted one, and Melody was on the small side for me. I love this red beast.' She patted the Thunderbird lovingly.

I could see that she did. I wondered whether Kent's small lanes would cherish it as much as she did, however. Passing places are for normal-size cars not this monster, delightful though it was. The 1958 model was the first of the larger four-passenger models, and Len and Zoe had already shot out to inspect its innards.

'Where do you live?' I asked Gran curiously. 'California?'

'No. Out near Wormslea on the Downs,' she said blithely. 'I need a car to get around.'

She was right. Wormslea is a very small village and probably the nearest it ever got to public transport was the First World War landing ground on its outskirts. A Thunderbird nearby must be livening up its life considerably.

'It was either this or a horse and cart,' she explained. 'The folks at my current residence would have found that difficult to cope with. Now, young man,' she addressed me briskly, 'I hear you have a Gordon-Keeble and a Lagonda. And this restoration garage. I need to see them all. Do you tweet?'

'Sometimes, but—'

'I'll follow you. Blog?'

'Yes, but—'

'I'll guest for you. Regularly, if you wish. Now, Daisy tells me you need me, so I came immediately. Besides, I thought you might like Juno.'

'Who?' I was thrown again.

She looked at me pityingly. 'No education nowadays. Thunderbird. Juno, goddess. Wife of Jupiter the Thunderer.'

I laughed. 'Stupid of me. Yes, I did want to meet you. Daisy tells me you knew the May Tree and the Charros band.'

She looked at me speculatively. 'You could say that. The murder. I thought as much. It was your wife that Carlos Mendez ran off with.'

'Yes. How well did you know the May Tree?'

She looked somewhat bewildered. 'Very well, thanks. I co-owned it with my husband.'

'James Fever?' I reeled. 'You bought the May Tree after Tony Wilson went inside?'

'Correct. I'm Belinda Fever, known to the band as the Feverbird. I bought Melody after James died. He'd have loved her *and* Juno. The father of Daisy's young man now owns the pub.'

'*Not* my young man,' Daisy said belligerently.

'Nonsense,' Gran informed her. 'You're ideally suited. I *like* Justin.'

Diplomacy was clearly not Gran's strong point. 'Carlos Mendez,' I said firmly to get back on track.

'I could do with a coffee.'

This took some time, and we were sitting in the garden together with refreshments by the time Gran Belinda was ready to impart whatever information she had. I was beginning to fear that was very little.

'So you're in the frame for Carlos's murder, Jack?' Belinda obviously believed in getting right to the point.

'Half in, half out. My ex-wife came down here to join Carlos.'

'And now you want to find out all you can about Carlos and the Charros. Didn't you know the band at the time?'

'No. I was too busy babysitting – the May Tree must have been Eva's territory.'

'Ah. I see now.' She nodded thoughtfully. 'Suppose you show me the Gordon-Keeble first?'

Was she deliberately employing delaying tactics? If so, she'd hit the right one. 'You drive a hard bargain,' I told her. Daisy, Belinda and I walked round to the barn where the Gordon-Keeble lives together with the Lagonda. 'You do things in style, Jack,' she commented. 'That rear arch needs looking at though.'

I hadn't noticed. Typical that I'd missed it. The cobbler's daughter goes unshod, as they say. For cobbler's daughter read garage owner's own wheels. I'm devoted to my classics – so devoted that I don't always *see* them when I look at them.

My respect for Belinda grew. She'd even heard the rumour

that there was another Gordon-Keeble in existence, in addition
to the accepted one hundred. 'I love legends, Jack, especially
car legends.'

'Have you ever driven one?' I asked. Mistake.

She brightened up. 'No. Shall we—'

My turn to set the conditions. 'Afterwards. Talk first.'

'Talk about Melody,' Daisy put in meaningfully.

I took the hint. Time to produce my nugget and blow it up
as much as I morally could or she would be on my case night
and day. Dave had told me that a Rose Taupe Morris Minor
had recently been seen on Bluebell Hill. Bluebell Hill is a
picturesque name for a road, and if one can forget the traffic
on this fast dual carriageway and think of the lane it had once
been years ago, winding itself up the Downs with woods on
either side, it still is. Prehistoric man certainly thought so.

'When are we going there?' Daisy demanded.

'*I'll* go as soon as possible. No point your coming with me
since there's no guarantee it will be seen there again.'

Daisy scowled, but gave way gracefully when I pointed out
that meant Melody might still be around in the neighbourhood
and hadn't been whisked off to foreign parts. 'OK then. Get
back to this dinosaur band of yours, but go over to Bluebell
Hill, Jack.'

I agreed I would, and then kicked off, as Belinda had
consented to delay her drive. 'Did you know Carlos well?'

'Of course. He used to come to the May Tree with his friend
Matt Wright, and after I'd known them some months Carlos
told me about his idea for the band. That would have been
about 1987. He was rather a nice young man then, about thirty
or so, and a first-class musician and leader, so I encouraged
them, with the result that the Carlos and the Charros band was
formed and often played at the May Tree. Carlos told me he
knew all about mariachi bands because his father ran one and
had often played in Kent. That's how he had first met Matt
and would stay with him occasionally. Then I think the family
went back to Mexico for a few years. Both Carlos's parents
were Mexican so he could talk and behave Mexico one hundred
per cent.' Belinda paused. 'Is this the kind of thing you want
to know?'

'Go right ahead.'

She obliged. 'Matt became one of the Charros with three other young men and the singer. They were all with other bands when he found them, but he persuaded them to take their luck with him and learn new tricks. He poached them one by one, telling them they could make a fortune, and they were well on their way to doing so. Carlos was always the leader, playing the vihuela. Josie – the singer – had a magnificent voice. I can still hear it in my head. Love songs, blues, rock – she excelled at them all. Carlos persuaded them all to give up their day jobs and play full time at weddings and other events. Then he grew bored, said he wanted wider horizons, and off he went with your wife. The band, being British-reared not Mexican, fell apart, and there they were, jobless. Not unnaturally they blamed Carlos.'

'Do you know where they are now?'

'Of course,' she replied, but did not offer any details. 'I was fond of them all. Dear Josie. She's the daughter of one of our former barmaids, Betty Gibson – we took her over with the pub. With her dark hair and eyes, Josie could have passed for Mexican or Spanish. Carlos taught her flamenco dancing – and other things.'

'Other dances?'

'The dance of life, my friend. Carlos was Josie's lover for three, maybe four years. He cast quite a spell, that one. Until he met his match.' She glanced at me, clearly amused. 'Eva Colby.' She was trying to goad me.

'A long time ago,' I said lightly, wondering if Eva had known of Josie's other role in Carlos's life – and vice versa.

'And now she is back and Carlos is dead.'

There was no innuendo in Belinda's voice but it brought the situation home to me in stark clarity. 'Where is Josie now?'

'After Carlos abandoned her, she drank,' Gran Fever said matter-of-factly. 'No more singing, no more bands. Now she is a trained live-in carer.'

'Locally?'

'Certainly. She's employed by an archaeologist, Dr Keith Fairbourne, to look after his father full time. He, too, was an archaeologist.'

'Not Ambrose Fairbourne?' I'd heard of him years ago. 'Specialized in Kentish history and archaeology and was always appearing on local radio and television?'

'Yes. He was a great man. Josie is very happy there.' She moved on, it seemed to me rather quickly. 'The other Charros suffered too. Jonathan Lamb who played the violin went through a very sad time, poor man. But he has recovered and runs an interior decoration business called The House of Lamb near Canterbury. He works with another member of the band, Clive Miller, who played bass guitar. He served a prison sentence for drugs after the band split up and Jonathan gave him a job. An unlikely partnership but it works well.'

'So they don't bear bitterness?'

'You must ask them.'

Her tone was matter of fact. Little speculation for Belinda Fever, I thought. Just the minimum. For the moment that suited me, although it suggested that if I needed to probe further it wouldn't be welcomed.

'That's two Charros and Josie. And there was Matt Wright as well.'

'Yes. Matt played the other guitar. He's had a hard time. Went to pieces after the band split up and never fully recovered. He does odd jobs when he's up to it, garden and house.'

'And the last?' I felt I was pushing even for the facts now, and I wondered why. What had her own relationship with Carlos been? She would have been older than he and apparently happily married, but had there been friction between them? Love even? What had been her attitude to Eva's conquest of Carlos?

'The last was Neil Watson. The other violin,' she replied.

'Where will I find him?'

A pause. Then she said: 'A question of faith, my friend. Neil killed himself after the band dispersed.'

I was shaken. 'And Carlos made the mistake of returning.'

'His death is not forgotten.'

FOUR

'**G**ran, that's *awful,*' Daisy said as I took in the implications of what Belinda had told us. And implications there were in plenty now it was clear that Carlos's actions were far from being buried in the mists of time.

'Yes,' Belinda agreed. Calm though she sounded, she must realize that this was highly relevant for Carlos's death. Four people – all with good reason to want their revenge.

'Have you told the police?' I asked. This sounded a crass question, but I needed to know.

'No. What should I tell them? I've no doubt they are by now fully aware of Carlos's past history with the band.'

'They are, but they might not know how strongly *it* still feels about Carlos.'

Belinda shrugged. 'They'll find out quickly enough if they want to. None of the Charros has anything to hide.'

I felt I was driving into muddy lanes here. Had Carlos deliberately chosen to stir up old emotions, or had he not realized what he might be running into? But how, I wondered, could his erstwhile colleagues have known he was back in their area? Had he told them or had they learned through the professional grapevine? Neither ticked enough boxes.

Belinda seemed to be more fully involved than her detachment suggested, so I probed further. 'Do the Charros still see each other?'

'At least once a year.'

Did I imagine a slight hesitation – and did it mean anything if so?

'On the ninth of July,' Belinda continued. 'That's the day on which Neil killed himself in 1992, and Jonathan Lamb hosts a lunch in his memory for those who knew him well.'

'That's a *long* time ago,' Daisy said in awe. 'I wasn't even *born* then.'

'A happy day for us all when you were.' Belinda smiled at Daisy.

I wasn't going to get deflected – if that had been Belinda's intention. 'Do you take part in the anniversary lunch?' I'd been watching her and reckoned it was worth a guess. To draw together friends – presumably all the Charros – to commemorate Neil was admirable from one point of view but surely strange from another. Why remind themselves so *formally* of an unhappy period in all their lives? It suggested that a wish for revenge might not be so unlikely after all. Not forgetting Neil was good, but not if it meant the Charros had not moved on in life.

'I go every year,' Belinda answered, 'and Betty Gibson comes too.' Her eyes dared me to ask why the barmaid and the late pub owner's widow should attend, with its implication that the May Tree was more a home to the Charros than simply a venue.

I accepted their challenge. 'Why? What's held you all together for so long?'

'I'm not sure I can answer that. Ask Jonathan. He's the prime mover.'

The Charros had failed as a band for reasons beyond most of their control, and Neil's memory was so treasured that it glued them together. Was the lunch just the loving remembrance it seemed or had it become a ritual that suggested more than that? I had an image of the weird suppers that a rich Parisian gourmet held centuries back for the mighty and wealthy of Paris. They began by entering a room in complete darkness from which they were ushered into another candlelit one, the central table of which was thoughtfully surmounted by a coffin. I couldn't believe the Charros' lunch was anything as way out as that, but nevertheless I wondered very much what did happen there.

I prowled restlessly around Frogs Hill after Belinda and Daisy eventually departed in Thunderbird and Volvo respectively – Daisy with much reluctance, not because she liked my company but because I was her only possible link to Melody. Belinda left me with a stern order to me to: 'Find Melody for Daisy.'

I had honoured my word and taken them both to the pub
in Piper's Green for lunch, driven in state in the Gordon-
Keeble. Daisy clearly thought the Gordon-Keeble was
second-best to the Lagonda, but Belinda was truly hooked,
and I allowed her to drive back to Frogs Hill, at her insistence.
I reckoned that anyone who could handle a Thunderbird on
the North Downs could cope with my beloved car. As I
explained, I'm very careful with the Gordon-Keeble owing to
its earlier accident, which, despite Len's magnificent restoration job, left it vulnerable. Every year he toils away murmuring
darkly that it's touch and go whether it will pass the MOT,
and every year it does. Of course it does, it's a Gordon-Keeble
– and Belinda had loved it.

She had not offered to give me the Charros' contact details,
but I was confident that I had enough information to track them
down easily enough. I decided to leave Josie for the moment
and tackle Jonathan Lamb, who was simple to trace because
of the House of Lamb design business. An affable recorded
voice informed me that the office was closed until Monday
morning but that I could ring or visit then.

There was no news from Cara, which was disappointing,
and no word from Eva, which was a relief. I don't know quite
what I was dreading, but somehow silence seemed a good
thing. Len and Zoe were still working flat out on the Alvis
despite the fact that it was well into the afternoon, and they
didn't need any interruptions from me – even if they'd noticed
I was around. So I decided to seek out Liz Potter, who runs
a garden centre on the outskirts of Piper's Green. She and I
are in the comfortable position of being amiable former lovers.
The only snag would arise if her nerd husband Colin was
on the scene, but with any luck he'd be chasing microbes in
a lab somewhere. He's some kind of scientist. Where Liz and
I are concerned, it is a case of all passion spent, as Milton put
it. Passion had reigned for a year and a half when I first
returned to England from the oil trade, although that included
passion of all sorts, including the occasional flying potted plant
during the latter stages. Her garden centre includes a good
café for lunch and coffee, so it is equally convenient for practical reasons, as well as for seeing Liz from time to time. Not

too often, though, or husband Colin takes the hump. Liz wouldn't care about that, but I did on her behalf. I am not his favourite person, even though she was not married to him or anyone during our affair and I, too, had been single.

I walked to the garden centre, deciding that the footpath route would do me good. I purposely left my mobile behind on the basis that any bad news could be avoided for a while longer. Liz is a busy person so I am never sure what my reception will be. Today, however, her wellington boots stopped in their tracks when she saw me. I hoped that there would be a grin of welcome but there wasn't. Instead she looked anxious.

'I've heard the news, Jack,' she began alarmingly. 'Come into the office if you want to talk.'

Even more alarming. Her office is a cubbyhole overlooking her attractive layout of tables, flower-beds and blooms, so it was a bad sign that she took me there and not, as usual, to the café. 'It'll be more private here,' she explained with a look of sympathy that I did not like at all. Liz's sympathy usually takes the form of 'I told you so'.

'What news?' I asked. 'About Carlos's murder?'

'Well, yes. Is it Eva?'

I went cold.

'It was on the radio,' she continued uncertainly, obviously having read my expression correctly. 'They said a woman had been arrested, and as she was his wife I assumed it was her and that you knew.'

'No,' I said numbly. 'I didn't.' All I could think was that it *could* be Eva and I'd been blithely ignorant of what was going on. Len and Zoe aren't great ones for listening to news broadcasts and nor am I.

'I'm sorry,' Liz said. 'Want to talk?'

'I don't think I can, Liz.' My brain seemed to be a crazy carousel of stray thoughts spinning round and round and up and down. Why hadn't Cara rung me? Why hadn't Brandon? How was Eva herself? Did she have anyone with her? Why hadn't *she* rung me?

'Old feelings rising?' Liz asked.

'Yes – *no*. Liz—'

'You feel involved? Responsibility?'

I managed to translate this into a coherent thought. 'Because of Cara, yes. It has to be unlikely that Eva will be charged. She might have *wanted* to kill Carlos, but she's too fond of her own skin to actually have shot him.' I wasn't sure I believed that, but I hoped it was true.

'Anything I can do?'

I reached out for Liz's hand. 'You're here, and that's good. Carlos had some girlfriend over here, so Eva claims. Maybe she did it, or else . . . Liz, I'll have to get going. Make some calls.'

'Make them here. I'll vanish.'

'Thanks, Liz, but no. I walked here, and the way back will give me time to—'

'To what, Jack?' she asked, as I paused. I'd been going to say 'time to think' but I wasn't sure it would work that way.

'No idea,' I admitted. 'Get my emotional armour on?'

'Knights of old galloping to the rescue? Pageboy here when required, Jack. You know that.'

I gave her a kiss and was halfway out of the door when she threw at me: 'What did you come here for, anyway? To buy a dozen red roses?'

I groaned. I was losing my grip. 'To ask if you know someone called Jonathan Lamb.'

'Yes. Not well though. House designer. Did some work for a chum of ours.'

'He was in Carlos's band, I'm told. Does the name Neil Watson mean anything to you?'

'No – wait a bit. There was some story about a lad in that band who killed himself.'

'That's it. What's Jonathan Lamb like? I'm going to see him on Monday.'

'Successful, smooth, likeable, clever, introverted, sharp – how much more do you want?'

'That's enough. Thanks, Liz.'

Once again I was already at the door when she called out: 'Jonathan Lamb, Jack. He and this Neil Watson were an item. That's why I remembered it. Jonathan's gay.'

So the reason for the annual lunch was established. Was it the reason for murder too?

* * *

By the time I reached Frogs Hill I was in control again. Brandon first. Result? DCI Brandon was not available, I was told. It was his weekend off. I told the sergeant that DCI Brandon *was* available this weekend and that the true answer was that he didn't fancy talking to Jack Colby. Try again. This time Brandon was there, a bad sign in itself, and I prepared myself for the worst.

He sounded remarkably human, however, and didn't try any of this 'can't discuss it' stuff. Well, not much. 'Early days,' he trotted out as usual. 'But I'm afraid it's true that Eva Mendez has been arrested.'

'Enough evidence to charge her with?'

'Waiting on the CPS.' Fair enough. The Crown Prosecution Service is there to give guidance over charging. Then Brandon added, 'Afraid there's not much chance we won't go ahead though.'

I thanked him – genuinely. Presumably, I had been and still might be on the suspect list and at the very least I was an interested party, and so Brandon was unlikely to keep me abreast of events from now on. Dave was another matter, however. Brandon could talk to him as a colleague in the Car Crime Unit, and Dave *might* talk to me. He knows by now that I can respect boundaries.

Dave and I get on well – and never had that been as important as now. He might know what was going on, especially as they work out of the same HQ at Charing. Not for the first time Dave was on voicemail. He, too, tries to guard his weekends like most of us, but he rang back quickly.

'Sorry, Jack. I know this must be a major headache for you. I've checked into it and at least Brandon isn't after you as a co-conspirator. Where were you on Monday night, incidentally? Joke,' he added hastily.

'What's he got on Eva?' I asked. 'He can't seriously be thinking Eva got it into her head to rush out of the hotel to Allington Lock and murder her husband.'

'Actually yes, Jack. He does. Your wife—'

'No longer my wife,' I replied automatically.

'Don't quibble,' Dave said dismissively. 'Mendez went out in his car that evening just before nine and the car was duly

found parked near where he was found. Your former wife lied
about not leaving the hotel. They've tracked down the taxi
that dropped her at the lock itself at about ten fifteen. I
gather that was on the other side of the river from the crime
scene. Hotel reports they'd had a flaming row during dinner,
loud enough to disturb the other customers and be heard by
the staff. Another taxi picked her up on the crime-scene side
of the river near the Kent Life museum at about eleven p.m.
Hotel reports her return there at about eleven thirty. Estimated
time of death for Carlos Mendez between nine and eleven
p.m. Not too bright, your Eva.'

I thought furiously. There must be a flaw in this. Dave was
right. It was a crazy story. For a start if Eva had been dropped
at Allington Lock itself she would not have thought about
crossing the river unless Carlos had specifically told her where
he was due to transact his 'business'. Then my heart sank as
I thought that it would be just like Eva to forget the details
and remember them too late, sending her rushing across . . .
No, I'd go no further.

'What about the pub?' I asked. 'Didn't anybody there see
or hear anything? There's a large outside seating area.'

'Apparently not. Brandon said the body was quite a way
from the pub, on the far side of the bridge and sluice and
hidden in undergrowth.'

'Right. It was. And the noise of the sluice meant no one
would have heard anything anyway. Of course. Very useful
spot for a murder.' My brain was spinning like a washing
machine without its cleansing properties. 'Did Eva pack a gun
in her luggage?' I still couldn't believe that.

'Don't know, but no gun's yet been found at the crime scene,
although they're still checking the river. Trouble is, Carlos
himself was in the habit of packing a Smith and Wesson with
his underwear. Evidence from the Mexican police is that he
always carried one.'

That was cautiously good news. Eva wouldn't have the nous
to be clever over removing the gun and hiding it somewhere
less than obvious. 'Trace evidence?' I asked. 'DNA?'

'Lab's still working on it. But there was an imprint of a
high heel or two in the earth. It doesn't look good, Jack.'

He was right, and we both knew it. 'What's her story?' I might as well know the worst.

'Guess what. She thought Carlos was meeting a woman so she admits she dashed out to find him. She thought he was in one of the moored boats on the lock side of the river, but he wasn't, so she crossed the bridge thinking he might have gone to one of those moored on the far side, but went nowhere near the point where he was found, and as there was no sign of him she then went home.'

Then went home. If anything more was needed to convince me that Eva's story was economical with the truth those words nailed it down. An Eva in pursuit of Carlos and a floozie would not have given up and just gone home. Never.

I waited impatiently for Monday, eager to get on with something, anything, that might help me get to the truth of the situation. Cara was Eva's next of kin, and former husbands did not rank in the list of those to be informed, even through Dave as intermediary. My fear was that Eva had indeed murdered Carlos. In vain I told myself how unlikely this was, because each time I did so, I remembered those intemperate rages of hers when she was beside herself with unfounded jealousy. She had not changed. Who else but Eva would even consider a tryst might be taking place on a towpath at nearly midnight in showery, cool Maytime?

Come to that, I still thought it was an odd place for a business meeting. Unless a boat was indeed involved. That would make sense – frightening sense. I reminded myself that both Carlos and Eva had been on the opposite bank to the lock, but there were boats on both sides of the river and they were an obvious line of enquiry that Brandon would be pursuing.

I repeatedly rang Cara without success or a return call and grew increasingly jittery. On her home landline, I did reach Harry, but he simply told me Cara wasn't there – either he was the uncommunicative sort or was protecting Cara's whereabouts on her own instructions. Even from her father? That really made me feel great, and even my two classics failed in their duty to comfort me.

When Sunday, Monday and several hours of Tuesday morning passed without news, I felt like a Ford deprived of its V8, empty and unable to move in any direction. And then Cara drove up, looking so drawn and white that all thought of reproach left me. She wasted no time.

'Eva's been charged, Dad.'

I hardly noticed her use of 'Dad'. The nightmare was upon us.

'She'll get bail, Cara,' I said firmly. No point uttering panaceas such as 'it's all a mistake'.

Luckily, she was still in 'coping' mode. 'I suppose they think she'll flee the country?'

She was right. That was possible. Because of her Spanish birth, Eva was an EU citizen, so she wouldn't get far by heading for Europe, but returning to South America might be on the cards. Nevertheless, as for fleeing: 'She couldn't find her own way out of a paper bag, let alone this mess,' I reassured Cara. 'Where is she?'

'Still with the police.'

'If she gets bail—' I couldn't frame the words. They sounded too inadequate, so selfish in this situation.

Cara understood anyway. 'She won't come here. Not suitable.'

I realized she was right, thank heavens. With the kind of restrictions there were likely to be on her bail if granted, Frogs Hill would hardly be ideal. So next came the vital question: 'Can you stay in Kent?'

'As much as I can.'

'At Frogs Hill?'

'I'd love to, but someone has to look after Eva. I can't inflict her on Harry, so I'll sort out something to rent in the Maidstone area.' She looked at me and grinned. 'Your face, Jack. It's a picture.'

'A bleak one, I imagine. I'm not doing much to help.'

'Wrong. You, Jack dear, are the one who is going to get us out of this mess. I don't believe Eva shot him, but she is going to be one hell of her own worst enemy while you're trying to prove it.'

I had my orders and I was happy with them, but I looked at her face and saw that despite the assurance the other Cara was hovering very close. 'Are you secretly afraid she *might* be guilty, sweetheart?'

Her relief was obvious. 'Yes.'

'So am I. But the likelihood is that she isn't. Which means I'll turn every stone I can upside down to find the toads that might be hiding beneath.'

She managed a giggle. 'I like toads.'

'So do I. But one of them might be in disguise.'

Seeing Cara had heartened me, and driving out to see my first potential toad that afternoon, I was just in the mood for Jonathan Lamb. I'd already decided he was a smooth cuss and probably a murderer, and no amount of telling myself I was somewhat in advance of the facts did any good. I had little doubt that I was following in Brandon's footsteps and that Lamb would probably slam the door in my face, but he'd find it a hard door to shut.

When I drew up at the House of Lamb, which was on the outskirts of Canterbury, it was clear that it was nothing like Liz's garden centre. Its declared aim, according to its website, was to consider interior and exterior as one, whether the interior was house or flat and the exterior was garden or patio and window sills. The building in front of me, combined with the neat parking area and small garden, bore this out with colourful window boxes echoed by tubs and flower plantings. There were several cars in the parking area, and I had little doubt that the Bristol 411 was Jonathan's, even if it didn't seem to go with my idea of a murderer. But as I have never made a study of murderers' cars, who was I to judge?

I gave my name to the receptionist (trying not to look too bullish), fully expecting the answer that I could take a running jump and lose myself. I was somewhat surprised therefore when Jonathan Lamb himself emerged and, with a welcoming smile, ushered me into his sanctum. A wolf in toad's clothing? I wasn't sure. He was in his mid forties, I guessed, smartly dressed but not the oily operator I had expected. His curly hair and rugged looks suggested he would be as at home on a country walk as in a five-star restaurant. Nor did his office display the clinical decor I expected. There were photos everywhere of designer houses and gardens, but they were good ones: attractive, rather than fighting the landscapes that surrounded them. Even the chair he offered me looked solid enough to take my weight rather than being a sophisticated piece of moulded plastic.

'I'm sorry to hear the news about Eva,' he said.

'You knew her?' I was surprised. I had imagined Carlos had kept his affair with Eva low profile. Stupid really. Eva would never be low profile.

'Oh yes. We all remember Eva Colby.'

'Was she that much in evidence at the May Tree?'

He considered this. 'No, but when she was there she left an impression, shall we say. She oozed, if you'll forgive me, trouble.'

'Did she pick on Carlos or vice versa?' I decided it would be prudent to leave my knowledge of Josie's role out of it for the moment.

'Difficult to say. Carlos fancied her, that was clear, but he liked money and I think he imagined she had more than she did. He was strapped for cash. The Charros were doing well but not well enough for him to create a new life for himself and Eva in the style to which they were both accustomed.'

'He managed it somehow. Probably with the help of Eva's relations. Incidentally, did she ring you to tell you she was back in Kent?'

'No. Nor,' he added, 'did Carlos. I imagine that's what you want to know, isn't it?' He looked at me ironically.

'Is it so obvious?'

'If it was my partner, even a former one, I'd do the same as you.'

I liked that. 'I'm rooting around trying to find a reason for Carlos's death. The police think they have got the measure of Eva, but something drew Carlos back here.'

'What you really mean is that you're fishing around to see who might have killed Carlos if she didn't.' He said it lightly and, I think, without intending to give offence. He couldn't do that, in fact, as it was true.

'Yes,' I answered him.

'And you think the answer lies in the Charros?'

'I amend that to Carlos's past.'

'Good. Well, you're on fertile ground with our former band. None of us had any reason to love him for what he did to us. He left us with mud on our white Charro suits. How could a Mexican band work without a Mexican? No way. So we had to hang up our whites and do the best we could in other fields. It was a tough time.'

I was aware that someone else had entered the room, and I looked round as Jonathan greeted him. 'Hi, Clive. Friend to see us. Eva Colby's husband. Clive was bass guitar, Jack.'

Clive Miller was no smooth Jonathan. He was a burly man also in his forties, but with suspicious eyes and a closed-in look that warned me it would take some time to get on easy terms with him. 'Once,' he grunted. 'Don't play a note now. What are *you* here for?'

The emphasis on the 'you' indicated he didn't see me as a potential chum.

'Because Eva's been charged—'

'With Mendez's murder. That scum. He deserved all he got.'

In my book very few people deserve to be murdered, and Carlos was not one of them, dislikable though he might have been.

'He wasn't top of my list of favourite people either,' I replied, 'and my marriage to Eva is history. But with her arrest and my daughter in a spin –' (forgive me, Cara) – 'I'm trying to gather all I can on Mendez's background.'

A long silence, then: 'You're with the police, aren't you?' Clive hurled at me.

'Car theft is my line, not murder. I help out in cases where classic cars are nicked. Specialist area. I like the Bristol, Jonathan.'

'Thank you,' Jonathan said, perhaps too politely. I was aware that I was very much under scrutiny from both of them.

Clive brushed the topic of cars aside, fixing me with a look that indicated his stocky barrel-like figure was ready for a punch-up and only Jonathan's presence was stopping him. 'So you thought you'd prefer to pin the murder on us? No way, mate, no way. That scumbag wouldn't have dared to show his face to us, let alone meet us. We'd be the last people to whom he'd announce his arrival. We heard it through the grapevine. He knew what his reception would have been if he'd come to see us. If it hadn't been for Jon here giving me a job I'd have been a complete washout. I did a spell in prison for drugs after he went and—'

Jonathan quickly intervened. 'Clive's right. Carlos would keep well away from us. And I've been lucky. Clive and I make a good team here. We're doing OK.'

'What about the rest of the band?' I wondered what Clive would have gone on to say.

Jonathan looked amused. 'If you're thinking of Matt Wright, don't bother. He can't plan his own breakfast, let alone a murder. And as for Josie, she's well established now and wouldn't give Carlos the time of day if he contacted her. Not that he would dare. All of us are anxious to leave things be, not stir them up.'

'So if he didn't contact any of you direct, what was the grapevine through which you heard the news?'

A pause, then Jonathan spoke. 'I didn't tell you, Clive. I thought the news Carlos was back might upset you. He did ring Josie to tell her he was coming down to promote business.'

I noted that Jonathan was no George Washington when it came to parting with information. If Carlos had used the word promote, however, did that imply he was simply trying to arrange more gigs rather than raise cash, I wondered. Somehow I didn't think so.

Clive took the information badly. 'Upset, Jon? Too bloody right I would have been *upset*. Bad enough knowing that creep was back, let alone having Josie put through the mincer again.'

'It's past history, Clive,' Jonathan murmured, then turned to me. 'Now, Jack, do think about it. Is it at all likely that after all this time any of us would get to the point of ruining our lives for a *second* time with an attack on Carlos?'

'Unlikely,' I agreed, just to please him, though I wondered just how upset Clive would have to be to go into action. Spur of the moment rage could surely not be ruled out.

'Carlos Mendez was a coward through and through. Right, Clive?' Jonathan said.

'Yes,' Clive snarled.

'It's worked out brilliantly my working with Clive here,' Jonathan continued. 'We have our own homes and our own partners, and Clive has two kids to whom I'm godfather. As I said, we're OK. And, what's more, we were there at our respective homes the night Carlos was killed, as we told the police when they came on the same errand as you.' His pleasant voice glossed over the underlying 'so get lost' message.

I decided I would put one last oar into these apparently untroubled waters. 'And Neil Watson?'

Jonathan seemed prepared for that and to have considered his matter-of-fact reply: 'Neil and I were lovers. When he killed himself I thought my world had ended. But it hadn't. And because of that I and the other Charros choose to honour him with a lunch each year. Does that make sense?'

It did – in a way.

I drove home to Frogs Hill contemplating what, if anything, I had achieved and where to go next. I now had a basis at least on which to work: a clear statement that all the Charros members stuck together. To which I needed to add Matt Wright – and Josie Gibson, the singer who no longer sang and whom Carlos had rung to say he'd be back. When I reached the Pits, contemplation was over. Len was upset and Zoe in a foul temper.

'Blame Miss Angel Face,' she said savagely. 'We're not going to get the Alvis finished today.'

So nothing new there, but how did Daisy come into it? 'Is Daisy still here?' I asked warily.

'No, but she was mooning around here all morning. She'd taken a day off work to so-called "help" you find that car of hers. She pestered Len for every bit of info he ever knew on Morris Minors.'

'Did she want anything in particular?'

'She didn't say, but the subtext was that she wanted results from you, Jack. *You.*'

Melody was back on the agenda for further action, if I could think of any. I had indeed gone to Bluebell Hill to see if by any chance a pinky-grey Morris Minor had by coincidence chosen the same time to share a major road with me. It had not, and I had put Melody aside with the crisis over Eva. Although I had not been able to take up Daisy's offer to hire me, the police had, and it was time I remembered that.

FIVE

Remembering Melody was all too easy. What proved more difficult over the next week was making progress on the case. I did my best. I was in touch with every Morris Minor and classic car club in the south-east of England. I scoured the Internet. I pestered Dave's Car Crime team about any Morris Minor reports and tried to establish whether either of the meagre two they had had reported could possibly be Melody masquerading under a quick paint job. Even I had to concede that neither of the two was the one I was seeking.

I had no choice. Daisy would have to be appeased. That meant I had to follow up a hunch so vague that I was still in two minds about even considering it, let alone mentioning it to the sunlight princess. With Eva now charged and on remand in Holloway prison, and Cara temporarily back in Suffolk, I was trying to sort fact from fiction over Mendez's murder. That had to be my priority, but I still needed to clear Melody off my plate.

The Pits, usually a source of economic anxiety because of its importance and the mortgage, became an escape route. The Alvis had departed and ceded its place to a 1950 Jowett Jupiter sports. This had arrived ignominiously on a low-loader, having defied the efforts of its owner and several specialists to diagnose why it refused to come out of its garage. To join discussions with Len and Zoe over their new patient was far preferable to following up dead ends in the Carlos case. Indeed, even Melody became an escape route compared with Eva's problems, and I launched myself with some pleasure into following up the hunch, even if it was pure fantasy on my part.

Considering the May Tree's name and despite my previous visits, I still harboured a childish image of lads and lasses in smocks frolicking in the sun under a blossoming tree on the green and once again was childishly disappointed at reality as

I arrived at the pub. No Shangri-La today, only spitting rain, empty tables, and a huge council recycling collection lorry looming up behind the chestnut tree, which looked damp and bedraggled and was fast approaching the end of its bloom. Tomorrow June would arrive, but there was a lack of cheer over the fast approaching summer. As I went inside the pub I saw a few lads and lasses in casual twenty-first century gear (not a smock to be seen), but I did spot Justin emerging to clear tables. Unfortunately, he spotted me too and immediately swung round to scuttle away – until I hailed him. He turned reluctantly round.

'Hi,' he said warily. 'Any news?'

'No. Have you?'

'Me? What do you mean?' No doubt about it, the lad was jittery.

'Huggett's barn,' I reminded him. 'Has Melody reappeared yet?'

He looked on more certain ground. 'Wouldn't expect her to, would you?'

'Actually, I would.' I took my gamble. 'It *was* you who ran off with Melody in the first place, wasn't it?'

Justin turned red, then white, then truculent as he managed to announce in one easy gasp: 'Dunnowhatyermean.'

'Come off it,' I said amiably. 'It was you who stole her.'

I'd never seen a jaw drop so dramatically. 'Not here,' he squeaked. 'I'm busy.'

Progress at last, and not a soul was taking any notice of us. 'So am I. Here. *Now.*'

He gave in. 'I didn't *steal* it,' he said mutinously.

'Took it then,' I agreed. 'Why?'

The poor lad seemed desperate, but as his eyes were so busy inspecting the ground he could find no answer for a while. Then: 'It's me and Daisy, see,' he muttered at last. 'I want to go serious.' His eyes, full of young hope, finally met mine.

'And that silly girl doesn't?' I prompted him.

His confidence increased slightly. 'She says I'm not her sort and she wants to see the world.'

'And so . . .' I prompted him again when he fell silent.

Then it came in a rush. 'I thought if I pinched Melody, I could, like, hunt for her, find her and bring her back to Daisy. Then she'd be grateful and we could go serious. I didn't steal it. I wanted to *find* Melody for her, but not with you around.'

Sometimes my hunches work. 'Right,' I said briskly. I quite understood why he hadn't wanted a third person present at Huggett's barn or wherever while the touching scene took place. 'That's understandable. So where is Melody now?'

'Don't know.'

'*What*?'

He looked as if he was about to burst into tears. 'Daisy went to the Old Bill, didn't she, so I got nervous. Couldn't take the car back just like that, so I put her in the car park at the Black Lion on the Canterbury road. A mate of mine works there, and if anyone asked he'd say it was his. I left one of the number plates in Huggett's, so as to make it all more mysterious and Daisy and me could talk over where Melody might be. Then I'd pretend to find Melody and drive her over to Daisy's in style.'

'So?' I asked grimly, when he came to a halt. 'What went wrong?'

'She's been nicked.'

I felt like howling in frustration and banging my head against a brick wall. I know the Black Lion. Its car park is a large one and all too accessible to anyone who fancied pinching a Morris Minor. Melody, it transpired, had disappeared only a few days after she had taken up residence there. Justin had abducted her on the ninth, handed her over to his chum four days later, and four days after that she had vanished again.

I pulled myself together, however, and offered to be peace-maker with Daisy. It was an offer Justin gratefully accepted, and so I called in at the Burchett Bakery on my way back to Frogs Hill. Daisy looked even lovelier at work. Clad in white overalls and surrounded by Chelsea buns, eclairs, pasties, loaves and jam tarts, she looked like Mother Earth's daughter – the object of every man's desire and the rewarder of none. I steeled myself to tell her the truth as soon as the shop was empty of customers, then duly broke the news to her and

waited for an explosion of outrage. It didn't come. Instead she
went dewy-eyed.

'He did that for me?' she breathed with awe.

'Yes.'

'Justie thought that up himself?'

'Yes.'

'Oh, the daft moron,' she said in loving tones.

'I'm afraid Melody really has gone, Daisy,' I warned her,
taken aback at this unexpectedly mild reaction.

'But Justie loves me.'

'Seems so,' I said, and assured her that my best efforts
would continue. Then I tiptoed out in order not to break her
idyllic dream of her future.

Women!

Frogs Hill brought me back to stark reality and failed to offer
its usual comfort when I returned. One look at Len and Zoe
made it clear that all was not going well with the Jowett.
Probably that was because, as I belatedly took in, Rob Lane
was there. Zoe's on-off boyfriend is the thorn in the Pits paradise but I don't enquire the current status of their relationship.
All I know is that he, as far as the Pits is concerned, is not
paradise but its counterpart.

'Sorry about Eva, Jack,' he told me condescendingly, leaning
against a freshly painted Sunbeam bonnet.

'So am I,' I replied neutrally.

'Anything I can do to help?'

An unusual offer from Rob so I bit back my instinctive
snarl, since he is a bull in a china shop in any situation.
'Thanks,' I said. 'Not at present though.'

'Met your daughter at the weekend,' he told me casually,
with the result that Zoe's suspicious head immediately popped
up above the bonnet of the Jowett.

'Cara?' I gaped at him. 'Where?'

'Through the Oate-Smiths. They farm out Stalisfield way.
They know Harry Bolting, so we dropped in there for the day.'

I always forget that for the agricultural community, which
spreads its net far and wide, Suffolk is no great distance from
Kent in respect of who knows who.

'Let me know if anything crops up.' Rob strode off grandly.

'I'm looking for a pinky-grey Morris Minor,' I called after him.

He stopped in his tracks. 'About time you got rid of that heap of useless metal called a Gordon-whatsit.'

I managed (just) to hold my peace, but only because I didn't want to delay his departure, much as I longed to hasten it with a well-placed boot. He continued his march as if he were the boss of the whole place. And if some work didn't get done round here soon, he well could be.

'Mortgage,' I said firmly to my trusty staff, neither of whom took the slightest bit of notice. After all, they had a Jowett to admire and diagnose.

'Meant to say, Jack—'

'Later, Len. Later. Unless it's important.'

He was already back studying the Jowett, however. The Jupiter had a horizontally-opposed flat 4 engine which unlike the VW and Porsche was water-cooled and this was clearly the focus of Len's attention. Far more important than what he'd meant to say to me.

Having done my duty by Melody for the moment, I was free to put one hundred per cent of my effort into the Carlos case, conscious that every hour I delayed could mean another hour in Holloway for Eva. I shut my mind to the possibility that whatever I found out might make no difference at all to Brandon's damning evidence. I made myself a coffee, took it into the Glory Boot, which is the best place of all for meditation, chewed at a prawn baguette from Daisy's bakery and thought through where I was with the Charros.

I reasoned to myself that if Carlos agreed to meet someone in the late evening at a lock on the River Medway, and then strolled along a towpath with him (or her), it had to be someone he knew well and trusted. Either that or *he* made the arrangements – perhaps, I speculated, with the intention of killing his companion at that lonely place. If so, his plan had gone amiss. Was that likely? He would have had to take his gun with him – OK, he could have brought it with him – but why would his then murderer not have left the gun at his side?

What was clear was that Carlos knew the person who killed him and, given that he was newly returned to the area, that meant it was probably someone from his past. Back to the Charros again. It was also possible that there was indeed a floozie involved and Eva's suspicions had been well founded. Or, I had to face it, it was possible it was Eva herself, guilty as charged. But a romantic stroll along a towpath didn't seem Eva's style, especially if she had actually planned to murder him. If she had followed Carlos in a jealous rage, however, I could see why Brandon believed he had a strong case. Bearing in mind that truth to Eva is a variable quality and that her story about remaining in the hotel the whole evening had been superseded by her new version, it could well be that this current tale for the police in which she dashed to Allington Lock but found no trace of Carlos was also untrue. Her 'true' story would depend on what put her in the most dramatic light at any one moment. Including, I thought grimly, the dock.

The only feedback I got through Dave was that no one at the lock or the pub had any recollection of seeing Carlos that evening, but I bore in mind that the lock-keeper was only on call for most of the evening, not physically present, and that pubs are crowded. Moreover this one had an outside seating area, so if Carlos himself had not bought the drinks he would not have attracted any attention.

Dave was also lukewarm on the Melody situation. 'Great,' he said unenthusiastically when I told him the news about Justin and the fact that Melody really had disappeared. 'So the Pink Panther is still at large. Well, Jack, you're on your own now. Budget.'

'Thanks,' I said, equally unenthusiastically. I wondered how I could pass that message on to Daisy. I had a vision of that beautiful angelic face dissolving into tears of disbelief that I could be thinking of abandoning her. With a heavy heart I realized there was no way I could do that, and nor could I let her pay for my services.

I was stuck – with Melody as the albatross around my neck.

I pulled myself together. If avenues were closed on Melody, there were certainly lanes aplenty on Carlos. Whatever their claim that they had all moved on, the band members were surely the key to his death. Nevertheless, something had brought him to Maidstone in the hope of money, and this dream seemed unlikely to be realized from the creation of a new band or a reunion of the old. Even if he could have been sure of a welcome from the Charros, its possibilities of success would have been limited. Time had moved on. But that annual lunch stuck out like a sore thumb. I'd heard explanations of why it was held, but I still was not convinced. For all Jonathan claimed that there were other reasons for Neil's suicide than the collapse of the band, a doubt remained. If, for instance, Neil's death had been because he and Jonathan had split up, it became understandable, but if that were the case then why should Jonathan, Clive, Matthew and Josie have an annual get-together, not to mention Belinda Fever and Betty Gibson? I had to find out and the sooner the better. I had a terrible vision of Eva growing old in prison, her once infuriating vibrancy sapping away.

It was time for the next step: Josie Gibson.

Gran Fever must have put in a good word for me, or perhaps the House of Lamb's phones had been busy, because Josie didn't sound surprised to hear from me.

'You'll have to come here,' she said somewhat belligerently. 'I'm looking after Dr Fairbourne.'

'Is he housebound?'

A pause. 'Could say that.'

Kent is a county full of surprises. One can be amongst sunny flat fields at one moment and plunged into the creepiest of woodland the next. Wychwood House was in the latter. It was near the hamlet of Delstead, about three miles north of Tickenden and six from Burchett Forstal. A single lane road snaked through the wood, and from that a gated track branched off to Wychwood House. I almost missed the gate because of the dense bushes and undergrowth shielding it, and I then drove past a mass of trees on either side of the track which kept the sun firmly at bay. The trees were aggressively green, flaunting their new summer leaves, and if someone had told me that Walt Disney's nastiest vultures were peering down at me I would have believed them. Even though I was in the

Alfa, the heavy silence percolated through to me, as though
everything and everyone were watching me, waiting to pounce.
Then I turned a corner – and there was Wychwood House.

The name Wychwood means a dwelling place in the wood
and has nothing to do with witches. You could have fooled
me. Granted, it would have to be a fairly rich witch to choose
to live here, but at first sight the house was Disney gone crazy.
There seemed no rhyme or reason to its gables, pinnacles,
turrets and roof lines, which were all set at odd angles as
though the builder had begun with a straightforward square
building and then built on pieces higgledy-piggledy as the
fancy took him. The red roofs with the black-and-white mock
timbered house beneath gave the whole building a crazy, yet
somewhat exotic appearance. Welcoming it was not.

There was a VW Polo parked in front of the house which
I took to be Josie's, but no other car was visible, although
there was a single garage to the right of the house where the
owner's car might be.

I walked up to the house, already with a sense of unease
about this visit. The night has a thousand eyes, as the poet
says, and so it seemed did Wychwood, each one of them
peering evilly out at me as I approached the door. When it
was opened, my first thought was that Josie Gibson could
have passed for a student witch quite easily, and I had to
discipline myself to rid myself of such unfair assumptions. I
could see that once she had been beautiful, with her dark hair
and dark eyes, and, as she told me to come in, her voice had
a husky quality that must once have been mesmerizing. Now
her lean face was lined and suspicious and her shoulder-length
hair, already greying, was lank and looked little cared for.

'You're Eva Colby's husband then,' she informed me accusingly as she led me through the witch's house. It was dark
and felt unused and unloved as we passed full bookshelves
that had a sad, unread look about them. There were few
personal signs to suggest that living people chatted in the
passageway or ate in the formal dining room we passed.

'We were married for a few years, yes,' I told her. 'Long
divorced.'

She did not comment, but even so I felt I had been judged

and found wanting as she led me into an equally cheerless living room with no sign of Ambrose Fairbourne. This room seemed to be her domain, judging by the photographs of herself when younger. No sign of one of Carlos, however, nor even of the Charros.

'So what are you after, then? Carlos got what was coming to him,' she remarked almost casually.

I decided not to ask whether she meant in the marriage or by his murder. 'Gathering background, to put myself in the picture.'

'Yeah, yeah. Jon told me. Well, we've nothing to hide, so why not?' The belligerence was back, but at least she was talking.

'I was told Carlos rang to tell you he was back in this country?'

That animated her. 'He had the cheek of the devil, that man. Rang me up, and when I told him to get lost he pretended he had the wrong number and hung up mighty quickly.' She looked at me almost defiantly. 'We none of us wanted nothing to do with him.'

'We?'

'The group, Mum, Mrs Fever, Matthew, Jon, Clive—'

'Mum being Betty Gibson, who worked at the May Tree?'

'She was working there when the band got set up. That's how I got into it. She knew I wanted to sing – it was an opportunity. That's what I thought, anyway. Four years I wasted there till your wife came barging in. What do you want to know all this for?' She glared at me.

'For my daughter's sake. Her mother's been charged, so naturally we both want to find out the reason Carlos came back here.'

'Leave it to the police. They've already been round to see us all, and they won't want you poking your nose in,' she snapped.

'Mrs Fever didn't have any such objections.'

'Belinda talked to you about the Charros?' She looked amazed. 'She normally keeps her mouth shut, does Belinda.'

'She told me what a wonderful singer you were.' I paused as I saw her eyes soften, then took mean advantage of it. 'She told me about your annual reunions. Do you also meet on other occasions?'

'Our business. No one else's,' she muttered.

'You said the Charros have nothing to hide.' I tried to sound bewildered and received a glare for my pains.

'They come over every so often. We have a bit of a sing-song for Dr Fairbourne.'

'Any plans for resurrecting the band?'

A cynical laugh now. 'Who'd want us? My voice has gone, anyway.'

Curiouser and curiouser – not just the annual reunion, but sing-songs. Then Josie became a lot more cooperative. 'Listen, we none of us have any time for Carlos after what he did, and we can't say we're sorry he's dead, but going out and shooting the guy twenty years later doesn't make much sense, does it?'

'No,' I agreed.

'So,' she said, grinning, 'I suppose there's no reason you and I shouldn't chat away like old friends. Except I know you're a copper's nark. So Mum says.'

'Why does she think that? I do freelance work for the car crime police, but that's hardly being a nark. Anyway, Carlos's death has nothing to do with that and a lot to do with me. Could I ask you how long your mother was at the May Tree?'

She debated for a moment or two then decided to cooperate. 'Started when she was eighteen. Year or so before the shoot-out. She met Tony when he was manager there.'

'Tony Wilson? The man who went inside for the shoot-out murder and robbery?'

'Right. When he came out in 'ninety-three she married him. Mum and my dad got divorced in the eighties, and Tony's wife did a vanishing act with the loot from the robbery in 'seventy-eight and he hasn't heard a whisper from her since, so he divorced her while he was in prison and then married Mum.'

'I'd like to meet her. Is that possible?' I asked. If she, like Belinda, was there through the Charros period, it could be helpful.

'Suppose so. I'll ask her. She holds no brief for Eva Colby though, any more than the rest of us. She'd no time for Carlos either. Mind you, it was Eva caused all the trouble, with her making a dead set for Carlos and filling him with talk of how rich she was. Money. Comes down to that. I grant you,' she added reluctantly, 'she was a bit of a looker too, your Eva.'

'Her riches were a slight exaggeration,' I said. 'Her relations are wealthy, as no doubt Carlos discovered, but they aren't given to throwing cash away.' I knew her father was a wealthy man, and Eva had had expectations, as they say, as well as a generous allowance from her grandparents. Whether they had materialized, I had no idea.

Josie cheered up considerably at this news. 'Poor old Carlos. Having to work for his money after all.'

'You liked him?' I realized too late I'd put my foot in it, but we all make mistakes. I'd been so busy thinking about Josie in the context of the band singer that I'd temporarily forgotten she'd been his lover too.

'Skunk,' she said unemotionally. 'We were an item for three years until your Eva came waggling her hips. You learn as you get older. But I took it hard then.'

'You still had your magnificent voice as an asset.'

'Had's the word. Croaking my way through a song or two when the Charros come over isn't how it was meant to be. Dr Fairbourne enjoys it though.'

I changed the subject quickly. 'Are you happy working here?'

'It's a job. Mum got it for me. She and Ambrose go way back. He liked his pint, did Dr Fairbourne. No more pubs for him though. Want to meet him?'

'I would.'

She led me into an overheated room at the rear of the house – presumably his study, as it was surrounded by books shelved on all four walls, leaving room only for the door in and for small patio doors overlooking the garden. There was a large desk with an old computer on it, photographs pushed into every available spot and two display cases with – from what little I could see from the doorway – archaeological finds. The room's occupant was in an armchair watching – or at least facing – a television screen. I saw the veins standing out starkly from the hands clutching the arms of his chair, the thinning hair and the gaunt face. His eyes remained closed as Josie went up to him.

'Ambrose,' she shouted. 'Visitor for you.'

His head turned towards me and I saw vacant eyes. 'Are you taking me to Eastry?' he asked eagerly.

'You told me early last week that you'd gone there on my day off, Ambrose,' Josie said quietly. 'Thursday.'

'Did I?' Then his face cleared. 'Oh yes, I went with Muriel.'

'Don't worry – he thinks everyone who comes here is about to take him to Eastry,' Josie said as Ambrose nodded off.

'Who's Muriel?' I whispered.

'His wife. Died donkey's years ago. Early seventies, I think.'

Now I understood. Ambrose Fairbourne, poor chap, had Alzheimer's.

His eyes promptly shot open. 'Are we going to Eastry or are we not?'

'Not today,' I told him regretfully.

He sighed. 'Tomorrow. We could go tomorrow.'

I agreed. It was easiest, and he clearly would not remember. What he would remember is the past. 'What's at Eastry?' I asked him. I did know the village, but telling me might give him pleasure. Eastry is a few miles inland from Sandwich, which is on the Kent coast near Deal and Dover and chiefly known for its golf and the Roman fortress of Richborough.

Dr Ambrose Fairbourne was only too eager to tell me about Eastry. Indeed, he looked shocked that I needed telling. 'In Anglo-Saxon times it was the capital of Kent,' he told me with almost personal pride. 'Not just a village – the whole area around it was then known as Eastry.' A pause while I wondered whether his archaeological memories had deserted him too. I could see that a whole shelf of the books in the study were written by him, but there would be no more, however good his memory for the past was. I thought he had stopped speaking, but he took us both by surprise.

'Murder!' he yelled.

'Whose?' I asked cautiously.

'King Egbert. Seventh century. Don't you know his palace was at Eastry?' He spoke with great indignation. 'Lambarde relates the story of the murder, admittedly based on Mathew of Westminster, who is now thought never to have existed, although the work cited, the *Flores Historiarum*, certainly does. The bodies are buried somewhere.'

'King Egbert's body?' I asked cautiously when he paused.

Ambrose beamed at me. 'Yes, young man. Probably in St Augustine's Abbey, but also there at Eastry. It is. It's there all right.'

'Who murdered the king?'

He stared at me aghast. 'No, no, *no*. You will never make a historian, young man. Legends spring from fact, however far removed. His nephews, or cousins – sources vary – Ethelbert and Ethelred. Some term him Ethelbright. The king murdered *them*, afraid they would take the throne from him. Or perhaps it was his steward Thunner on his behalf.' He half rose from his chair, and his arm swept through an arc. 'The bodies were hidden, but a great shining beam of light showed where they lay. The ley line. That's the answer, my friend. The true answer. Egbert gave land for an abbey to their sister – minster not abbey – in restitution and became a good Christian.' A pause, and a sly look. 'Grave goods. Gold.'

Josie was giving me no help, so I had to proceed cautiously. 'Buried treasure?'

'Certainly. Gold.'

I thought I saw where this was going. 'Is this something to do with the legendary golden statue of the Norse god Woden thought to be buried near Woodnesborough?' I knew it was only a mile or so from Eastry. 'And the prehistoric golden Ringlemere cup was found near there too.' If I'd hoped to please him with my feeble knowledge of the subject, I'd failed miserably.

Ambrose frowned. 'Eastry. It's there at Eastry.'

'Of course,' I said hastily.

'They say,' he told me confidentially, 'that the bodies were moved to Romsey abbey. The king lies elsewhere, but I shall find him.'

'Of course.'

'That's settled then,' he said briskly. 'Tomorrow we'll go to Eastry, young man. You'll pack my equipment, Josie?'

'Yes, Ambrose. It's always ready.'

'Then I'll leave it to you. You're both dismissed.' He changed his mind. 'No, stay. I don't get many visitors. I had one yesterday or the day before, and there will be one tomorrow too. I'm sure of that. I'm going to Eastry. Do you know it?'

'A little,' I said. 'Tell me about it.' While he did so and his eye was not on me, I stole a look at some of the photographs of a younger, healthier Ambrose. One was at a book launch, another a wedding photo with his wife – mid nineteen fifties? – and another with her, standing by, yes, a grey Morris Minor 1000 outside an unmistakable May Tree Inn. I put that one as late sixties or early seventies, judging by the clothes.

'Do you remember Carlos and the Charros?' I shot at a whim, after I'd thanked him for telling me about Eastry again.

He looked doubtfully at Josie. 'Do I?'

'Yes, Ambrose. Remember? I was the singer and we performed at the May Tree Inn.' She took one of the photos to remind him. 'You liked that pub.'

'Bang, bang,' he said, beaming. 'Murder. Egbert, Eastry. Let's talk of graves, of worms and epitaphs. King Richard the Second. I shall go tomorrow – with you, if you like, young man.'

I extricated myself with promises I would try to keep, though I doubted if he would remember them even as long as it took to leave the room. 'Does his son live near?' I asked Josie as she showed me out.

'Not that far. Canterbury. He's an archaeologist too. Keith has power of attorney or I'd never get paid. I live in with a relief at weekends and if I'm lucky a day off. It's a roof over my head, and Mum's not far away. She and Tony come over regular.'

'I saw the wedding photo of his wife. Was she the Morris Minor fan?'

'Yes. Both of them, really. She must have been dotty about them, because there are quite a few pics of that Minor. Ambrose thinks he still has one sometimes, poor lamb.'

'He doesn't have one though?'

A short laugh. 'No way. He's seventy-eight now and been like this for eight or nine years and hasn't driven since. There's still a car in the garage – a Renault estate – in which Keith takes him out sometimes. Ambrose likes familiar things.'

I went away saddened. It was only later I remembered that I hadn't asked her about Matt Wright, the fourth member of the former Charros.

SIX

I tried to concentrate on Matt, but I couldn't get a fix on him as memories of Daisy's indignant face kept coming back to me. Try as I could to wedge Melody into a spare corner of my mind where she wouldn't get lost but would stay quietly until I got round to her, my brain was forever doing U-turns much neater than she could ever achieve. I told myself once again that Carlos's murder came first, otherwise I would have been drifting round Kent in the forlorn hope of pinning down a lost car. I would assuage my conscience by trying Bluebell Hill one more time, however, as soon as I could fit it in.

The plan worked, because as I drove through the gates of Frogs Hill I realized that I had been focusing so much on the Charros that I had overlooked one possible factor. The May Tree itself, whose living history did not begin with the band. Barmaid Betty Gibson went back much further than that, and even Carlos had known the pub when he visited Matt before the band was formed. Matt, too, had been a regular at the pub.

Belinda had given me Matt's mobile number but I had tried it several times without success. Messages left on voicemail brought no response, which was frustrating to say the least. He was an odd-job man so why not reply to phone messages? Had he been warned about me? If so, why? I remembered Josie's casual reference to the missing 'loot' from the May Tree Shoot-Out in 1978. Was it stretching imagination too far to wonder whether Carlos or his chum Matt had discovered where it was? Could that have been the root of the 'business' meeting at the lock? A meeting with – my ignition fired up – *Tony's missing wife*? Carlos specialized in wives. Suppose he'd run into her before or after Eva's explosion into his life, perhaps in Mexico? It was possible, although unlikely, that either through her or otherwise he had got information on the whereabouts of the proceeds from the raid that had caused the shoot-out, and so it was worth considering.

Try home resources first – that was Dad's maxim. So I did. I marched into the Pits in a meaningful manner, which received the usual amount of attention – none – so I resorted to cunning.

'Nice work there, Len. Glad you solved the Jowett mystery.'

This resulted in an immediate reaction – well, as immediate as Len ever gets. We had lift-off on the communication front. He blushed. 'Only used my eyes. We all have them. Rust round the engine blocks. Water leaks through the cracks. Just got to strip the engine down, weld and remachine the block, reassemble, then realign the engine.'

I made duly impressed noises, then said as casually as I could: 'You were around these parts in 'seventy-eight, weren't you, Len?' I could see his eyes still on the Jowett, however. He was itching to get started.

'No. At Brands.'

He'd worked at Brands Hatch racing circuit for many years, but that's in West Kent and quite a way in towards London. 'But were you living around here at the time of the May Tree Shoot-Out?'

He nodded. Len saves on words that way, so that he can get back to welding things that matter all the quicker.

'What happened to the gang that carried out the raid? That was local, wasn't it? I know Tony Wilson went inside for shooting one of them, but what happened to the wife and the others in the gang?'

Len shot an agonized look at the Jowett. 'Tried to tell you the other day that Vic Trent's a mate of mine.' That said it all, I thought. Take care. 'There were four of them,' Len continued, 'and the missus. Vic did a shortish stretch inside, then opened a corner shop. The organizer, Brian Thompson, landed up dead, Tony went down for it, and Frank Watson did a runner.'

'With the loot?'

'That's the story. And . . .' Len paused and wiped his hands on the special rag from which he will never be parted and which must have more residual oil on it than a leaking sump. It's his way of playing for time. 'Took Wilson's missus with him,' he finished.

The missus had to wait. I'd just done a belated U-turn. 'Frank Watson? Any relation to Neil?' If ever a breath was bated, mine was.

'His dad.'

I reeled at this connection, although I wasn't sure why, save that it was a coincidence that might not be one. Did it get me anywhere? I'd no idea, but I'd run with it and see what happened. 'Is he living round here now?' Silly question, I suppose.

'Ran as hard and far as he could get was the general opinion.'

Or not, I thought. With his son Neil here, Frank could have been a lot nearer – at least at the time of his son's death. I tried not to put jump-leads on my theorizing. What, after all, did this tell me about Carlos's death? Not much, unless of course Frank Watson was still around and blamed him for Neil's death. Could Carlos have discovered his presence and decided to make hay with a touch of blackmail? Carlos did not strike me as the soul of bravery, however, and he would not have risked going within a thousand miles of Frank if Neil had killed himself because Carlos had dumped the Charros. Nevertheless, the story of Watson and Son must have some mileage. Like those carsickness prevention strips that cars used to trail from the chassis to the road, there were trailing ends around – and my job was to pick them up one by one. This one was still attached.

'What about Wilson's missus?' I asked, grasping another one. 'Did she really go off with Frank?'

Could Carlos have tracked her down? Had he met her alone, with a sob story about Frank having abandoned her? Sheer speculation, but there might be a glimmer of gold somewhere.

Len considered my question while the rag received the last vestiges of oil. 'Joannie Wilson,' he said at last, 'made off with the haul from the raid during the hullabaloo over the shooting, so Vic says. When the cops arrived, she wasn't there, and nor was Frank.'

'Doesn't necessarily mean they went together,' I pointed out.

'Vic said Joannie had the stuff in the boot of her car, and she was thick with Frank all along. Planned. They'd have gone anyway, and the shoot-out was a bonus.'

'Did they go in the same car, or was his car left in the car park?' I asked.

No reply. Len had finished communication for the day. No matter. I knew now that I wanted to make the early acquaintance of Mr and Mrs Tony Wilson. Especially Mrs, since she linked both eras, the shoot-out and the band. The theory about Carlos might have something to it, I thought hopefully, unless this was a red herring and the loot had in fact been snaffled by Betty to keep until Tony's release, so that they could enjoy a happy old age together?

It was a week before I could get to see them, as they were away on holiday. I wasn't going to risk a chat with them on the phone, because I like seeing the body language and the whites of people's eyes. I realized, however, that they might well refuse to see me, as neither the May Tree nor Carlos could be subjects dear to their hearts. Josie and Belinda must have given me a clean bill of health, however, because when I did speak to them Betty was charm itself. Indeed, I thought uneasily, it was almost *too* easy to follow up the Charros and their connections – almost as though they were passing me round like an unwanted parcel.

I was told to ignore the satnav and follow the route that Betty gave me. I needed their instructions because their home was in the village of Boyfield, out in the wilds, with the nearest town being Sittingbourne. On the Downs the elements like to remind you that they are in charge. Winds blow, rain falls in torrents, the sun beams relentlessly on the sweating inhabitants below and the snow shows no mercy. All the same, I could appreciate why someone who had been behind bars for fifteen years might relish the isolation of a village such as this. Not that the house in which Tony and Betty Wilson lived was itself isolated, as it was in a small development. Number fourteen Jubilee Crescent had double electric gates with a lion at each end (stone), staring keenly down at all comers on behalf of the modest bungalow they guarded so zealously.

The gates were the only sign of prosperity, however, and the chances of Tony and Betty Wilson living on the proceeds of the shoot-out looked slimmer. There was a sign by them suggesting we beware of the dog, but the gates were open so

I drove in to where an old four by four was parked side by side with a newer Fiesta. The Wilsons came out to greet me with a bouncy spaniel called, Josie said, Don. Whereas Betty was, like her daughter, grey-haired and wary, Tony was the opposite, outgoing and genial – at least he appeared so to me.

'Come in,' he said cordially. 'First prize for finding us.'

I calculated he must be about sixty-five now, and he showed few of the usual signs of the serious ex-con. No wariness here.

'Tell us again why you've come,' he suggested, after we were settled in a pristine living room. It overlooked a neat rear garden complete with patio and built-in barbecue, and together they sent out a message that their lives were in order, no matter what strife lay behind. 'We've been out of touch with the latest news about the Mendez murder, just got back from our jamboree.'

'Cruise round the world?' I joked.

'Week in Marbella. Can't beat it.'

Again, hardly in line with their living off the fat of a missing fortune.

'We know Eva's been charged,' Betty put in, 'but what's happening now?'

'Waiting for a trial date. You knew Eva?'

'Oh yes. No offence meant, but she thought she owned the place. You should have seen her swanning about, Tony.'

'Otherwise engaged.' Tony grinned. 'I was inside – missed all that and Carlos too.'

'He was a no-gooder,' Betty said savagely. 'He and your Eva made a good fit. Hope you don't mind my saying that, Jack.'

'Go ahead,' I said. 'We were divorced twenty years ago, and there were no bruised hearts.' Had there been? I suddenly wondered. Is that why I felt so obstinate about trying to clear her name? Was it just for Cara or for me too? Whether or not it was, any bruise I was currently nursing was due to Louise, not Eva. Louise had disappeared from my life with sadness on both sides, she to pursue her career on stage and screen and me to try to forget her. She was succeeding, I wasn't.

Betty took up my invitation to go ahead with alacrity. 'She was a first-class bitch – to women, anyway. Carlos chased anything in skirts if he thought there was money around. He had a thing about flamboyant women like Eva. He spent money like water so he was always looking for the next one.'

'He must have met more than his match in Eva then,' I pointed out. 'They were still together after twenty years.'

'Then she must have had money,' Betty said flatly.

'Possibly,' I conceded. 'Were you there when the band was set up?'

'Of course. I knew them all. Matt and Carlos were familiar faces by then. I suggested Josie, and Carlos brought in the other three.'

Time to dig deeper. 'One of whom was Neil Watson, son of Frank.'

Tony looked up and the geniality vanished. 'You've been doing your homework, Jack. Yes, the son was called Neil. But it's Mendez's murder that your Eva's up for. What's that got to do with Frank Watson?'

Keep right on going, I told myself. 'So far as I know, nothing. But Carlos came back to Maidstone, so Eva claims, on some business deal to raise cash. Eva's motive for killing him, according to the police, and indeed her own statements suggest it, was that another woman was involved. So I need to find out why Carlos came back and for what. No woman has yet been found and the business deal could be Eva's fantasy, but I need to know.'

'But what's Frank got to do with it?' Tony said belligerently. 'He vanished off the face of the earth long before this band got going.'

'Tony's right.' Betty shot him an anxious glance. 'I can confirm he wasn't around then, and I remember Frank Watson from the night of the shoot-out.'

I was under joint attack now.

'Neil killed himself when Carlos left them in the lurch. It could be that his father still feels strongly, wherever he is.'

Tony snorted. 'Frank? It was 1992 when his son died, wasn't it, Bet? You told me about it when we met up again in 'ninety-three. Frank wasn't even on the horizon then, and he isn't now, more's the pity. I'd like to have a few words with him.'

'Neil is not forgotten,' I persisted. 'There's an anniversary lunch each year to which you go, Mrs Wilson. Does Frank go too?'

'Talk sense,' Betty said with a snort. 'I just said he's vanished. Is it likely he'd be around these parts? And if he was at the lunch, believe me, I'd know. What's more, there's a price on his head.'

'So the police know he went off with the spoils of the raid after the shoot-out?' I asked, as innocently as I could.

I thought I heard a pin drop – but it was only their heavy breathing in the silence that followed.

'Not just the cash,' Betty said at last. 'He took Joannie with him, Tony's first wife.'

'I'm sorry,' I said, seeing his face react. I meant it. He was obviously happily married again, and I had miscalculated as to how strongly he might still feel about his first wife.

'Water under the bridge.' Tony shrugged. 'Except that Bets and me could be living the life o' Reilly if we had the cash now. He can keep Joannie.'

Bravado, I wondered. 'Cash?' I queried. 'I thought it was a collection that you hijacked?'

'Right,' Tony said. 'The Crowshaw Collection. We had it all worked out how to get it turned into cash soonest, though. Some of it was gold coins, some goblets and stuff. Been in the family for centuries. Not all gold but enough of it was to make the headlines. The arrangement Brian made, him being the organizer, was that Frank was to get the coins melted down, Joannie was going to get over the Channel soonest with the other stuff and we'd all meet up in Calais. Didn't work out like that.'

The Crowshaw Collection – I'd done my homework so I knew the story by now. The Martinford family at Crowshaw Manor had kept the collection for so long that the question of treasure trove didn't seem to arise, probably because whichever ancestor had dug it up, he'd kept mum and gloated over it in secret. In more needy times the family had to sell it to keep the manor going and decided to raise money on the open market on the continent, rather than going to the British Museum – which is why there wasn't much public sympathy for them when the raiders hijacked the lot.

'Is it possible that Carlos discovered Frank and Joannie are back in this country and thought he'd like some of the cash?' I asked.

'Every now and then a rumour goes round but nothing firm,' Tony replied, 'and I make sure there's nothing to it.'

'Has any of the haul come on the market in these years?'

'I'd know if it had.' Tony grinned. 'Always been interested in gold and stuff. I reckon we all are, eh?'

'We usually admire it in museums,' I said somewhat drily, reminding myself he'd done fifteen years for murder over this haul.

'Take your point,' he said cheerfully. 'But this trove of treasure wasn't in a museum. It was up for grabs. The family was short of filthy lucre and so were we. We found out by bribing the security firm what day it was leaving and that was that. Brian was a good planner, I'll say that for him. Only the four of us, but it went like clockwork. You know Crowshaw Manor? It's at Cranes Bottom, right in the middle of nowhere and between the A2 and the M20 so whichever way the security van took to Dover it had to go through a tangle of more or less single track lanes to reach a major highway.

'From the manor there were three choices: easiest turn right and up to the A2, next easiest turn left and work a way round to either the M20 or to another road to Dover, and thirdly straight up and round a very wiggly narrow route indeed to the A2. Four of us, four cars – all of which we nicked for the purpose. All three roads blocked by one of the cars sideways across it, fourway hazard blinkers going like the clappers, drivers mysteriously absent. First two of the roads, those to the right and left, were blocked only ten yards or so from the manor, so the security van with the goods had to turn back and take the third, which was blocked a quarter of a mile or so up, near enough to a turn-off so that cars coming in the opposite direction could find another way round. Not that there was much other traffic around. My car blocked the third road at the top near the turn-off and I was hidden safely in the bushes. Meanwhile car four, Brian's, followed the security van after it set off up road three to hem it in when it reached the blocked car. It was a doddle.'

Tony looked rather pleased with himself. 'Brian and I strolled up to the van,' he continued, 'and since we had the sense to dress like policemen, albeit masked ones, the guards kindly rolled the windows down so we could spray them with tear gas. Must have wondered what was going on up to that point. Then we helped ourselves to the stuff, the other two having joined us, and we put it into my car, and off we went back to the four separate places we'd left our own cars, peeling off one by one, so we could all drive separately back to the May Tree to sort ourselves out.'

'And what happened there?' I asked, bearing in mind one of the four had died as a result.

Tony sighed. 'You're worse than the flaming cops. Brian threw his weight around. That was the cause of it. He was already getting a bigger percentage of the final takings than the rest of us, but he announced he was taking more. I objected, so did the other two. Things turned nasty as we all pitched in. Brian produced his shooter, the other tried to stop him and I grabbed my piece that I'd kept handy at the hijack just in case. Only grabbed it to warn him off, not to use. But a right old kerfuffle took place, when Brian decided to shoot me. Vic got in the way and caught one in his leg, and somehow Brian got shot with my gun. Accidental, like. There was a lot of noise in the pub that night, so with the racket going on outside the shots didn't attract instant attention, us being at the back of the pub, but then folks started coming. We'd transferred the stuff earlier to Joannie's car as being the least likely to get attention as she drove through Dover. So there I was all alone with no sign of Joannie, no sign of Frank, Brian lying dead, Vic wounded – and no sign of the goods. I spent so much time hunting for Joannie that I was still there when the cops came.'

I was beginning to feel decidedly chilly at a story that had more holes in it than Emmental cheese, but luckily Tony didn't seem to need any comment from me as he continued: 'Someone must have called them, even though everyone was running around like headless chickens.'

'Even me,' Betty said ruefully.

'I thought as I was the pub manager I might escape notice

in the crowd,' Tony added. 'Fat chance. But it was an accident. Self defence, anyway. But the jury didn't see it that way.'

'Vic got off lightly,' Betty said disapprovingly. 'Tony cleared him, didn't you, love?'

Tony shrugged. 'He got a year or two for the robbery, but he didn't have nothing to do with Brian's death. Now Frank . . .'

'He was a nasty piece of work,' Betty said. 'True, it was the only time I ever met him, but I didn't take to him.'

'What was he like to look at?' I asked.

'Nothing remarkable that I could see,' Tony said. 'Only remarkable thing was how unremarkable he was. Joannie must have thought differently.'

'Weren't you surprised not to hear from him again, Tony?' I asked.

'I wasn't expecting a letter of apology sent to Maidstone prison. Not after he hopped it with Joannie and the loot.'

'And you're certain that's what happened?'

'Rock sure. Frank's first wife divorced him a couple of years earlier and he was missing it, so he decided to skedaddle with Joannie. I'd seen them together – just never put two and two together about what they was planning.'

I turned to Betty. 'Yet his son Neil, who must have been pretty young, then turns up at the May Tree in 1987. Didn't you think it was a coincidence? Did you wonder if Frank would appear?'

'He wouldn't dare show his face there, even though Tony was still in jail. Anyway, as far as I remember, Neil was at uni in Kent and sharing a flat with Jon Lamb.'

'I'd like to lay my eyes on Frank again,' Tony said. 'I really would. Just a couple of questions for him: where's Joannie, and where's my share of the booty? Still, we do all right, don't we, Betty?'

She patted his hand. 'Should do. We've been together long enough.'

Touching this might have been, but the burning issue for me was still outstanding. 'Could there be *any* link between Carlos and Frank and Joannie? If he'd met them somewhere – South America, for example.' I was getting desperate now as once again I seemed to be heading nowhere. 'Does that ring any bells with you, Betty? I'm sure you would have remembered it.'

'I'm sure I would too,' she flashed back wryly. 'No bells rung though. Carlos was more likely to have told Neil if he'd met his dad,' she pointed out, 'not me. He knew Tony was in prison and how he felt about Frank.'

I grasped this straw. 'Or he might have told other gang members. I'm trying to get hold of Matt Wright, but I've had no luck with the phone.'

'Matt's not good with phones. Best place to find him is at Wychwood House. He does a lot of odd jobs there.'

So where had all that taken me, save round in a circle back to Wychwood? It was just possible that Carlos had got a line on where Frank Watson was, with or without Joannie or the proceeds of the Crowshaw Collection. Blackmail was the sort of crime I envisaged Carlos having been very good at, but in Maidstone? Neither Frank nor Joannie were likely to have returned here – not if they valued their lives.

Thanks to Betty Wilson I could now contact Matt Wright at least, although I was still somewhat uneasy that everyone I met in connection with Carlos seemed very *affable*. They all seemed ready enough to provide facts, but the picture these presented remained fuzzy.

When I rang Wychwood House, Josie, however, was once more far from welcoming. 'Why do you want to meet Matt?' she asked suspiciously.

'Same reason as I wanted to meet you, Josie.'

A long pause, then: 'He'll be here tomorrow doing the garden.'

So once again I drove to Wychwood, and once again I had that weird feeling as I passed through the woods. This was no pleasant shady summer scene. There was still a heaviness about it that made me even gladder that my home was Frogs Hill. Perhaps it was merely a reflection of my mood, I told myself. I was no nearer to that magic point at which I sense I have nailed a problem down, even if it wasn't yet solved. On the contrary, I was all too aware that in Holloway women's prison Eva was on remand awaiting trial, and so far I had no real leads to give Brandon (even if he hadn't asked for them).

A white van was in the forecourt and so was Josie's Polo, which was a reassuring sight. As before, there was no sign of Ambrose in the house as Josie, looking practical in jeans and a tank top, led me through to the large kitchen, which overlooked the garden.

'Matt's out there,' she told me, and through the window I could hear the lawn mower thundering along and see the man behind it. Matt was tall, in his fifties, with thinning hair, a paunch and a general air of hopelessness even about the way he shuffled his trainers over the grass.

'He'll be coming in for coffee any minute,' Josie told me. She looked slightly more human when I told her I had enjoyed meeting Tony and her mother yesterday, although I thought 'enjoy' was a relative word considering Tony had served a long sentence for murder.

'I'll go out to meet Matt,' I told Josie. I wanted to speak to him alone, not because I expected any great revelations man to man, but one never knows.

The garden was overhung by trees at its rear and on one side, which gave it a closed-in effect that the regular flower beds and neat bushes did little to alleviate. Perhaps its lack of personality stemmed from the fact that Ambrose had been divorced from life for many years. A garden can tell when it's not of much interest to its owners – I gathered that from Louise when she saw mine, save that mine was not regular and neat but had taken the opposite course to Ambrose's.

Matt gave me an impersonal nod when he saw me coming, and I watched as he finished mowing the lawn and sweeping up the cuttings. He took great care over this task, as though by so doing he gave himself a reason for living.

'Josie says you've come about Carlos,' he said as he finalized the last bag of grass. 'He got his comeuppance, that's all,' he added, without waiting for a word from me.

'It's a tough comeuppance, despite what he did to you.'

He disregarded this. 'Your wife's in for it, isn't she?'

'*His* wife, no longer mine. Yes. She's on remand.'

'You'd reason enough to do him in,' Matt commented dispassionately. 'So did I. Only, I never did.'

'Nor me. But I haven't harboured a grudge against Carlos all these years.'

'I have.' Matt scowled. 'Look at me. Odd-job man. I was a fool to believe him. Number One in the charts, he said. That's us, the Charros. In our dreams.'

'And you were the first, weren't you? His friend before the band existed.'

'Thought I was. Went to hear his dad's band when I was still a kid, got to know Carlos, and when he came back to Kent he stayed with me and my parents. Told me I was great on the guitar. I was with another band then. After we started the band, Carlos rented an annexe we had. When he was with Josie it was fine, but after your wife got her hands on him – well, he dumped the lot of us.'

'Did you play for anyone else afterwards?'

He snorted. 'Never had the chance. The band I was in before I joined the Charros hit the charts a year or two after the Charros split up. I could have been with them. All very well for Jonathan. He had other skills to fall back on. But me? No way. Done for in the music world, done for outside. And look what happened to Neil. He bore a *grudge*, as you call it.'

'Clive's done well with Jonathan though.'

'Yeah. Jon picked him up after his year inside.'

'That wasn't Carlos's fault.'

'Who do you think put him inside, then? Carlos shopped him. Didn't they tell you? Carlos took the dope himself and then split on Clive to get out of paying for it. You didn't find that out – and you call yourself a cop?'

'I don't, in fact, but thanks for the information.' Time to look again at Clive Miller. True, he was in a happy business relationship with Jonathan and had a family life, but if he had met Carlos on a dark night on a towpath and they fell out . . .

'And Neil,' Matt added with satisfaction, now he thought he had got the better of me. 'He had a *grudge* all right. Gave up his postgrad course to follow Carlos's drum.'

'Was his father around at the time?' It would be interesting to find out if Neil's parentage was generally known.

'Eh?' Matt stared hard at me. 'Not that I know of.'

'His father was Frank Watson. Met him?' I held my breath. Those lunches . . . .

'No,' said Matt simply. 'Know the police have been to see me about Carlos, do you? Wanted to know where I was that night.'

'It's not surprising. They're interested in all the Charros.'

'I was at home. My mobile *palace*,' he told me with satisfaction. 'Alone. But if I'd known someone was going to have a go at Carlos, I'd have gone along to help. I had a *grudge*, you see.'

I ignored the sarcasm, and Matt, highly pleased with himself, walked off to get his money and coffee. I followed him, only to have the door shut in my face. I wasn't going to leave without speaking to Josie again, and perhaps Ambrose too, so I decided to hang on. Memory is a strange thing. On buried treasure and gold, Ambrose could still be spot on, and that meant that his memory might still be intact about Carlos and the May Tree.

To pass the time I wandered round the side of the house where the sun did not reach. It felt chilly and forbidding. By the pricking of my thumbs . . . I thought of the witches' chant in *Macbeth* – or should I say the Scottish Play, for fear of bringing bad luck my way? My thumbs were pricking too, which was ridiculous when I had only to walk through that kitchen door to be in the house with at least three other people. But I didn't do it. Instead I decided to wait until Josie was free and have a wander round while I did so. I might find an old car or two. All sorts of such buried treasures lie in barns and sheds, unused and unloved, when their owners have grown old or replaced them with newer models. There are plenty lying hidden to make car lovers drool in ecstasy if only they could catch sight of them. Keeping cars in barns is like keeping a precious art painting on one's private wall.

As I reached the front of the house I could see the doors of the double garage were open and Ambrose's Renault inside. It was an Espace and dated (judging by the number plate) 2001. Then I strolled over to a track through the woods on the far side of the house, and my spirits rose as I saw fresh

tyre marks in the mud. Hidden classics? Then I realized no
one here would be *driving* a classic. I toyed with the idea
that one might be hidden in the half shed, half barn that I
spotted some way along the track and decided it was worth a
look. The barn was side on to me as I mooched up to it to
satisfy my curiosity. The wooden door was ajar and I couldn't
resist. I went to peer inside. An old Bugatti, maybe?

I froze. No Bugatti. It was a Morris Minor 1000. I remembered the photo of the Morris Minor that had belonged to
Ambrose and his wife, but this one did not look neglected.
Far from it. It was shiny and polished and loved. And then I
did a double take. I'd been asleep at the switch.

It was *pinky-grey*, I was facing its rear end and there was
no number plate. Feeling as though I were taking part in a
fantasy nightmare, I forced my way past the side of the car
to the front to see if there was a number plate there. Not only
were my thumbs pricking, but my whole body had joined
them. I was also uncomfortably aware that if those doors closed
on me, I might be done for. In this weird household no one
would bother to search for me. I'm not usually claustrophobic
but a sudden surge of life made me want to be out of here
– and fast. I bent down and saw a familiar number plate.

I'd found Melody.

I had no time to think about my discovery, no time to
contemplate, because a shadow fell across the car and a
pleasant voice said: 'May I help you?'

It was Ambrose Fairbourne who stood blocking my path
out, and I had to fight irrational panic as I saw his vacant eyes
and the non-focused smile on his lips.

'I was just admiring your wife's car,' I said, thinking this
might appease him. It didn't.

His face was transformed with fury. 'It was her. *It wasn't
there.* It's *there.* Do you hear me, sir?'

I was at the wrong end of the garage as he advanced on
me, lug wrench in hand raised high.

SEVEN

I was trapped. This was no idle flourish. Ambrose meant business, and I was his target. My best chance was to make a dash for it along one side of Melody while he advanced up the other, but even then he could hurl that iron wrench at me, and the demented have a power that often seems beyond their normal physical strength.

The problem was that Ambrose did *not* advance. He stayed where he was. Lug wrench poised. The hunter waiting for his captive prey, knowing he has all the time in the world. He just smiled – not a smile for me but *at* me, as though not sure what he was doing or who I was. I could be there all day, I realized, while he played this game and I yelled in vain for Josie or Matt. Somehow I had to make a move. Attracting attention would bring swift retribution from Ambrose, so I'd take it very gently, step by step . . .

'Not bad these Moggies, are they?' I began chattily, using the Minor's nickname in the hope of showing him I was an aficionado. 'Of course, they have a few faults – the rusty floor pans, bonnets that fly up without warning – and I do like this Rose Taupe colour. Not too good on the gearbox but one can overlook that because of the durable engine.' I gave Melody a casual pat, and I was relieved to see that at least Ambrose appeared to be listening. 'I'm not surprised you like this car so much,' I continued. 'Do you belong to one of the Minor clubs?'

Silence. I was past Melody's bonnet and almost at the door handle, inching my way along, and Ambrose had not yet moved.

Nor had the wrench in his hand.

He was watching me very, very carefully. Another foot – perhaps a bit more – and I would be able to make a successful grab for the wrench. Inch by inch. Eyes first on the car and then slightly turning to him. One more time should do it . . .

Too much, too soon. A screech of fury, and the wrench crashed on the concrete floor where I had been standing but no longer was, thanks to a speedy jump backwards. It missed me by millimetres, but even as I recovered he had leapt round with amazing agility to grab hold of it again. He swung it back up in the air once more and waved it around.

'I am Egbert,' he crooned. 'King of Kent . . .'

I bowed my head, desperately thinking of my best response. Try the innocuous. 'And I your loyal subject,' I tried.

Another screech. 'You are a traitor, Cousin Ethelred. You seek my crown.'

Not good. Ethelred had ended up as a corpse together with his brother somewhere under the royal Saxon palace floor. I scrabbled in my memory for the rest of the story. It might be my only lifeline.

'Great King –' a small detached part of my mind was listening to this charade, not mocking but urging me on – 'you then regretted your actions in killing me and gave land to Ethelred's sister to build a nunnery.' Or was it an abbey, or a minster? Or was she Egbert's sister or aunt or niece? I couldn't remember. Oddly, this seemed of the utmost importance, and so it might be if he took it so seriously.

Ambrose stared at me for a moment, clearly debating my words. Then – I could hardly believe it – the wrench descended and he conceded in a relatively normal voice: 'That is true.' He seemed slightly puzzled. 'Are you seeking gold, young man?'

No prizes for the answer to this one. 'No,' I said promptly.

'But you know where they lie?'

'No.' I was less certain of the answer this time.

'A pity. Gold is the greatest gift the earth gives us.'

Except life, I thought to myself, thankful that I still had mine. For how long was not yet certain.

'The earth gives,' he continued, 'and it takes back in grave goods. Gold gleams still – earth cannot tarnish it. It will emerge from its hiding place, as shining as the day it left when buried. It is his belt-mount, given to me, Egbert.'

'Where is its hiding place?' I ventured.

The wrench rose again although not so immediately threatening. He was more intent on gold.

'It is *mine*. I am King of Kent, not you, and I am dead and shall retain my own. The burial place is known only to me. So you, young man, can't have it.' The wrench was laid aside again and I inched closer to a point where I could make a stab at preventing his grasping it once more. 'We have a duty to the grave,' he continued earnestly. 'A duty to protect its whereabouts. Eastry – kindly take me there, young man.'

'Not in this car,' I said firmly. Melody was staying where she was. Again I'd made the wrong move, however. I'm always lousy at chess. I braced myself as he looked so furious that the wrench became an issue again. 'This car doesn't work,' I added hastily. 'Is it yours?'

'Doesn't work? A strange way of putting it. Everything belongs to the king, but you may have this car if you so wish.'

'Now?' I couldn't believe my luck.

'No. After we have been to Eastry.'

Back to square one. 'In this car?'

Another screech of fury was the answer to that. 'No. It's not the right one.'

'I'll return in my Gordon-Keeble and then we can go.' I was secure in the knowledge that he would not remember this offer.

His eyes lit up. 'An excellent choice, Ethelred. A car fit for me, King Egbert.'

On this harmonious note, however, the cavalry belatedly arrived in the form of Josie, who was clearly relieved to see her charge. 'I've been looking everywhere for you, Ambrose.' Then she took in my presence – and Melody's. 'What's *this* doing here? Ambrose?' She turned back to him accusingly.

'It's not mine,' he said, visibly cowering. 'I don't think so anyway. It's his.' He pointed to me, and I shook my head when she turned back to me.

'Have you ever seen this car here before?' I asked her.

'No. The barn's falling down and I never come here. What are you so interested for?' She glared at me. 'This is none of your business.'

'It is very much my business. It's a stolen car, and it's a case I've been working on for the police.' Credentials established, I turned to Ambrose. 'Do you know how long the car has been here, Dr Fairbourne?' Not a chance that he would, of course.

He simply stared at me and shook his head. At least King Egbert had vanished.

'And you've no idea how it came here, Josie?' I continued. 'Have you ever seen it before?'

Ambrose forestalled her. 'I have. At Eastry. It's King Egbert's car.'

'He hasn't a clue,' Josie said wearily – but kindly, I thought.

'Would you have heard if it had been driven here during the night?' I asked her.

'I might not have done. My room's at the back of the house,' she said. 'If I'm in the garden I don't always hear cars arriving. Or if I'm out, of course. I can leave Ambrose quite a bit of the time without having to get a relief or drag Mum over here. He's physically safe enough and doesn't play with fires and that sort of thing. And, anyway, there's a back way to this place – the track eventually joins the lane to Chilham. The car could have come that way.'

I know enough about the workings of rural communities to appreciate that however deserted and remote a place might seem somebody will always know every detail about it. Even so, the 'somebody' who deposited Melody here would either come by the back route or Josie would surely have to be involved, otherwise the risk of being seen would be too great.

'I'll have to report this to the police,' I explained to her. 'Then they'll come to collect it.'

'Good,' said King Egbert decisively. 'Have a word with the court steward too. Ask for Thunner.'

I recalled he was the chap who looked after the slaughter of King Egbert's victims, so I thought I'd pass on that one. I wondered whether to bow in thanks to His Majesty, but settled for a nod instead. Ambrose Fairbourne didn't even notice me pick up the wrench and carry it off with me.

The Visitors Centre at Holloway prison in London proved a welcome stepping stone to facing the ordeal of my first visit to Eva. It was a Saturday, and with children playing, refreshments and friendly staff it seemed like a family gathering

– which I suppose it was. Different rules apply to remand prisoners, but I'd booked an appointment to visit Eva for three fifteen in the afternoon. Here in the Centre, however, it still seemed unreal. That all changed when I finally got to see Eva. I'd wondered how her ordeal was affecting her. Would she still be the same overbearing flamboyant egocentric woman I had known so well or would she be in total collapse? She was neither. For the first time I could see in her the girl I had fallen for hook, line and sinker, when I was twenty or so. Since our divorce, I had assumed that I'd fallen for her only because of her sex appeal, but nothing is ever as simple as that. Now I remembered the loving loyalty, her courage, sheer warmth and love of life – not that they were visible today, but without the outer shell the human being could be glimpsed. Or so I told myself when I saw her drawn face, devoid of her usual heavy make-up. Her opening remarks were not encouraging.

'When do you get me out of this place, Jack?'

'As soon as the police drop their charges.' I didn't think using the word 'if' was a great idea.

'You find out who did it. You promised.' Her voice rose, and I hushed her.

'I promised to try and I'm doing so. But you changed your story, Eva, and even now I'm not sure what the true story is.' This was not the best of places for an interrogation but I had to make a stab at getting some kind of 'truth'.

A sigh of impatience. 'I tell the lawyer I not go to the towpath. I go to the lock, then I go to the pub and Carlos not there, so I go back to hotel.'

'That doesn't seem like you, Eva. You'd go *on* looking for him. He told you where he was going, didn't he?'

'The lock. He not say more or when he leave.'

'Brandon thinks he might have been meeting someone on a boat. Did you tell him that?'

'I not know. Perhaps. He had woman there.'

I pressed on. 'So you would have gone to look at all the boats moored around there.'

'I go see the boats. I not see Carlos. He hiding under bed, perhaps. With woman. Not see, so I go across bridge but not to towpath. *Not see him.*'

'Did you tell the police you checked the boats?'

'They not ask.'

That I found hard to believe. 'Carlos told you it was a business deal – did he give you any idea what kind of business?'

'Woman business,' she told me scornfully.

'Why would he arrange to meet her on a towpath, Eva?
A little unromantic, isn't it? Even if he'd gone first to meet
her on a boat, they'd hardly walk in the semi-dark along that
towpath.'

'Carlos afraid of me,' she told me complacently. 'Hide on
towpath with woman. Perhaps a man too,' she added placatingly. Eva was always good at adapting to what she thought
you might want to hear.

I clutched my head. 'Talk to your solicitor, Eva. Tell *him*
the truth, even if you can't tell me.'

'Of course I tell the truth. Carlos met on boat with woman.'

'But you said you didn't know that for sure, and when you
checked the boats he wasn't there.'

'No, he hide under bed – with woman.'

I was going round in circles, and I would get no further.
Assuming Eva was not guilty, I had to go on digging away at
Carlos's past. I took a deep breath. 'Where did you first meet
Carlos, Eva?'

She beamed at me, so I was on safe territory. 'I met darling
Carlos in 1990 at May Tree. Lovely, lovely place.'

'Did he ever tell you how he got to know about the May
Tree?'

'He went there with Matt. He build up band with him.'

I tried to remember Matt's exact words. There was something
I couldn't quite get a grip on. Something he said about Carlos
coming *back* to Kent in 1987, something about his father and
his band. Belinda had mentioned it too. 'Had Carlos visited
the May Tree before going there with Matt?'

'How would I know?' She gave a shrug. I remembered those
lovely shoulders of hers. . . . how I used to kiss them. To my
dismay, I again felt a moment's desire, but it was a desire born
of memory not of today. Now I could only feel pity, not love
or passion.

'Did he ever mention knowing a Frank Watson?' I asked

her. 'There was a lot of money missing –' (the simplest way to put it) – 'after the valuable haul from a raid in the seventies. There was a fight over it at the May Tree, and this Frank Watson ran away with the cash as well as with the landlord's wife.'

Eva was always impatient when the conversation moved away from herself. 'Yes, yes. Man in the Charros band.'

'That was *Neil* Watson.'

'Perhaps.' Another shrug.

'Did you know him well?' It was like chipping at stone.

'He was gay. Why should he be my lover?'

A typical Eva turnaround.

Another chip at the rock. 'Did Carlos ever talk of the seventies' raid or the missing money? Did Neil ever seem to have a father around?'

Eva had had enough and banged her still beautiful hand on the table.

'How would I know his father, Jack? You talk stupid. What that to do with me?'

Aware of the guards' interested eyes on us, I changed the subject but even so ended the visit defeated. Eva was still giving out the same familiar message from the ivory tower in which she had always lived – herself. Only, the ivory tower was now physical as well as emotional.

I had left another message on Dave's voicemail as I left Wychwood House asking him to send his team over to pick up Melody, but there had been no reply by the time I left for London. That was frustrating in itself. I found a brief message when I had checked my phone after leaving Eva but it was only an irritated, 'Call me, Jack,' from Dave (he doesn't believe in texts). I had tried, but the bird must have flown for the weekend.

Frogs Hill was deserted when I reached it that evening – rather to my relief, as I had thought I might find Daisy patiently waiting for me. I'd left her a message giving her the good news and telling her to wait for the police to contact her. Nevertheless, I confessed to a secret hope that she might have driven up in Melody to thank me. Len and Zoe leave at midday

on Saturdays unless there's a really interesting job – as they
see it – such as rebuilding a carburettor.

There was no Daisy. The sun was beginning to sink towards
its bed in the west, and I felt flat. There was no loving human
being to welcome me, and for once the Gordon-Keeble and
Lagonda failed to work their magic. If Louise . . . No. Stupid
to think that way. Louise had moved on in her life, and so
should I. In a way I had, but not fast enough, and seeing Eva
again had set me back a few notches.

I checked the landline, even though it was a weekend and
was rewarded by finding two calls. Cara? I thought hopefully.
She'd been very quiet. No such luck. The first was from Dave.
I assumed it was merely to say mission accomplished over
Melody and hopefully that he had another commission for me.
It was not. Dave was hopping mad. Instead of his usual laconic,
'Call me, Jack,' his message came over loud and clear and
very annoyed.

'What the blazes is going on, Jack? When the team got
there, the bird had flown. Barn was empty. No one there knew
a thing about its going – or said they didn't. You sure it was
there in the first place? Neither the woman nor the old man
seemed too sure of anything. Can't go after them for theft in
the circumstances, but we'll keep an eye on them. Don't call
me back. Just leave the job to us for the next few days. OK?'

Melody vanished? I was completely flummoxed. Just what
could the link between Wychwood and Melody be? Only, it
occurred to me, Belinda Fever who was hardly likely to be
playing a joke by nicking her own former car from her granddaughter. Had Ambrose pinched it from the Black Lion car
park and taken it to Wychwood under the impression it was
his? Highly improbable, especially as he wouldn't know how
to dispose of it unless Josie had helped him. One step further.
Had she helped him nick it just to please her employer by
arousing his memories of old times? Not very likely. Had
Ambrose forgotten Melody wasn't his and taken her on a
jaunt somewhere? If so, where was Melody now? I conceded
that it was possible to lose a car even when one is in one's
right mind, let alone in Ambrose's state, but if he had just
abandoned the car somewhere, how did he get back home?

Had he and Josie disposed of Melody altogether? If so, where? And more importantly why? Had she driven it to give him the jaunt to Eastry he wanted? If so, why not tell the police?

Then I remembered the second call, and sure enough, it was from Daisy. A simple message recorded twenty minutes before I arrived: 'In the pub, Jack.'

I took one look at my lonely kitchen and the possibilities presented by my fridge and freezer for eating that evening and left for Piper's Green. That's where our terrific and only pub is. As I walked in, I expected to see the whole bar in rapt contemplation of Daisy's beauty, but I didn't. This might have been the case if Daisy had been alone, but Justin was with her, looking more miserable than ever. Even Daisy looked downcast.

'It's not my fault,' Justin said instantly as I approached.

'I know that, Justie,' Daisy said patiently.

'I take it that you've heard the news and that Melody isn't back in Huggett's barn,' I said as jovially as I could.

Justin wasn't doing jovial today. He shook his head.

'The police said you'd found her, Jack.' Daisy's lovely eyes looked accusingly at me.

'I did, but I wasn't authorized to drive it away then and there. The police have to do that.'

'I think,' Daisy informed me crossly, 'that there's something seriously weird going on.'

'I agree. It's possible that the owner of the house has something to do with it, because he's elderly, has Alzheimer's and loves Morris Minors.' Even if he had, I remembered he had shown no sign that he thought Melody was his.

Daisy's eyes lit up. 'Are you going to talk to him or shall I?'

'Not you, Daisy. And the police have told me to steer clear of it.'

'They can't tell me to do that,' she said with a beatific smile. 'Or Justie.'

I froze. 'Don't either of you go anywhere near him.' I spoke so sharply, they actually paid attention.

'Why not? It's my car,' Daisy said mutinously.

'Because,' I told her, 'the case is in police hands. Secondly,

it may have links to a murder case, and thirdly, the owner is
unpredictable to the point of danger. *Keep away.*'

Daisy considered this. 'All right. I'll keep away from where
Melody was found, but I won't keep away from you, Jack.'
Another beatific smile – or rather a triumphant grin.

'And nor will I,' Justin said valiantly, but he was disregarded.
I got the message. Daisy was on the warpath and would continue
to haunt me – and not for my blue eyes or manly build.

Back to my juggling act between Melody and the Carlos trail.
I'd met the three surviving Charros and the singer. It seemed
to me there was something missing, however. The bare facts
of the relationships amongst them didn't add up to a whole.
I'd asked to see Clive on the Monday but was not totally
surprised when I arrived that Jonathan was with him – on
guard. That was obvious, for all the fuss they made of me by
serving me an espresso and biscuits and chatting merrily on
any subject other than Carlos Mendez.

'About Carlos,' I interrupted firmly.

Silence, then Jonathan took the stage. 'I gather you've met
Josie and Matt, so I presume you are now convinced that the
remaining Charros are not operating a Mafia vendetta after
twenty years?' he said lightly but not mockingly.

'That's Sherlock country,' I replied equally lightly. 'I'm just
trying to find out what happened.'

'I'm sure,' Jonathan said more seriously, 'that only your
Eva can tell you that. We don't blame you for trying, however.'

'Thanks.'

'So what can we do for you this time? We're at full attention, but only because we want to get this matter sorted out
once and for all. Josie is pretty upset at having it all raked up
again.'

'It wasn't me who killed Carlos,' I reminded them, 'so don't
blame me.'

'Nor, believe it or not, was it any of the former Charros.'

'You all knew he was back, and you all had very good
reason to hate him.'

A glance at Clive, who sat sullenly mute, then Jonathan
answered: 'He made no secret of his return, because he knew

he had nothing to fear from us. Not even from Josie, whose life was so badly affected by his actions.'

'They affected yours and Clive's too,' I pointed out.

'What's that supposed to mean?' Clive growled.

'I suppose,' Jonathan said, 'he's heard the story that it was Carlos who gave you away to the police, Clive.'

Another growl. 'Never knew whether he did nor not.'

'There was no evidence of it,' Jonathan told me smoothly. 'Only suspicion.'

Suspicion can be a powerful driving force, I thought. Moreover, there were motives that went far beyond the mere dissolution of the band – motives that might be relevant to the anniversary lunch, now only a month away.

'Did you know Frank Watson?' I asked out of the blue – with interesting results.

'*Frank*?' No doubt about it, Jonathan was shaken.

'Is he still alive?' I asked.

He took a fraction too long to reply: 'Neil died in 1992 when he was twenty-two. I imagine his father must then have been in his mid-forties. He could well be alive. I've no idea. Have you, Clive?'

Clive took his cue and shook his head.

'The police file on the May Tree Shoot-Out must still be open,' I commented.

'Probably.' Jonathan said no more, but for the first time I sensed I was in the driving seat.

'Frank Watson is thought to have escaped from the shoot-out, taking the priceless Crowshaw Collection with him,' I pointed out. 'If he *was* back in this country or had never left it, then it's possible that Carlos discovered that in the 1980s and decided he'd like some of it in the form of blackmail. You were living with Neil at the time of his death, so he must have talked about his father, and if he was around you would have met him.'

Jonathan had recovered his sangfroid now. 'I don't recall it, but it's an interesting theory. The snag is that Neil was living with me and not at his home, wherever that was, and I don't recall Neil telling me adventure stories about his father being a gangster. Anyway, Frank Watson was hardly likely to stick around in England if the police were still after him. Neil just told me his father took him to South America when he was about eight, and he lived there until he came back to Kent – *alone* – to go to university. He lived in lodgings and then with me.'

So Neil had kept mum about his father and Jonathan had obviously never made the connection – or had he? I tried a parting shot. 'Frank Watson had every reason to want Carlos dead if he believed Neil had died because of him – and if Carlos was blackmailing him, even more reason.'

'That,' murmured Jonathan, 'is true. The only problem with that theory is that you haven't the slightest evidence that Frank Watson *is* back in England.'

I returned to Frogs Hill expecting to join Len and Zoe in a truly interesting quest to restore life to a Karmann Ghia, a car for which I've always had a special affection. Dad had an affinity with Karmann Ghias, and that's important in a classic car. My plans were foiled – once again by Daisy. She was sitting on the wall, contemplating her smart black boots.

'*There* you are,' she said brightly. 'This is my day off so I thought I'd come over. What's the news?'

'Nothing on Melody.' I had rung Dave's team early that morning, fearing she would be on my trail. 'Too soon.'

'Not for me, Jack. Have you been out hunting for her?'

Honesty is the best policy. 'I'm afraid not. The police—'

'Then I'll go and beard that old chap at – um – Wychwood, is it?'

'*No!*'

She grinned at me. 'Then you go, Jack.'

Actually, why not? I'd go.

My heart sank, but on the other hand I needed an excuse to go to Wychwood again. Preferably not now, it was true. But I faced reality with a grim determination. The mystery of the missing Melody needed my urgent attention.

EIGHT

planned to tackle Wychwood unannounced. At the very least, if both Josie and Ambrose were out I could nose around the old barn again to try to figure out whether I had indeed been hallucinating. I might have had Melody so much on my mind that I saw her everywhere. I dismissed that notion right away and concentrated on why it had been so necessary for Melody to disappear again. The most likely reason was that I had seen her. The next most likely was that Ambrose might have taken her on a solo local jaunt and forgotten to bring her back. I thought I could rule that out, however, as even in his demented state he had shown no liking for her.

So back to the first possible explanation. Why was Melody so precious that she had to disappear quickly in case I (or the police) removed her forcibly? She had looked a straightforward Morris Minor 1000 to me. In good nick, true, but then a great many Moggies could answer that criterion. The colour? Striking, but not so unusual that an enthusiast could not get any Minor resprayed in Rose Taupe more easily than by stealing Melody.

Tentatively, then, I put Melody's disappearance down to my arrival on the scene. Which meant what? First, the possibility that someone did not want Daisy to have her car back – very unlikely – or wanted it themselves (more likely). The second possibility was that I represented a link to the police and – stretching it – to Carlos's murder. That would mean that Melody had some kind of connection with Josie, her mother, Belinda Fever, and therefore the Charros. The drawback to that theory was that by the time Melody disappeared I had already seen the car and had had every opportunity to mull over its connections to Wychwood. The barn door was being shut *after* I had seen what was inside.

Could Melody be linked to Carlos's death? He had been

killed late on a Monday evening in mid May, and Melody had
been stolen four days earlier – first, by Justin, whom I had great
difficulty in imagining could be mixed up in a murder. It had
been *after* Carlos's death that Melody had disappeared from
Justin's friend's 'guardianship'. She could have been stolen
for a day, perhaps, without the friend being aware of her
absence from the car park, but could not have had a role in
the murder because of the timing. What threat could Melody
present now? Was someone's DNA plastered all over her? Was
Josie in the frame? How would she have known of the car's
theft in the first place, unless of course she was responsible
for it? Presumably, Gran Fever did not know about Melody's
disappearance from the barn, and I did not want to be the one
to tell her.

This case, I thought savagely as I drove to Wychwood
through the rain, was, as Churchill famously said about Russia,
a riddle wrapped in a mystery inside an enigma. I couldn't
even define the case itself. Was it Carlos's murder? A hunt for
the missing Crowshaw Collection? Or the theft of a Morris
Minor?

Rain, rain everywhere. It dripped from the trees as I passed
them, it fell on to the muddy track, it beat on the windscreen
in triumph. Fields were becoming ponds, ponds could consider
themselves lakes, the green leaves of June were battered with
serious rain. No summer showers here. As I turned the last
corner of the track, Wychwood House presented a dismal sight
indeed with trees looming over two sides of it, encouraged by
the late spring rain.

It was raining so hard that I ran from the Alfa to the door,
pulling my jacket hood over my head and not pausing to look
around me. There was no reply to the bell, and it was only
then that I turned round and took in the significance of the
cars parked there. I had not even noticed there were any as I
arrived. I recognized Matt's van and Josie's Polo. The third
car I had seen recently at the House of Lamb. It was Jonathan's
Bristol. Its presence was *very* interesting, and unless their
owners had gone on a long country walk in the rain they were
all in the house.

When there was still no reply to the bell, I persuaded myself that it was legitimate in the interests of the case for me to squelch up the track to the barn despite the fact that I would undoubtedly get even wetter. I regretted it the moment I got there. The door was padlocked. By forcing my way through the long wet grass and weeds I managed to find a crack through which I at least managed to establish that Melody had not returned to her temporary home. I harboured a vision of a fairy tale ending whereby Belinda had quietly 'rescued' the car to restore it to Daisy personally, and without much hope I fished in my pocket for my phone.

Belinda picked up immediately and sounded amused. 'Me? Rescue Melody from a fate worse than death at Wychwood? Good gracious, Jack. That sounds such a delightful scenario, but I am afraid I have to disappoint you. And, it seems, Daisy.' A pause. 'Did you say that you're at Wychwood now?'

'Yes, and so, I believe, are the Charros, all present and correct.'

'Not quite,' she reminded me briskly. 'Don't forget Neil.'

She was right. Neil, the unseen but much remembered Charro. As I turned down the track again I began to feel like the goodie cowboy riding into town to face the baddies lined up waiting for him. Unlike a cowboy, however, I was part walking, part running because of the rain, and all I had to face was a former singer, a gardener, two interior designers and Ambrose. It didn't sound too bad, put that way.

This time the door was opened so promptly that I wondered if Belinda had warned them of my arrival. Perhaps she had, because an unsurprised and stony-faced Josie barred the entrance.

'It's not convenient,' she informed me.

'I'm not here to see you or your guests, Josie. I'd like to speak to Dr Fairbourne.'

'You can't. He's with us.'

'Police work,' I reminded her gently. 'This missing Morris Minor.'

She glared at me for a moment, but then said: 'You'd better come in, I suppose. We'd more or less finished, anyway.'

What they had finished she did not explain as she led the way to the living room, where Ambrose was indeed present. He was comfortably huddled in front of an unseasonal fire

and looked very pleased to see me. Perhaps it was only the
boiling temperature of the room that made the others seem
uncomfortable at my arrival.

'Good to see you all again,' I told them cheerily.

This welcome did not seem to be reciprocated. Matt was
slumped on the sofa with Josie, and Clive was perched tensely
on the edge of an armchair. Jonathan had taken an upright
chair as befitted what I assumed he thought his role: leader
of the pack.

'Just an impromptu get-together to plan the anniversary
lunch,' he told me graciously. 'Time is marching on and the
ninth of July is less than a month away.'

I murmured something appropriate without implying that a
lunch for half a dozen or so guests could hardly take that
much planning. Then I turned to Ambrose. 'Do you attend the
lunch too, Dr Fairbourne?' I gave myself a mental pat on
the back for a rare neat chess move on my part. Ambrose had
no reason to be involved in this discussion, so why was he
here? I awaited his or someone else's response. What's more,
where was Belinda if this was about the lunch?

A beaming vacant smile from Ambrose was the only
response I received.

'What can we do for you this time, Jack?' Jonathan enquired
with only a slight emphasis on the 'this'.

'I'm here about the disappearing Morris Minor.'

A look of relief on their faces. They all seemed to know
about it because Clive immediately sprang to the defensive:
'Nothing to do with us.'

'Of course not,' I murmured. 'I just needed to check with
Josie and Dr Fairbourne on the exact time we were together
in the barn with the car.'

'Why?' Josie snapped. 'You were there. You know.'

I shrugged. 'Form-filling. You're witnesses.'

'Josie told us it was Rose Taupe,' Jonathan commented.
'Great colour, great car.'

'It is,' I agreed. 'You had a Morris Minor once, Dr Fairbourne,
although I know the one we saw in that barn wasn't yours.'

'Did I have one?' Ambrose looked puzzled.

'You had several, judging by your photos.'

'Photos?' Then he sprang into life. 'Yes, I had a grey one. Muriel and I used to drive it to Eastry. And I had a blue one too.'

'But never a Rose Taupe Minor?'

'No.' A pause. 'And it wasn't hers either.'

'His wife's,' Josie amplified.

Ambrose's words about the Minor had been slightly different earlier, I recalled, which implied he must have several stories running through his head at the same time. 'Is the barn usually locked?'

'No. Usually nothing in it to steal,' Josie replied. 'Police told us to padlock it. Security. I'll let you know if that car turns up again. You can have the key if you're bothered and check it yourself.'

'Best kept with you. Thanks anyway.'

Matt sniggered. 'Anything to oblige, Mr Sort of Policeman.'

The general bonhomie was out of place for this group, as if they knew they were winning. But winning what?

'We wouldn't hear it even if it did come back,' Josie commented. 'We sleep tight, don't we, Ambrose?'

'Don't like Rose Taupe,' Ambrose broke in. 'Josie, why was that thing in the barn?'

No one answered, and their faces were devoid of any expression. If anyone here knew the answer to Ambrose's question I wasn't going to hear it.

I was afraid I might find Daisy when I reached Frogs Hill again, but fate was kind to me. Very kind. It was my daughter who was awaiting me in the farmhouse, albeit an unhappy looking Cara.

'My day has suddenly brightened up,' I told her.

'It has a long way to go for me.'

This didn't sound good. 'Why didn't you tell me you were coming?'

'I didn't know I was, until Eva summoned me.'

'You've seen her?' Gruelling though that must have been, it surely would not account for Cara looking so very miserable.

'She called me. So I went, like a fool, though I was glad I made the effort. She's not in good shape, and you know what the statistics are about people on remand. Depression and—'

'Not Eva,' I broke in. 'However depressed she wouldn't kill herself.' Nevertheless, if I had needed any proof that speed was essential this was it.

'She said she was worried you might have the wrong impression of what happened that night.'

Here we go again, I thought. 'Which presumably she has now confessed to you was not true,' I said grimly. 'What's the story?'

'She isn't actually sure that Carlos did come down to Maidstone with a floozie or plan to meet one here.'

'Nothing surprising there. Good job Brandon's only arrested her and not a troupe of lap dancers,' I said wryly.

'Eva's quite enough for him to cope with,' Cara said fervently. 'She told me she rang Carlos about an hour after he stormed out of the hotel restaurant and left for Allington Lock. He said he was on the towpath at the lock and wouldn't be back that night because he was staying on a boat. She decided this deal included at least one woman for a rave-up, so she called a taxi and went to the lock. Couldn't find him on a boat so she went over to the towpath and walked along it in the Maidstone direction. No sign of him there so she went the other way past the weir and found him dead. Out of shock she did a runner and was picked up by a taxi she called when she was nearly back at Maidstone. She was seen by a couple on the main road while she waited for the taxi. They identified her to the police.'

This was beginning to sound like the unwelcome truth at last. No wonder Brandon thought he had enough to charge her. She could easily have left trace evidence at the scene, and running away was not going to help her case one little bit. I only hoped it *was* the truth this time, and that she hadn't had a row with him and killed him herself. 'What about the gun?' I blurted out to get all the bad news over at once.

'She says she didn't see one,' Cara told me.

Not much help either way. If Brandon's river search found nothing he would theorize that she had pinched Carlos's gun and afterwards secreted it somewhere in the hotel or its grounds. Not good.

'And what's with you, Cara?' I asked quietly. 'Trouble at the farm?' She was not her usual confident self.

She managed a grin. 'Not exactly. Only a tiff with Harry. He says he needs my help on the farm at this time of year, not my rushing off to London every two minutes. My *other* boss is fine with it though.'

'Does Harry have a point?'

'*You* rushed after Eva. So should I.'

'I only want to stop her putting her head straight into the noose – not literally, thank heavens, nowadays. I haven't achieved much else.' Yet, I told myself without conviction.

'That's why I've come. To help.'

'Then Harry's being unreasonable.'

She cheered up immediately. 'The trouble is, Dad, I'm not used to being – well – tied.'

I thought of Louise, who had untied herself from me to follow her star rather than throw in her lot with me, and I wanted to do all I could to prevent its happening to my daughter. The roles were reversed in her case, but basically it was the same situation: two people who love each other apparently going their separate ways.

'There must be a compromise between you two,' I said. 'You just have to find it.' I'd never told Cara about what happened between Louise and me, but I did so now. I didn't want the story plastered all over the tabloids, given that Louise is a celeb, but I could trust Cara.

'Didn't you try to work out a compromise with her?' she asked when I'd finished.

'There wasn't time.'

'Could you now?'

'It takes two.'

I could tell Cara was going into control mood again. Sure enough, out it came: 'Maybe I'd better go to see your Louise,' she said. 'Perhaps we could work something out together.'

'Don't,' I said through clenched teeth, 'do that, Cara. I'll sort out my own problems.'

'Or not.'

'Then I'll have to live with it. OK by you?' I was getting rattled.

She studied me. 'Now I see where I got it from.'

'Got what?'

'Obstinacy.'

'So?' I glared at her.

Cara sighed happily. 'We're having a row. Now I *know* I have a father.'

'Try having one with Harry. Get it out on the table.'

'I will. Thanks, Dad.'

I was so moved at not one but *two* 'Dads' that I ruined the moment. 'And, my pet, we can both tackle Eva.'

Much happier – both of us – I waved Cara off on her way the next morning: first to London to see Eva and then back to Suffolk. I even felt up to tackling Daisy, so I took the Lagonda over to Burchett Forstal bakery. There she was reigning supreme amongst the farmhouse loaves and stuffed rolls, wielding her tongs like a sceptre.

I waited for a while until she was alone in the shop and took advantage of a brief lull to go inside.

'Any news?' she asked breathlessly. 'I have to give the old heap back to Justie's dad soon,' she pointed out, no doubt having read my expression correctly.

'No news. I went to Wychwood yesterday but we're no further on, and nor are the police.'

'So why can't *you* find her?' she asked miserably.

'Because a car detective doesn't have a hidden magnet that draws us to the very car we're looking for. We have to wait for sighting reports of abandoned cars or other unusual signs, plus keep up the watch on the ferries.' Mistake.

'You mean Melody might have gone out to *Russia* or somewhere?' she shrieked.

'It's possible, but I don't think so in Melody's case.'

'Why not?' she demanded hopefully. 'Because she's so special?'

'Firstly because the Morris Minor is not much of an international car so demand would not be high, and secondly my seeing her at Wychwood House suggests it's not an ordinary theft.'

'No theft is ordinary to the victim,' she said sulkily with a wisdom beyond her years.

'That's true. In some cases it's not to the thief either.'

'What do you mean?'

'Look at Justin, who stole Melody in the first place. Melody meant something to him because you mean something to him.'

A peal of laughter. 'The idiot. Well, I don't mean anything to this bloke at Wychwood House. I've never met him.'

'No, but your Gran owned the May Tree and he was one of her customers.'

Daisy shrugged. 'Maybe, but it's all local, isn't it? Everyone knows the May Tree.'

Including Josie and her mother and all the Charros. But I always came back to the stumbling block. Belinda Fever was not going to steal a car she'd given to her granddaughter. And yet . . . that seemed such a neat solution.

'Fancy a ride in a Lagonda?' I asked Daisy. 'Lunch out?'

'Cheers. Yes, if I'm quick. The relief comes in at twelve. Just us?'

'With your Gran, Daisy.'

It was a perfect picture. A pub, a green, a duck pond – and the Lagonda. Not to mention the Thunderbird in which Belinda duly purred up. The purr was enhanced by a roar of approval from Daisy and me, both standing up to cheer her in. Daisy went one better and leapt on the bench to reinforce the message. The couple of ducks strolling around on land marked their disapproval by retreating to the pond.

Belinda then proceeded to do the perfect Gran act by tottering over, sitting down with a sigh and demanding a cup of tea – or a non-alcoholic beer would do, she amended. 'To what do I owe this honour, Jack?' she asked. 'Merely doing your duty by a dotty old woman?'

'Duty, yes. Far from dotty, far from old.'

'That should be a compliment. What makes me think it isn't? Why the duty, Jack?' The thoughtful eyes met mine head on, although Daisy merely looked bewildered.

'I found Melody in an old barn at Wychwood House.'

Daisy's attention was immediately one hundred per cent on us both.

'So you said,' Belinda said calmly.

'She's vanished again.'

'You said that too.'

'Do you know Wychwood House?'

'Of course, but I would hardly walk up there and run off with Melody.'

'You know Josie and Ambrose well, though.'

'As much as one can know him nowadays, yes.'

'You knew him before the Alzheimer's struck?'

'He was a customer at the May Tree all the time I was there. That's from 1980, which is a fair while ago. You know all this, Jack.' Belinda was getting impatient.

Good. That meant I might get somewhere. 'Do you know him well enough to ask him and Josie if Melody could be left there for a few days?'

Daisy was open mouthed with shock, but Belinda was right there. 'I don't know what planet you're on, Jack, but it's not the same one as I am. Steal Melody? You really think I'd upset Daisy by doing such a thing? I thought Justin had stolen her.'

'Her disappearance from Wychwood is no ordinary theft, Belinda.'

'But Gran had nothing to do with it, Jack,' wailed Daisy.

Belinda ignored her. This was between her and me. 'You've got a very strange bee in your bonnet, Jack, and it's stung you this time.'

'All the Charros were at Wychwood just after Melody disappeared. Why?'

She was looking at me with pity. 'You're trying hard, Jack, but you're still way out. Look elsewhere. Not at me. And for goodness sake, let's have lunch.'

I'd mishandled this discussion big time, even though we patched things up over lunch. I'd had a hunch about Melody and Belinda that had been punctured like a tyre on a bed of nails. Furthermore I'd upset Daisy and, worst of all, I didn't know where I was going with this. The key lay in Wychwood, I was sure, but the key to what? Melody? Carlos's death, or Frank Watson? Or perhaps all three. Just one would do at present.

If the key to this puzzle did lie at Wychwood, the odds were it included Ambrose as well as Josie. I didn't know much about Alzheimer's but I suspected it wasn't a condition that left much room for considered deception. If, however, I could hit the right note and gain some rapport with Ambrose I might get somewhere – provided I could avoid that lug wrench.

I spent some time studying Eastry, since I reasoned that was the way to get Ambrose's attention – even if he performed another reincarnation of King Egbert. I mugged up on its archaeology and history, discovering there had been no less than three major digs there in relatively recent times: one in late 1970 at Eastry House, which from its finds proved to be an Anglo Saxon burial ground, of which there are now several known in the vicinity of the village; the second dig was in 1980 at Eastry Court, next to the church. This was specifically in search of the Anglo-Saxon royal palace. The results of that were inconclusive from the finds; the palace might have been there, or it might not.

The third dig, as recently as 2006, was by television's famed *Time Team* presented by Tony Robinson; this had pinpointed Highborough Hill to the north-east of the village, and the dig there had led to further digs again in the village itself. Once again, Eastry Court failed to reveal any conclusive evidence, and from the overall effort the surest result was that the hill site had been a ritual meeting place. Christianity had come to Kent at the end of the sixth century, but it had obviously taken time to change over completely from pre-Christian faiths and rituals, as there was little doubt that inhabitants would hedge their bets with only gradual merging of the two.

Had Ambrose been involved with the Eastry digs? It was highly possible, at least for the first two, although his chief claim to fame, I had discovered, had been an Anglo-Saxon hoard found in Suffolk. And yet: 'Are you going to take me to Eastry?' he had asked when I first met him. Not Suffolk. Was it Eastry's royal palace or the burial grounds that attracted him, or both? Had he dug there, or did he wish he had done so? I remembered his quoting Shakespeare: 'Let's talk of graves, of worms and epitaphs.' Buried treasure and King Egbert. Grave goods rather than buried treasure? For a king they would be treasure indeed. Was I at last on the right track? I could find no evidence that Egbert had been buried at St

Augustine's in Canterbury, which had been founded with the
express intention of providing a burial place for the Kings of
Kent and was now in ruins. That did not mean Egbert was not
buried there, but Ambrose might well have – or had – his own
theories as to where the grave was.

'Ambrose, you've got your wish,' I breathed to myself. 'I'm
going to take you to Eastry.'

Fridays were thought to be unlucky in earlier times, and this
was a Friday. On some days misfortune seems to hang around
in the air from the time one fires the engine by simply getting
out of bed, but this did not seem to be the case when three
days later I drove through the woods to Wychwood again. I
was beginning to have doubts on the merits of this mission,
however. Even if Ambrose did want to go to Eastry, what
relevance could that possibly have to Carlos, the Charros and
Frank Watson? Looked at from that angle, this mission was
only a crazy whim. I reminded myself that Ambrose had been
a May Tree regular, and Carlos had paid regular visits too.
Did they overlap? Even if they did, however, Ambrose, for all
his large house, did not seem to be a rich man, so he could
hardly qualify for Carlos's 'business meeting'.

I almost changed my mind about going to Wychwood, but
as I was so near I steeled myself to go ahead. What was so
wrong about humouring an old man's whim, even if it did
not have relevance to my case? It was gone midday when I
reached the house, and the door was opened immediately.
Josie looked distraught and was only too pleased to see me.

'He's gone,' she cried. 'I can't find Ambrose.'

'I'll help you look,' I offered. 'He's probably just wandered
off.'

She shook her head. 'He wouldn't do that. It's his lunchtime,
and he knows that when it's my shopping morning I bring
some back with me. He's always waiting for me. But today
he wasn't, and I've searched everywhere I can think of.'

This sounded bad. 'Has his Renault gone?' If he thought
he could still drive, there might be trouble ahead. As his son
sometimes took him out in it, there would be petrol in the car,
so Ambrose might have seized the opportunity.

She took the point, and we raced over to the garage. I pulled the door down, and she peered inside. 'No, the Renault's here, thank heavens. But he's not in the house, so he must be out here somewhere.'

'We'll call the police to keep a lookout but I expect he'll come back in his own time.' I didn't even convince myself, and it was clear a major hunt was necessary.

Josie disregarded me. 'He'd never miss lunch. He must have hurt himself.'

'We'll check the grounds. What about the old barn where I found the car? That's been on his mind recently. He might have walked up there.'

She clutched at this straw and, as we hurried along the track without a sign of him, all sorts of wild scenarios – or not so wild – chased through my mind. Would we find a king in full regalia, a Saxon warrior, a monk . . .? Was he digging trenches looking for his precious Anglo-Saxon remains?

I ran ahead and saw the doors were closed. 'I can't see any sign of him around,' I called back to her.

'Where is he then?' Josie wailed.

The doors weren't locked so I pulled them open – and found Ambrose.

No King Egbert now. No Melody either.

Ambrose Fairbourne lay spreadeagled on his back with distorted blue lips, through which his tongue bulged, specks of blood on his face, eyes staring sightlessly upwards, his neck—

He had been strangled.

NINE

I was barely aware of Josie at my side as I knelt to check there was no life left in him. The only sound was that of her deep rasping breaths. I registered that she was trying to hold back panic, but even as I went to help her, her screams began, piercing through me with almost physical pain. I put my arm round her and half pulled, half pushed her out of that terrible place until we were some ten yards down the track and surrounded by the greenery of the trees rustling in the cool breeze. I waited a moment or two until her breathing was more regular, then pointed further down the track to where I could see a fallen tree trunk.

'Over there,' I said gently. 'Sit down while I ring the police. Then I'll come to join you.'

Josie said nothing, but looked at me with humbling gratitude. In nightmare situations such as this it is a relief when someone takes the initiative, and in this case I had no choice. It had to be me. I watched as she followed my instructions, and I rang for the emergency services. I double-checked that Josie was still sitting on the trunk, then forced myself back to the barn. I'd often met violence in the past, but this time the poignancy and pointlessness of this crime overwhelmed me. Who on earth would want so badly the death of an old man suffering from Alzheimer's, when his active participation in this world was past? Was Ambrose wealthier than he had seemed? Was this a case of his heirs wanting to gain their inheritance more quickly than nature had planned? I clutched at this scenario, but his son seemed to have an established career of his own so it hardly seemed likely.

Had Ambrose disturbed a casual intruder? But why would any casual intruder want to break into a garage that a peek through a crack would reveal was empty? I checked the padlock without touching it, but it did not look forced, so Ambrose must have unlocked it himself unless it had once again been left open. Was his killer someone who wanted the Morris Minor and didn't know that it was no longer there? Why *kill* Ambrose though? Casual intruders would probably be local and news of Ambrose's condition would have spread, which meant they would know that they had nothing to fear from leaving him alive to tell the tale. That's what logic told me, but life is not always logical and nor are inflamed emotional reactions.

Ambrose had been strangled manually, as far as I could see. There was no sign of a ligature but that would need closer examination. I remained in one spot at the door, partly not to disturb the crime scene any more than I had already done and partly to ensure that Josie was still sitting on the tree trunk. I could see that she was. In Ambrose's weak condition, physically as well as mentally, it was conceivable a woman might have been his killer, but that was for the police to work out. The idea that Josie might have killed him repelled me, not just because of the nature of the crime but because I had begun to have an unexpected liking for her. I could see no motive – quite the contrary – but nevertheless she was undoubtedly in the best position to kill him. Her alibi that she was shopping would need witnesses to convince the police. However, if she wanted Ambrose to die there were easier ways than strangulation for her to kill him – *if* she had any reason to do so. For the life of me I couldn't see what she had to gain from his death. Years ago Carlos had deprived her of one career avenue, and Ambrose's death would mean the end of a job that seemed to suit her well.

I walked along the track to join her, still pondering why Ambrose might have come to the barn. I sat down at Josie's side, but the wood felt cold to the touch – unless it was me who was cold. She was a pathetic sight: long grey cardigan over jeans and T-shirt, lank hair, and a weather-lined face that at the moment was sagging under all the cares of the world. She looked in a terrifying state of confusion, and no wonder, with all that must be running through her mind. I put my arm round her and she seemed glad of it, although in a world of her own which must be spinning out of control. Was that through shock at the discovery of Ambrose's body or – I had to consider – the horror at facing what she herself had done or brought about? Had the Charros' visit two days earlier anything to do with this? Is that what the meeting had been about? Again I could not think of a single reason linking the two events, but the coincidence could not be ignored, for all its sinister implications.

'The police will be here soon,' I said to Josie, just to make contact. 'I think I hear sirens.' I couldn't, but it seemed to break the ice.

'Who would have wanted to kill him?' she blurted out.

It was a rhetorical question, so I didn't answer it directly. 'He's been dead some while,' I told her. When I had briefly touched it, the body seemed already to be slightly cooling. 'How long were you out?'

'Left about nine thirty,' she said dully.

Blood cools at about one and a half degrees centigrade in an hour in average conditions, if I remembered correctly. So if I was right, Ambrose could have died not long after Josie had left and certainly more than an hour ago. I hesitated whether to continue or not, but as she had made the first move, I decided to keep the conversation going, without pushing her.

'Was he OK when you left – nothing unusual?' I asked, making it sound a casual enquiry.

'No. I helped get him up as usual. Eight o'clock. Gave him his breakfast. Got off to the supermarket, did the shopping as always, but when I got back he wasn't there.'

I thought she was going to break down again, so I raced ahead as fast as I could. 'As far as you know, was anyone coming to visit or sit with him?'

'Like I told you,' she told me dully, 'he's safe enough for short periods. Matt said he might come to do some work on the garden.'

'Did he do so?'

'No sign of him, but then there wouldn't be. He doesn't care if I'm out. He knows I'll pay him next time. Haven't had time to see if he's done work or not.' Her voice broke, perhaps because she realized there would be no next time.

'What reason might Ambrose have to walk up to that barn?'

'Only bloody Eastry,' she replied without rancour. 'I kept

telling him that Morris Minor wasn't there any more, but he
kept on going on about it and going to Eastry, so he might
have gone to the barn instead of the garage where the Renault
is. The garage is locked too but I think he knew where I keep
the keys. He might have got mixed up, thinking the Renault
was up there.' She jerked her head towards the barn, then
shuddered, perhaps thinking of what *was* up there. 'He's
supposed to take another test before he drives again but he
couldn't drive a pedal bike the way he was.'

'Did you do the shopping alone?' A step too far because
she glared at me.

'With my mum. Sainsbury's. Any objection?'

'Good choice,' I said placatingly.

She didn't miss the implication though. 'And if you think
I'd kill old Ambrose, what do you think I am? A flaming
maniac? Why would I? I've – had – a job and a place to live.
What am I going to do now, eh? You tell me that!'

Her voice reached a screech but, fortunately for me and
perhaps for her, I could now hear the sirens and they were
close by. I'd rung Brandon as well as dialling 999, and my
guess was that as Brandon might see the possible link with
Carlos's death he would gear up straightaway to come with
his full team. It was time to move, to my relief. While one is
doing one doesn't have to *think* so much, and so for me the
image of Ambrose's body might retreat for a while.

Taking Josie with me, I went down the track to the front
of the house, where there was as yet only one police car
drawing up. A female PC was first to emerge, followed by her
male partner. I didn't know either of them, but they told me
that, as I had predicted, Brandon was on his way. I led the
male PC to the crime scene, leaving Josie with his partner.
The constable looked so green as he quickly emerged from
the barn that I wondered whether this was his first serious
crime scene. Certainly, I found myself more or less in charge
and told him to stay at the barn while I joined the other two.

From then on it was like any gathering of people: slow
build-up and then suddenly everything's happening at once.
One minute I was wondering whether to launch into a full
explanation of who I was and what I was doing here, the next

there was a blare of sirens and I was directing traffic for parking. The die was cast now. It would all begin in earnest, and it was out of my hands. Cars and vans parked, disgorging uniform, plain clothes and civilians alike. I briefly saw Brandon, who nodded at me, then got down to work. Josie and I were the outsiders, banished to remain by the house as cordon tape, medics, pathologists, and photographers took over. We were spare wheels as the machinery of the crime scene revved into action. I had a ridiculous longing to yell, '*Stop*,' and pretend that none of this had happened and that Ambrose was once again smiling vacantly by the fire.

'Let's go inside,' I told Josie abruptly, unable to watch any longer.

She managed a grin of sorts. 'Do my job? Make coffee?'

'We'll do it together.'

Brandon was remarkably unquestioning of my discovery of the crime scene when he finally got round to me. It wasn't the first time I'd happened to be present at one, but he was too sensible to make a point over that. Been there, done that, start from here was his approach. It took some three hours before he started in on *me* in earnest. I'd given my story several times in brief both to him and other officers before this grilling really began. Ambrose's body had not yet been removed, so it was going to be a long haul. Josie and I had lunched on a coffee plus a sandwich she insisted on making for me with surprising energy. 'It'll help,' she snapped when I resisted. It did help, and I had told her so. She was the first to be interrogated in full – unsurprisingly – and it was late afternoon by the time she emerged (in tears) and I took her place.

'Any particular reason you were here today, Jack?' Brandon asked me.

I was still 'Jack' to him, I noted, so I might not yet be at the top of the list of suspects – yet.

I had my answer ready. 'Job for Dave Jennings. It was in that barn that Daisy Croft's Morris Minor was last seen.'

'And you thought it might have come back? Exceptionally industrious of you to check.'

So he didn't believe me. Hardly surprising, I suppose. 'This is a car that does more disappearing acts than the traditional lady in the cabinet trick,' I explained. 'It's an interesting case and—'

'What else?' he cut in.

'I thought it might have links to the Mendez murder.'

'So you said on the phone. Tell me more,' Brandon said grimly. '*After* you've explained why you're poking your nose into my case.'

I saw red, but managed to subdue that to pink when I replied. 'You can't expect me to take a cruise to the Bahamas while my ex-wife is banged up in Holloway. She's probably not guilty of anything except acute jealousy and not being able to distinguish reality from fantasy.'

'You could be right,' Brandon agreed more amiably. 'Unfortunately, until we and the CPS have solid evidence to the contrary and can therefore delete the "probably" we've no choice.'

That sounded cautiously good news. 'Are you still working on it? You're on to something – someone? Found the gun?'

'No to all of those,' he said dampeningly, 'and we've checked the river and round the hotel grounds. Trace evidence in plenty, so she now admits she saw him on the towpath though she claims he was already dead.'

I was torn, glad that Eva had at least admitted to her presence at the scene, but terrified that she still had further to go: that she had killed him. In vain I reminded myself that if Eva had gone provided with a gun, whether hers or Carlos's, and then used it, she wouldn't have had the sense to take care over hiding it. She would have chucked it straight into the river or even left it by the body. 'I've some new leads,' I began too eagerly.

A step too far. Brandon was on to me like a flash in DCI mode, brooking no flimflam. 'That's the reason you came here, isn't it?'

'No. I did want to check on the car, but my main reason was to take Ambrose to the haunts of his former Kentish archaeological interests. At Eastry.'

That caught him off balance. 'Very generous of you. Why?'

'He wanted to go.'

Brandon eyed me speculatively, but obviously decided to leave Eastry lying fallow. '*Why* check on the car?'

'Because, as I explained, I think it's connected somehow to Carlos's death.'

'How?' he whipped back like a busted fan belt.

I had no choice now. 'Josie was the singer in Carlos's band. You were following up the former members. Did you talk to all of them?'

He nodded. 'We did. Including Josie Gibson. But it seems unlikely that any of them would rush to Allington Lock to kill Mendez after so long. Ambrose Fairbourne's murder is a different matter, especially if you're right and that Morris Minor has any link to it.'

'It's certainly one heck of a coincidence its turning up here if it doesn't.'

'Likely or not, it could be Miss Gibson was complicit in the theft – and it was serious enough for someone, if not her, to kill Fairbourne because he got in the way.'

I felt my stomach turn over, but despite my personal reactions it had to be considered. 'Before Daisy Croft,' I told Brandon firmly, 'the Morris belonged to Belinda Fever, her grandmother, who was owner of the May Tree Inn at the time the Mendez band was formed.'

He frowned. 'Very cosy circle, as Miss Gibson was with the band at that time. We've nothing to suggest a Minor was involved in Mendez's murder though. He drove an old Ford Granada there.'

'His killer could have come in the Morris. It's an unusual colour,' I pointed out. 'Pinky-grey. Might have been spotted?'

'Timing?' Brandon asked.

I thought back. Justin had taken Melody on May the ninth, moved her on the thirteenth to her new 'home' at the Black Lion, and on the seventeenth she had vanished again. Those eight days included the evening of Carlos's murder, the thirteenth. It was theoretically possible that she had been 'borrowed' from the car park just for the purposes of Carlos's murderer and then returned a few hours later, but in that case why had she been taken again four days later?

'Just about possible but unlikely.'

'OK, Jack. Leave it to us. I'll liaise with Dave.'

Colby not required, I realized. Tough. 'What about the boat angle?'

'No sign of one that would fit the bill, all checked. Nor any evidence of Carlos having been on the lock side of the river.'

'There are moorings back in the Maidstone direction on the side Carlos was found.'

Brandon dismissed this right away. 'We checked those too.'

I was getting desperate. 'Suppose there *wasn't* a boat?'

A beady look. 'A ploy? Why? How?'

'The towpath was an odd place to suggest as a meeting point. The killer lures Carlos there with talk of locks and a boat for entertainment or discussion, whichever. But that doesn't mean there had to *be* a boat.'

'Agreed. That's the conclusion we reached.'

I was too wrapped up in this to stop now. 'Mendez's car was found in the lane down to the river on the side his body was found. The killer suggested they met there for a drink and chat and then that they would go over the bridge to the boat – which didn't exist. No problem, as he'd planned to kill Carlos anyway.'

'Agreed. We got there as well,' Brandon repeated, deadpan. 'Any ideas on how he got Carlos to stroll along the towpath in semi darkness on the weir side of the bridge though?'

'No,' I admitted. 'Unless the killer suggested they strolled out to see if the boat had come through the lock, because a chum was bringing it through.'

'Possible, but weak,' Brandon conceded. 'Thanks, Jack. So now all I have to do,' he added, 'is to find out why Mendez was killed and who killed him. No problem. Luckily, we already have someone who has motive, opportunity, left evidence, and has lied like blazes from the word go.' He spoke dispassionately, not sarcastically, and I had to see his point of view.

'The Charros also had motive enough.'

'As I said, it's a long time to cherish the idea of revenge.'

'Refreshed by a memorial annual lunch?' I was heartened by seeing his expression change. 'As you know,' I continued, 'one of the band committed suicide, thought to be because Carlos's actions had ruined his life.'

Brandon dismissed this angle – rather regretfully, it seemed to me. 'Too way out, Jack.'

'Even though those involved were at Wychwood House on Tuesday – a mere three days ago – and one of them was possibly here this morning, Matt Wright?'

A split-second freeze, then: 'Miss Gibson told us about Wright. We're following that up. Now –' he came to the salient point . . . for him – 'how do *you* know about the band being here on Tuesday?'

'I called here unexpectedly.'

'I'll let that go for the moment. What were they here for?'

'They said it was to discuss the anniversary lunch. That's on the ninth of July.'

'What were *you* here for?'

'To talk to Ambrose Fairbourne.'

'Did you do so?'

'Not for long. He was with them.'

'To discuss a lunch? He had Alzheimer's. What did *you* want to talk about to him?'

'The Morris Minor.'

'And today it was an archaeological trip? Pull the other one,' he snapped.

'I can't. I thought the two might overlap and his archaeological life might have something to do with Carlos's murder.'

Silence. 'Did you work out what it was?' he asked at last.

'No. I found his body. The only obvious connection is the May Tree Inn at Tickenden. Ambrose was a regular there even before Carlos formed his band.'

'I still don't see it,' Brandon said flatly. 'Evidence?'

'None. Except the coincidence of the May Tree Inn.'

'Any other golden nuggets you'd like to dig up while I'm here?'

'Yes. Does the name Frank Watson mean anything to you? He was the father of Neil, the Charro who committed suicide. Frank Watson ran off with the loot of the Crowshaw Collection in 1978. That had a lot of golden nuggets.'

A flicker of interest from Brandon. 'Does Fairbourne link into this?'

'Not as far as I know, but Carlos—'

Brandon sighed. 'OK, Jack. That's enough. You're free to go.'

I wasn't sure whether this was good or bad news, but I didn't argue. 'Is Josie free too?' I explained to him that I would like to drive her over to stay with her mother, and he raised no objection provided he had the address. Josie must have found it tough enough living in Wychwood House with only Ambrose as company, but without him – even if there were police around – I could see she was in no state to stay here alone.

I negotiated the security system at Jubilee Crescent, Boyfield, with Josie and patted the spaniel Don, as he was indicating he was the official Cerberus and considered the house his own property. Betty came rushing out of the house, and it was a relief to hand Josie over to her care. I wasn't too sure that Betty was the caring sort, but Josie was happy, which was the point of the exercise. They made an odd contrast: Betty extrovert, lively and in control, compared with Josie who looked almost the elder of the two.

'What's this all about, Jack?' Betty said anxiously over Josie's shoulder as her daughter clung to her. I hadn't explained fully on the phone and did so now.

'Murdering that old man?' she exclaimed in horror. 'Josie, you poor girl. Finding him like that. And all the while you and me were at the supermarket. Poor old Ambrose. You'd never think it, Jack, but Ambrose was a real looker when I first went to the May Tree in 'seventy-seven. Tony said they used to come to the pub together, Ambrose and his wife, in that car of theirs. Ambrose adored Muriel, and then she went and died of cancer. He was a real flirt after that, but it didn't mean anything. Everyone made a fuss of him though, especially the women, but it took time for him to get over it.'

'He looked rather dashing in his photos,' I agreed as I followed them inside the house. 'Was he a regular during the period Carlos formed the band and while it played there?'

'Sure. He was still around.'

Could that have been the reason Ambrose was in the room with the Charros on Tuesday, or had that been simply because it was easier for Josie to keep an eye on him?

'Did he still have a Morris Minor then?'

'Couldn't say after all this time. I think he had one for a year or two when I first went to the pub, but then he moved on to Renaults.'

'What's all this about then?' Tony came in to join us, looking anxious, and when Betty explained, he tactfully indicated that we should leave mother and daughter together in favour of a beer in the conservatory. It was a non-alcoholic one for me, which won me no plaudits from Tony, who was born into a different generation. He took me (with Don barking enthusiastically) into their garden, which looked out over the Downs farmland to the blue and grey haze of the Channel far beyond.

'Josie and you found the old chap's body then?' he asked.

'I'm afraid so. A shock for us both. I'd only gone there to chat about archaeology with him.'

'Keen on that, are you?'

'Only because he was. I promised to take him to Eastry one day.'

He spluttered with laughter. 'You and everyone who came to the house. He was fixated on it. Thought he knew exactly where the king was buried, along with his treasure. Poor old sod. Josie said he never got over finding the Suffolk hoard and was convinced there was another one waiting for him.'

'And could there have been?'

'Wouldn't know. Not my game.'

'Did he talk to you about it?'

'Talked to everyone – if you can call it talking. He'd got a house full of archaeological stuff of one sort or another. But it never produced this treasure for him. I felt sorry for the old chap. I know what losing a mint of cash means.'

I seized this opportunity. 'You mean Frank Watson. Did Ambrose know him?'

'Not that I know of. He might have seen him that night. Good old Frank, eh? When Betty told me she thought Joannie had scarpered with the loot I couldn't believe it, especially when she said she reckoned that it had been planned all along. Then I found that Frank had gone too. You know how life can change so sudden? One minute we were celebrating and discussing how to divvy up the cash after the stuff had been smelted down, the next I was left with a dead body, no wife, no loot, police storming around and handcuffs.'

I almost felt sorry for him. 'Do you have any idea about where your wife and Frank went?'

'We all have *ideas*, but precious little to back it up. Vic reckons it was South America. I thought maybe Australia. Joannie liked it there. The cops kept Vic and me apart after we were carted off in the hope that one of us would spill the beans as to where the booty went. If only I knew, I told 'em.'

And then it happened. It was one of those glorious moments when one's brain produces the fruits it has slowly been ripening. South America – Carlos! Matt had mentioned Carlos knowing the May Tree well before the band was formed, and there had been mention of his father's *band*. There had been a lot of noise, Tony told me, in the pub that evening. Could it possibly be that Carlos was there with his father's band on the night of the shoot-out? Surely he'd have been too young – no, he wouldn't. He could have been twenty-one or twenty-two in 1978. I tried not to make too much of this and keep control but . . .

'Was there a band playing that evening?' I asked.

Tony laughed. 'Look, chum, I had other things on my mind than music that evening. Might have been.'

He went on to grill me about the murder, but eventually he decided it was time, as he said, 'To join the ladies.' I was relieved to see that Betty had worked some kind of magic and Josie was looking much more composed.

'Jack's still on about Frankie boy, Bet,' Tony joked. 'He's hoping to find him skulking around carrying the collection in his back pocket.'

'That would be good,' I agreed. 'Did you see Frank Watson leave that night, Betty?' I took a chance. 'And the band too?'

'He's got this thing about there being a band around, Betty. Can you remember? Jazz, was it?'

Betty looked puzzled. 'Jazz? No, general Latin-American. Vicente Mendez, that was his name. Carlos's dad. That's what gave Carlos the idea for the Charros. Last time we ever saw Vicente – he had been a bit of a regular before that, but he hopped it when the police were called. He didn't like police,

Carlos said, so they all disappeared sharpish, including Carlos. You got back at five or so, Tony, but you were in the back room while the band got set up about seven – and the balloon went up about nine if I remember rightly.'

'I do,' Tony said feelingly. 'Accident, that's all it was. Are you telling me Carlos was there then?'

Betty was looking uneasy. 'Far as I remember he was. He'd been several times with his dad. But that was years before the Charros, Jack.'

Tony had been brooding. 'That kid?' he said. 'I'm beginning to remember him now. Greasy kid, he was. He took a shine to Joannie but he wasn't her type. Too young, whereas Frankie boy was right up her street. He'd split up with his wife a year or two earlier and was ripe for a bit of Joannie and the cash to go with her. Vic and I were the dumb ones. We went inside, and Frank had a nest egg for life.'

'Do you think he and Joannie are still alive?' I asked.

'Not,' Tony said with great simplicity, 'if Vic and I catch up with them. But we've no handle on where they are, so we let it be, let it be.'

'Was Carlos actually playing in the band that evening, Betty?'

'Sometimes he played, I think. Not always. Can't remember that far back for sure. I think he helped me and Joannie at the bar for a while.'

'But he left with the band?'

'Didn't see any of them go,' she told me. 'I was too busy looking for Joannie, worrying about Tony, dealing with the police and all that. Some of the customers hung on, lot of them went. I remember Ambrose going at a very early stage, said goodbye and that if anyone needed him he'd be at home. Then the police arrived and stopped any more departures. The band had gone by then and Carlos too – I didn't see him again, anyway.'

'If you were all going to meet up again across the Channel, what happened to Frankie's car, do you think? Was it still in the car park?'

'No idea, mate,' Tony said. 'Otherwise engaged. Fools, weren't we? We all trusted Joannie, even Brian. We thought, like I said, we'd all join Joannie in Calais in our separate cars. *Her* plan, I reckon, was to depart with Frankie somewhere up north while things calmed down, but after the shoot-out it changed, I reckon. Her car was found at Dover though, so I reckon they were over the channel and down to Spain soonest. It was Frankie started the row with Brian about the share of booty. He didn't know Brian was carrying – probably thought he could turn it into a punch-up so he could slip out with Joannie and drive off into the sunlight.'

I was glad I wasn't Brandon trying to sort the wood from the trees in this kind of story. 'Didn't you follow that line up to try to trace Frank when you heard about Neil's death, Tony?'

'How, Jack?' Tony said simply. 'Didn't hear about it till Betty told me, and anyway he'd long gone. Don't go getting any ideas that I'm still in the network,' he joked.

'Are you?'

Tony chuckled. 'No way. I make the odd phone call to Vic and a couple of others from the old days. But I'm sixty-five now, a respectable retired publican married to a lovely wife I'm crazy about. If I ran into Frank or Joannie I'd like a few words with them, but that's not likely now, is it? They're in Barbados or somewhere, I reckon,' he said without rancour. 'But Betty and I do all right. Can't ask for more, can you? World isn't run that way.'

Its isolated position perched on the Greensand Ridge is one of the blessings of Frogs Hill. I can feel detached from the world, as though divided from it by a pane of glass. I can see, but am not connected. Just what I needed that evening. The Pits was closed, so the next place to try to get my thoughts in order was the double barn-cum-garage where I keep the Lagonda and Gordon-Keeble. Today, however late home as I was, bed held no attractions as my mind was racing like a magneto, so I made my way straight to the Glory Boot. This has a smell of its own: accumulated dust, oil and a fragrance I can only sum up as 'the past', as defined by classic cars of course. Here I can stare for hours on end not only at the automobilia but also at the Giovanni paintings, which can be summed up as classics in fantasy land. My particular favourite is a robin blue Karmann Ghia set in an azure sky with a hint of mountains below.

The Glory Boot also has another attraction – it has no phone. All mobiles, iPods, iPads have to be left outside – mentally, at least. Len and Zoe know better than to come here unannounced, and so I'm left with my own thoughts, helped along by considerations of what my father would have contributed. He still does in a way. Tonight, however, Dad seemed determined to fight my every effort to arrange the tragic death of Ambrose Fairbourne into a pattern that included Carlos Mendez.

I could hardly blame Dad, because Eva had been – and for me still was – a family problem. Both my parents had suffered under her reign, even though thankfully Eva and I had not lived at Frogs Hill, although we did live near enough to visit. Too near for my parents' taste, although that instantly changed when Cara was born.

I sat down on a Corbeau bucket seat that Dad had once used in the Tulip Rally and thought about Ambrose – and, for good measure, Carlos. Carlos had been present at the shoot-out, and now it seemed Ambrose was there as well. Could they have met there? Even if they had, so what? It got me nowhere if they were all together one evening in the late seventies and met again ten years later when Carlos and the Charros was born. There was no sign of any treasure around by then. It had long vanished with Joannie and good old Frank.

I felt a mental nudge from Dad. 'And another thing, son . . .' he whispered, in imitation of his favourite catchphrase from *Columbo* times. Another thing? About Frank? I wondered. Could be, Dad, I agreed. Treasure was one thing, but Frank must have felt strongly about the death of his son. *So what is 'the thing', Dad?* But I was greeted only by silence.

TEN

I t's all very well staying silent, Dad, I thought gloomily as I shut the Glory Boot door behind me, but why not give me a break? Even Kafka could not find his way through the impenetrable mist that currently enveloped me. In fairy tales, princes who fought their way through brambly hedges were rewarded by a beautiful princess beyond. I was painfully aware that my bank manager would not consider me a prince, and furthermore I doubted if I could rely on Louise returning to play my sleeping princess. I was also uncomfortably aware that celibacy was rapidly becoming a way of life. It's nice to dream, but unlike Louise's return, the threat of Eva's was no inducement to continue my mission. What *was* an inducement was the thought that Cara was my partner in our joint efforts. I remained convinced that there was more to this case than a jealous woman's revenge, and coupled with my concern for Eva herself, that drove me on.

So where now? It was all very well to decide to track down Frank Watson, but where should I start, as the House of Lamb's door had been gently but firmly shut? I wasn't the only person after Watson. At the slightest hint of his whereabouts, his former partners in crime would be on his trail long before me. So would the police. An unusually sympathetic Dave had conveyed the news to me that the file was still open although there had been no leads since a sighting in Rio in 1980. Should I begin with Vic Trent? No, he would have no more information than Tony did, so I put him way down my list of 'jobs to do'.

And also featured on that list was Melody.

Over the next few days Daisy took to alternately texting me (with a mournful 'missing Mel' as a subtle reminder) and just 'popping in', as she put it. Nice as it was to see her bright face, it was driving me round the bend – and Len and Zoe were ahead of me.

It was the following Wednesday before there was a break-through of sorts – in the form of Dave.

'There you are,' he told me irritably and unnecessarily as he rang me at breakfast-time.

'I am,' I agreed.

'I spend a lot of time running after you. This Morris Minor of yours . . .'

'Of Daisy Croft's, to be exact – and featuring in a murder case.'

'Don't I know it. First you, then Brandon after me. It's back.'

I was knocked off balance. 'What?' I asked stupidly.

'*Back*. Found. By *my* team.'

'Where? The middle of the Hindu Kush?' I, too, can do stroppy.

'Wormslea Retirement home. Know it?'

I did. 'Belinda Fever lives there.'

'And that's good?' Dave barked impatiently.

'It was she who gave the car to Daisy in the first place. Belinda's her grandmother.'

'Bully for Gran. Off her trolley, is she? Pinched it back?'

'No and no.'

'Either way, the job's truly over this time, Jack. *We* take over now.' He must have heard me gathering breath. 'And if you're about to pontificate that there's something weird going on, save your breath. I agree. That's why *we're* taking over. You're fired.'

Great. Could the day get worse? It could. What, I wondered wearily, was going on? I didn't have long to wait for the next stage. A cloud of smoke rivalled only by Zoe's Fiesta announced the arrival of Daisy in her Volvo.

'Boss says I should come straightaway,' she told me breath-lessly. 'He'll make up the rolls for me. Let's go.'

I was lost. 'Where?'

'Gran's, of course! Melody's there.'

Back on target. 'Then so are the police.'

'*Why*?' she wailed. 'They haven't taken her away, have they?'

'It's a murder case, Daisy, and Melody is mixed up with it.'

'But she's mine.' Her face was a study in indignation.

I took pity on her and unlocked the Alfa. 'Hop in. I'll take you up there. We might get there in time.'

'For what?'

'They'll probably take her for tests.'

'Get going, kiddo,' she ordered me grimly as she slammed the Alfa door and fastened her seat belt. 'First Justin, now the police. Time someone realized that car's *mine*.'

With Daisy bouncing in anticipation beside me, even I began to get into the Melody mood as we swung through the lanes with the sun deigning to beam on us. I half expected Melody to have vanished again by the time we reached Wormslea and perhaps Daisy did too, because we both breathed a sigh of relief when we saw her pinky-grey curves parked in the gateway to the field opposite the home.

I was about to joke that the description of pinky-grey curves for Melody was highly suitable for a village called Wormslea, when I saw Belinda. She was standing grimly by Melody with her arms folded. The reason was not difficult to fathom. There was a low-leader just approaching from the lane to Bredgar and two police cars already parked there. Dave's or Brandon's men, I wondered. It had to be one of them with this speed and degree of response.

'Can't you do anything about this, Jack?' Belinda demanded as Daisy flung her arms around her, sobbing at this new threat.

'No,' I said sadly. 'I wish I could.' Melody had been missing for nearly two weeks this time. Where had she been and why?

'Why has she got to go?' Daisy sobbed.

'Checking for evidence,' I tried to explain, not for the first time.

'Evidence of *what*?' Belinda said scornfully.

'That,' I said seriously, 'is the question.'

I went over to talk to the police, introduced myself and enquired their own provenance. This made a difference. If they were Dave's men, that meant one thing; if Brandon's CID team, quite another. It meant Brandon was taking on the task of seeking alternative solutions to Carlos's murder in earnest. Nevertheless, it opened up a can of pinky-grey worms and I would fairly and squarely be one of the fishermen. Whose men were they? They were Brandon's.

When I returned to join Daisy and Belinda, Daisy said: 'Well? What's the answer?'

'Not yet known,' I said glibly, since it seemed a good catch-all answer. 'There might be fingerprints, DNA and so on.' Plus nastier things than that, but I decided not to elaborate.

Daisy looked at me in scorn. 'Then they'll arrest you. You touched her, didn't you, when you found her in the barn, so your mitts will be plastered all over Melody. Anyway, that's not the point. Melody's *mine*. She's, like, part of me.'

'Does she mean more than Justin to you?' I asked curiously.

She hesitated. 'Yeah, well, there's that. He's OK is Justie. And his dad did lend me the old crock.'

'Never call a car an old crock if you're relying on it to get you home.'

'There's always you, Jack.' She grinned at me.

Between Belinda and Daisy I didn't get back to Frogs Hill until lunchtime, and even then it was a while before I had reassured Daisy sufficiently to persuade her to leave again in the 'old crock'. I'd promised Len I would nip over to Headcorn on an errand for him, but Daisy's departure had been even further delayed when she insisted we clamber over the fence at the end of my garden so that she could investigate the meadow beyond. It was mine and used to be rented out, but it's been lying fallow for a couple of years and wild flowers have taken advantage of it to bloom in profusion. There were, Daisy assured me ecstatically, thousand upon thousand of ox-eye daisies there, and why had I not gone there to admire them? Everyone had a duty to do so, as they were named after her. To please her I did my duty by them, and it was indeed a world away from murder to consider how they flourished regardless however much mankind tried to stop them. Eva and Carlos vanished into the background of my mind as I wondered how many battles had been fought over the ground beneath our feet over the centuries. Poppies and ox-eye daisies grew where once warriors had fallen and armies had raped and pillaged.

My enjoyable detour had a good result in that had I gone

out on the Headcorn mission (to pick up a spare radiator shell from a chum of Len's) I would have missed the call from Wychwood House. It was from Ambrose Fairbourne's son.

Dr Keith Fairbourne took after his late father with his academic, lean face and slight build, but there was a liveliness there that I had naturally never seen in Ambrose. A BMW estate was parked outside Wychwood House, which was a hopeful sign. Good cars often translate into likeable owners.

'It's good of you to come over,' he welcomed me. 'The police are fine but Josie suggested you could give me a broader picture now that things are calming down – somewhat,' he added drily.

I uttered appropriate condolences as he ushered me through to the room where I had last seen the Charros and Ambrose together. 'Is Josie living back here again?' I asked.

'Yes. Temporarily, at least. She's out at the moment, but she's coping, with Matt Wright's help. Know him?'

I said I did. Brandon had not mentioned Matt again, so I presumed he was not suspected of involvement in Ambrose's murder. 'Are you planning to move here?' I asked Keith.

He grinned. 'I'd have to get divorced first. My wife wouldn't hear of it. She thinks the place is creepy.'

'Don't you?'

'I'm used to it, but I haven't lived in Wychwood myself for a very long time. But at present I have to be here. There's a lot to sort out, and Josie's a great help.'

'Have the police said when the funeral can take place?'

'No idea. I hope soon because with the long vacation coming up I can act fairly speedily. You know, I still can't believe he was murdered. Who would want to kill an old man with Alzheimer's? Do you have any ideas? Josie explained the situation over your ex-wife and this other murder, and I'm sorry about that. Do *you* think there's a link? The police won't discuss it with me. Understandable, I suppose, but frustrating.'

'Eva's my very ex-wife, so I'm in the same position. It's hard to believe she could be guilty, however.' I hesitated over whether to elaborate on any possible connection between the two murders, but as Josie was a common factor I thought I should, although I would soft-pedal on the Charros. Keith Fairbourne listened intently.

'So far the car is the only firm evidence of a link. The rest is theory.'

Keith blinked. 'Car?'

'A stolen Morris Minor. It was found here. Didn't Josie or the police tell you?'

'They may have done. I didn't take it in, thanks to everything else going on. Is it important?'

'It could be.' I told him the whole story, and he heaved a sigh.

'My parents were always crazy about the Morris Minor 1000. Do the police think it possible my father stole the one you found in the barn? He sold the one he had when my mother was alive and bought one of the newer models. One of the last batch, I think, but he switched to Renaults in the late seventies.'

'It's possible he stole the Moggy, although the state he was in makes it highly unlikely he could have planned the theft.'

Keith looked dubious. 'He hadn't driven for years, so he couldn't have helped himself to it from very far away.'

'It had a local owner.'

'Ah. Did Josie know anything about it?'

'She says not.' I didn't emphasize the 'says' but he took the point.

'Equally unlikely that *she* would steal a car – she's got a perfectly good Polo. Unless you think she stole it for my father's sake?'

'I doubt that.'

'What happened to this car in the barn?'

'It vanished and has now turned up again. Reasons not known.'

'And its owner?'

'A girl who works in the bakery at Burchett Forstal. Before that it belonged to Belinda Fever who used to run the May Tree Inn with her husband James from the late seventies until the mid-nineties. Did you know them?'

'Only a dim recollection. My mother died in 1971, and I

was brought up largely by my aunt in Canterbury as my father couldn't cart a six year old around wherever he decided to dig. I came here quite often as a child, but pubs weren't included in the entertainment.'

'You don't remember the Carlos and the Charros band then? It was formed of local people in 1987 and collapsed in 1991.'

'I was at university doing my PhD in 1987 so those years come under the "dim recollection" heading.' A sudden smile. 'I do remember a sexy barmaid – Josie's mother, I understand. So, tell me, Jack, what do the May Tree and Morris Minor have to do with my father's death?'

'Not yet known,' I admitted. 'I suppose this is rather like a dig. You go down through the layers, sort out the finds and hope you've struck gold.'

'A bad comparison.' He grinned. 'Gold is the metal least affected by its surroundings. You know it almost as soon as you see it. I imagine that isn't the case with the murders of my father and this Carlos, which is why the context is vital.'

He was right. With Ambrose's death a whole new field was opening up, and whether or not it had any relevance to Carlos's death was a priority task. I might have to dig deep but this, I thought, was the man who might give me some answers. 'Your father seems to be chiefly known for the hoard he found in Suffolk, so why was it he so constantly talked of Eastry? At least in latter times.'

He grimaced. 'Poor old dad also assumed he was king of Kent in latter times.'

'I know.' I didn't think politic to tell him how. 'Why Eastry though, when as far as I can see none of the digs there have produced evidence either way that Egbert's royal palace was there, only that Eastry had a gathering point at Highborough Hill and that there was an Anglo-Saxon settlement there?'

'Easy one,' Keith said promptly. 'Dad *was* convinced the palace was at Eastry, despite the absence of proof, but it wasn't the palace that he was after. It was Egbert's grave and grave goods. Egbert is thought to have been killed by an arrow in July 673. He was a staunch Christian, murderer or not, but in the seventh century the two religions, old and new, would still have been overlapping. Egbert's father had issued a decree outlawing paganism and its rites, but that doesn't mean the two didn't carry on side by side for a while, unofficially. The probability is that Egbert was buried in what was known as St Mary's Oratory, a chapel beside the first St Augustine abbey church in Canterbury, both of which then disappeared under the present cathedral. His father was buried in St Mary's, and his great forefather Ethelbert had specifically built the abbey church for the bodies of the kings of Kent as well as the archbishops.'

'So where does Eastry come in?'

'The village is so close to Woodnesborough, the heart of the old Viking religion, that my father believed there might also have been a second burial in Eastry with Viking rites as a "just-in-case" measure – although this second burial would probably only have had a single bone or other such relic together with the grave goods which would buy him his passage to Valhalla according to Viking ritual.'

'Overlapping of the two religions, yes, but this sounds a step too far,' I commented.

'I thought so too. But that's the excitement of archaeology. We can never know for sure what happened, only degrees of probability.'

'So Ambrose was focusing on the four known Anglo-Saxon graveyards in Eastry?'

'No way. Our Egbert was a king and had to be buried like one, if the old gods were to allow him in.'

'Which meant?'

'Heard of ley lines?'

'Everyone has, I imagine. And your father –' I suddenly remembered – 'mentioned one once. Do they exist though?'

'Who can be sure? The evidence seems strong enough. Dad was brought up by my grandfather on Alfred Watkins. Watkins was no archaeologist by training, but when he was sixty-five he came up with the theory of the ley system, his name for ancient trackways, which were punctuated at sight-line points with mounds, castles, churches etc., and he published two books on it in the early 1920s. The theory sounds reasonable enough, but it shook the archaeological world up like a mini Galileo round-earth concept. Mounds, moats, beacons and mark stones fall into straight lines, interconnected at vital points, with the traces of old trackways still to be seen. Mounds, Jack, *mounds.*'

'There was a track running through Eastry?'

'My father believed so. The Roman road runs straight through the village of course, but the track he thought existed would have connected the churches of Eastry, Northbourne and Great Mongeham; there's an intersection of several tracks at that point, one probably leading to Upper Deal, which in those days was much closer to the sea than it is now.'

'And the churches align?'

'Yes and no. The current Eastry Church, which is early thirteenth century, is at the side of the old manor house, Eastry Court. A straight line from the church to the current Great Mongeham church doesn't connect with the current Northbourne church though. What it does go through is Northbourne Court, where there was an old Augustinian chapel or abbey. According to *William Thorne's Chronicle of St Augustine's*, the land was given to it by Egbert's forefathers in 618.'

Interesting, but time to get back to Egbert. 'But the mound? I don't see how a track between the Christian churches fits with a Viking burial.'

'Because the tracks preceded Christianity, and the burial mounds played an important part on them. Dad at first thought Egbert's mound would be on Highborough Hill, which was towards Woodnesborough, and of course the word borough stems from barrow. That theory would fit nicely with the *Time Team* 2006 dig – which Dad was too far gone to appreciate – but it didn't work out, and in any case Dad had already changed his mind over Highborough. He believed Egbert's grave was on the track to the south-east of the village, which ran from Eastry along the rising ground known as the Lynch and then continued on to Northbourne. He picked on a stretch of it called Woodlea Hill, which he discovered was once called Kinlea Hill – which suggested a king's mound to Dad. All he had to do was find the grave.'

'Did he dig there?'

'Of course. Woodlea covers quite a long area of hillside, and a mound isn't necessarily at the highest point but on the slopes. When he and my mother were hunting for Egbert's grave, the technology wasn't as good as it is now, but even so he found it – or so he thought. But the dig produced nothing and he dug elsewhere. Again nothing. Whenever I asked after that, he'd say: "It's there, Keith, it's there all right," but so far as I know he never did find it. That's the reason that when the Alzheimer's took hold Eastry became the one subject on which he was fixated.'

'Has that left you to take over from him?'

Another grimace. 'No. I'm a Roman man, and as a side issue I have to confess to a fascination with King Arthur, so far as that's possible. There are lots of later legends about Arthur in Kent, but less evidence. A major monastic library was burnt down in the so-called Dark Ages, and who knows what treasures disappeared with it? That's my fantasy, just as Dad's was Eastry.' Keith paused. 'But I can't see that this can have any bearing on Dad's death, unless you think he did find his treasure and was sitting on it. If so, let me disillusion you. He was a highly moral man of firm beliefs where archaeology and buried treasure were concerned.'

'You mean he would have turned over the grave goods as treasure trove?'

'Not necessarily. He was far more likely to have left them where they were. For a start, grave goods aren't always considered treasure trove, because that presumes that the owner intended to pop back and collect his buried treasure some time. That's not the case with grave goods. Dad believed that grave goods should remain with the departed, not go into a museum.'

I blinked at that. 'An unusual way of going about things.'

'My father was an unusual man. Anyway, I doubt if he was murdered for the key to King Egbert's grave. He would never let on where it was, even if he'd found it.'

'Even to you?'

Keith smiled. 'Even to me.'

'So the grave goods are not –' I realized too late this was a naff question – 'in this house?'

'Absolutely not. Want to look round, though?' he asked me. I did. How could I resist this witch's domain?

It proved to be a fascinating place, just made for youngsters,

I thought. Staircases short and long popped up in unexpected places, doors revealed rooms so small or so large that opening one was a constant surprise.

'It would have been a great place to grow up in,' Keith said rather wistfully, 'although it terrified me when I was very young and actually living here. Visits were fun when I grew up a bit, exploring dark attics and finding new corners and staircases. And there's one room you'll really like.' He led me round a staircase or two and flung open a door on to a musty dusty room which was completely empty.

Except for one thing. A large painting of a grey Morris Minor 1000, parked on a grassy slope with a younger Ambrose standing by it, one hand possessively on the bonnet. It was painted with loving care.

'My mother's work,' Keith told me. 'When she died Dad moved it in here because it reminded him too much of her.'

It was so evocative that I wondered whether Ambrose was, after all, the cause of Melody's presence here. I remembered his outburst: 'It's not hers . . .'

Then it occurred to me that Ambrose's precise words were: 'It's not *her*,' not 'hers'. Maybe I had misheard. 'Just one question,' I said.

'Go ahead.'

'Did your father ever talk about a Frank Watson or the May Tree Shoot-out?'

'Not that I can remember. Is it important?'

'It could be.'

With Brandon's reluctant consent I'd read the police file on Frank Watson. There was little in the file that I could follow up, however. All possible sightings bar one had been dismissed, whether in South America, Australia or nearer to home. I tried Vic Trent's number to see if he could add anything to Tony's story but there was no reply.

I came to two conclusions. First, the obvious one: if Frank Watson was back in England he would have changed his appearance (although time alone would have done that) and his name. Second: the only way I was going to get any further was through Jonathan Lamb, who wasn't going to tell me anything without a struggle, especially about the anniversary lunch. Phone? Drop in?

I duly dropped in on the protector of the Charros' memory and found him in the outer office. No receptionist today. 'Just wanted to tell you the Morris Minor has been found,' I said, beaming.

He wasn't deceived. An eyebrow was raised. 'Good of you, Jack. I'd invite you in for another chat but—'

'The police have the car.'

A charming smile. 'I'm glad it's in such safe hands. They've been here too. They wanted to know why we were at Wychwood House two days before Ambrose was killed, as I am sure you had mentioned to them.'

'Unfortunately, I had to.' I can do charming too.

'We explained we were discussing the lunch and that Josie wanted to keep an eye on Ambrose so we brought him into the same room as we were.'

'Did you mention to the police that Frank Watson attends these lunches every year?' Nothing like a shot in the dark.

The smile vanished. 'No Frank Watson, and you're out of bounds, Jack. You're not the police.'

'No, but I can set them on to that track.' I pushed further. 'It seems strange that you've had no contact with him since Neil's death.'

'Why? Neil and his father didn't get on that well.' A red spot on Jonathan's cheeks suggested I might be getting warmer – or that he was getting ready to throw me out. Or both.

'There must have been inheritance issues, for a start.'

'There weren't.'

'Frank Watson had as much reason to dislike Carlos as you did. It's highly relevant whether he attends that lunch.'

He stared at me for a moment. 'You've made your point, Jack.' A pause. 'Let me explain. Neil and I lived together. Frank had grabbed Neil and taken him with him when he left the country in 1978 and went to South America, as all good crooks seem to do. When Neil returned in the late eighties, it was against his father's wishes. When Neil died, Frank went over the top. Carlos was also in South America by then, but Frank never caught up with him. He couldn't trace him and nor could we remaining Charros, even if we had wished to chase him across the world. Frank eventually calmed down, and we lost touch.'

'Then how do you know he isn't in this country and that his hatred of Carlos didn't revive again when he discovered that Carlos was back?'

'Because he had indeed been here in England since Neil's death. He'd found religion and been ordained.'

I sighed. 'And where is he now? Priests can lose control like anyone else.'

'The last I heard he had a church somewhere in Dorset. I don't know where, but there's been silence for the last decade or so.'

'Under his own name?'

'I don't know. It's a common one, so he might have risked using it. He'd be a fair age now, so he's probably retired. Or possibly,' he added gravely, 'dead.'

ELEVEN

I felt envious of Zoe and Len. Zoe was working with loving care on a Lanchester, which was a long-term restoration job, and Len was busy assessing a 1935 Frazer-Nash Colmore. I know that look on his face. It means he is about to mount his speedy white charger on a mission of salvation – except that the word speedy doesn't apply to Frogs Hill. It was clear my presence was redundant.

The idea of work on the office accounts, which was badly needed, did not appeal to me, although at the moment the Pits represented my sole source of income. Even Melody was no longer missing. As for my non-paid work of private (unwanted, unasked) assistant to Brandon, I was at stalemate. I'd checked with the invaluable *Crockford's Clerical Directory* and there were several Watsons, none of whom could have been my quarry, and in any case I could hardly imagine a man of the cloth beetling over to Maidstone from the West Country to wreak twenty-year-old vengeance on Carlos. Even if Jonathan had been in touch with Watson, how would the death of Ambrose Fairbourne fit into that scenario, let alone the theft of Melody?

Nevertheless, I had felt obliged to tell Brandon about this possible lead. He gave it low priority, which made me feel even more like a spare wheel.

'But what connection does Watson have with Ambrose Fairbourne?' he asked when I rang him.

'Not known,' I admitted, 'except that Fairbourne was present during the 1978 shoot-out.'

'Actively or passively?'

I was forced to admit I had nothing to suggest that he had taken any active part, and indeed the contrary. 'Ambrose was into digging stuff up, not helping to pinch it like Watson,' I told Brandon. 'Nevertheless, it is a coincidence that he and Mendez both knew the pub.'

A pause, the sort that is full of meaning. 'I'll look into it,' he had finally said.

What he meant was that I could get lost along with my daft theories. So on the Monday morning I had gone to bury my head both physically and mentally in the Pits. It must have worked some magic because when Len and I came up for air from the Frazer-Nash, Zoe actually asked me how the case was going. I told them, including the Frank Watson tale.

Len grunted. 'Vic told me a lot about that bloke. Don't see him as a man of the cloth.'

'That's just the point, isn't it?' Zoe argued. 'Turning your life around full circle.'

Len fixed her with a beady eye. 'You can give a Beetle a Porsche engine, but it doesn't make it a Porsche.'

These words of wisdom dumbfounded us both. Nevertheless, I thought, at least some of the original Frank Watson must remain after his conversion, even if there was plenty of the newly arrived good stuff to make him battle against the idea of murder. The fact that he would have to travel a hundred and fifty miles or so to carry out the murder, if he even knew about Carlos's arrival, would add more weight to dissuading him from action.

In the afternoon came the good news – or relatively good.

'Hey!' Zoe suddenly cried out.

I'd heard a toot on a horn and a car driving up, but had been too busy with the Lanchester to which Len had reverted after delivering his Solomon's judgement on the Frazer-Nash. Now I realized it wasn't any old engine arriving. It could be *the* engine. I rushed outside and saw a vision of a pinky-grey Morris Minor 1000 from which a joyful Daisy was leaping out.

'Got it back, Jack. See, Len? Hey, Zoe. Take a look at this!'

We all duly admired Melody's curves and grace. At first sight she didn't seem to have suffered at all either from the thief or the police. If cars could smile, Melody would be beaming.

'Didn't get nicked again?' Zoe joked.

Daisy sighed happily. 'She's under twenty-four-hour guard.'

'Where are you keeping her?' I asked warily. 'Not Huggett's barn, I trust.'

'No way. We're going to rent a garage for her, and she's nailed to our drive till then.'

I was busy examining the lady. 'She doesn't seem to have suffered at all,' I concluded.

'Bit of a scratch on one of the doors, that's all. Gran says she'll pay for it. Justie knows a chap who'll do it on the cheap.'

I bit my tongue over the wisdom of employing chaps 'who'll do it on the cheap' in connection with classic cars. Melody was a classic – she was a survivor. I even felt privileged to be part of her life.

'Is Justin still in the picture?' I asked.

''Course he is,' Daisy said airily. 'Want to come for a spin in her, Jack?'

Spinning wasn't quite the verb I'd use about a Minor, with its comfortable cruising speed of forty mph, but I could hardly say no to Daisy's offer. 'Where to?' I asked cautiously. Knowing Daisy we might be off to Scotland.

'Gran's place,' she told me. 'Got to show her Melody's really back.'

So off we went for our spin. It was a tonic to be next to Daisy on a summer's day with the sun actually shining for once. If he played his cards right, Justin was going to have a very happy life ahead. The purr of Melody's engine, her growl of excitement when she accelerated, was almost hypnotic. I can't say she was as comfortable as my Gordon-Keeble or even the Alfa, but she provided the comfort of a familiar home – and what more could one ask? She was a happy car. One could slip into her driving seat with the sense of familiarity of a pair of slippers.

Gran Fever was already waiting for us when we drove through the Wormslea Retirement Home Gates. She was dressed as befitted a sunny day in sky-blue trousers, blouse and beret.

'Very suave,' I greeted her as we drew up.

'Coming, Gran?' Daisy yelled at her.

'Only if I'm at the wheel,' she bartered as we got out to greet her.

Daisy's face fell. 'Don't you trust me?'

'Of course, but it would give pleasure to an old lady.' Gran performed a mock tremble, and Daisy giggled.

'And that means Jack won't have to sit in the back,' she said.

For which I was truly grateful. This was a two-door model, and my six foot plus a bit wouldn't fit too easily into the Minor's rear seating, delightful though Melody is.

'Where are we going?' Daisy called out as Gran set off in fine style, scaring not only the horses but me too.

'Cream tea,' Gran yelled over Daisy's screams of delight as we took a corner too fast. Too fast for Melody that is, but luckily nothing was coming in the opposite direction, and in the adjacent field the sheep who had assumed Belinda was making straight for them stopped their mad dash for safety. We drove rather more sedately to an idyllic spot out where a pond surrounded by grass, converted old stables and craft shops provided a venue eminently suitable for a Morris Minor decanting three customers bent on a cream tea at the café.

'And no one can run off with Melody,' Daisy said with satisfaction. 'We can have a table outside and watch her.'

'I doubt if any car thieves drop by on chance on a Friday mid afternoon,' I told her.

'Don't you believe it,' Belinda replied. 'Car thieves don't come with a special hat on marked "owners beware". They could be anywhere.' Her mock sombre tones didn't go down well with Daisy, who took it seriously.

'I'm going to have my tea *in* Melody then.'

We dissuaded her, albeit with some difficulty, and settled down to tuck into our scones, jam and cream. I looked round at the assembled mums, chums and retired folk and thought that Belinda was right. We judge too much by appearances. All the same, I'd lay long odds that Melody was safe here.

'This,' Belinda informed me rather than Daisy, 'is a good place to chat about murder.'

Belinda had obviously planned this rendezvous, and I was all attention as to why. All I had to do was wait. I had my own questions ready. 'Why?' I asked.

'Agatha Christie would approve of such a teatime topic.'

'Murder in general?'

'Murder in particular. The death of Ambrose Fairbourne. What are the police doing about it, Jack?'

I had expected better of Belinda. 'Following up leads.'

'What are *you* doing about it?'

Getting warmer. 'Following up leads.'

'Such as?'

I could not allow Belinda to set the pace. Not today. 'I see why you're concerned about Carlos's death,' I said, adding jam to the butter on my scone with studied concentration, 'but what's your concern over Ambrose? Because of Josie's involvement?'

No disconcerting Belinda. A slight look of surprise. 'Melody was found at his home, and certainly I'm concerned that Josie might be suspected of having something to do with that.'

'Melody was also found in Huggett's barn and then stolen from a car park. Do those interest you too?'

She carefully poured another cup of tea and failed to answer.

So I continued: 'And the link between Wychwood House and the Charros . . . Does that interest you too?' I enquired.

The tea still took all her attention.

'The link,' I pushed gently.

'I barely knew Ambrose Fairbourne.'

'Although he was one of your regular customers at the May Tree?'

'How well do you know regular customers to your repair shop, Jack?'

The Pits a repair shop? It was a specialist restoration centre, as she knew full well. But she would not succeed in goading me. 'Was Frank Watson another regular customer?'

She looked startled at the switch in subject, but the hand that held the teacup looked steady enough. 'Who?'

'Neil Watson's father.'

She frowned. 'Why should I know him? Did he come to listen to the Charros?'

'I doubt it. He was involved in the 1978 May Tree Shoot-Out. Betty and Tony Wilson believe he escaped with the booty from the raid and the former Mrs Tony Wilson. Betty doesn't remember him during the Charros' time, it's true, but Neil must have talked about him.'

'Perhaps he did.' Belinda was in full command again. 'But the shoot-out was before my time, so I doubt if I took it in – interesting though it all sounds. And I don't recall Neil having a father around during the Charros period, any more than Betty does. There must be a price on this Frank Watson's head, so he would hardly be hanging round the pub ten years or so later.'

'Jonathan Lamb told me he was a clergyman in Dorset.'

'Then why ask me?' She was beginning to get riled – and that could be good.

'I always need two reliable sources,' I parried.

'Try *Crockford's*,' she flashed back. 'Ideal for tracking down clergymen.' Then she relaxed. 'I can't see where this is getting us, Jack. If Frank Watson has disappeared, whether to South America or Dorset or heaven, he's unlikely to be around here murdering Ambrose Fairbourne or even Carlos. You're on the wrong trail, Jack.'

'Or the wrong crime,' I whipped back. Everyone seemed determined to ignore the element of Frank Watson in these two murder cases. Was it 'everyone' who was barking up the wrong tree or me?

'I'm lost,' Daisy said crossly.

Her Gran ignored her and so did I. The battle going on between Belinda and myself had to take precedence. 'Ambrose Fairbourne was a regular customer by the time you took over the pub. He might have mentioned the shoot-out to you. Carlos was present too.'

'How on earth would I remember?' she snapped.

'Because they both continued to have connections to the May Tree.'

'Not so. Carlos wasn't a regular during my time. I only met him not long before he formed the band.'

I'd made a false move and tried to recover quickly. 'Carlos and Ambrose could have met before the shoot-out though. Ambrose had been a regular for years before that, and Carlos had visited the pub with his father's band.'

It was a weak recovery though – I knew it, and Belinda

spotted it. That made me press on even more rashly. 'With both Ambrose and Carlos there that evening, either or both of them could have known what happened to Watson and the Crowshaw Collection, couldn't they?'

'I'm not psychic, Jack. They would hardly tell me about it, would they?' Belinda laughed, clearly knowing she had won – temporarily.

Canterbury is a magnificent city, and just walking through it gives one a sense of perspective. It did so today, as I realized that even after three days I was still nursing hurt pride where Frank Watson was concerned. I told myself that Canterbury had flourished under the Romans, had a cathedral church under the Anglo-Saxons and another under the Normans; in comparison with that my pride was hardly a major issue.

The cathedral we know today is mainly twelfth-century workmanship. With Thomas Becket's tomb safely in the crypt and his shrine erected, the age of pilgrimage to the city had begun. The cathedral had survived the dissolution of the monasteries and even the second world war bombs only dented it slightly. Pilgrims used to approach the cathedral on their knees, their horses presumably parked elsewhere, as is today's motor traffic wherever possible. Even the large shops that now dominate one end of the St Peter's Street can't diminish the cathedral's glory. And just outside the old city walls St Augustine's Abbey, where King Egbert might or might not have been buried, lies in ruins.

I was here on another mission for the Pits, but as my route took me past the library I made a spur-of-the-moment detour to the reference section. I remembered Belinda's reference to Watson possibly having retired to heaven, and that *Crockford's* has a list of recently dead clergy which I hadn't yet checked. What did I hope for? That I would find nothing, or that Frank Watson would be amongst the list of the recently deceased? The search produced nothing. Which meant what? Either he had changed his name when he was ordained, or he had died soon after his ordination and that he – and all clues to his treasure – were indeed in heaven.

I drove home in low spirits. Where next? Only one choice.

The Pits. At least I had fulfilled Len's mission, and I was able to hand him the ignition coil he wanted for the Frazer-Nash. He thanked me and turned back to the job. Once again I was not needed.

'When will it be ready to go?' I asked, determined to remain one of the party.

'Don't know,' Zoe sang out. Len didn't even reply.

Them that asks no questions isn't told a lie, I thought, remembering Dad's beloved Kipling poem. Kipling always has a word for it, he would say. I felt obstinate though. I *had* to ask questions about Carlos Mendez and Ambrose Fairbourne. Even if—

I stopped right there. I *had* been told a lie. By Jonathan Lamb.

My first sight of Eva the next day shocked me. She looked even more subdued and listless than on my previous visit. I thought of what I had read about the mental state of prisoners on remand, and I could see it in Eva.

'Is good that you come, Jack,' she told me, and I think she meant it, although her face had hardly lit up in welcome.

'Has Cara visited you?'

'Yes. She is good daughter. You good husband.'

She sounded like an automaton and now was not the time to remind her I was not her husband.

'How's the food here?' I started with this banal approach, deciding to delay the serious issues for the moment.

She shrugged. 'I still live.'

'When you're out of here I'll treat you to all the paella you want.' It had been a standard joke between us in our marriage that she liked no food but paella.

She tried to smile. 'When *do* I get out of here, Jack?'

'I hope soon,' I said more confidently than I felt, 'but I need your help.'

'How I help? I help you already.'

I struggled on. 'Did Carlos ever talk to you about his life before he met you?'

She looked at me as though I were out of my mind. 'We were married long time. Of course he talk.'

'Did he mention having known the May Tree Inn when he was much younger and before he joined the Charros?'

She frowned. 'He said he and Matt knew the pub well.'

Careful, I warned myself. Eva was already growing bored. I remembered the signs. If she could not see a direct connection to her, her attention span was limited.

'Did he ever talk about a night when there was a gunfight at the pub?'

'Why you want to know?' Her voice began to rise.

'Concentrate, Eva. It might get you out of here.'

She paid attention to that, at any rate. 'Perhaps. He say his father play there until one time there was trouble and he not go back for years. They go to America. Then Carlos come back here and start band and have that woman. Then he met *me*.'

Charming! I thought of poor Josie. 'Good, Eva,' I encouraged her. 'Did he have money when you met him or talk about a man who had run off after the night of the trouble at the May Tree?'

'I no remember. Perhaps.'

Press on regardless. 'Does the name Frank Watson mean anything to you? Or Tony Wilson, Vic Trent?'

'No.'

I sighed with desperation. 'Did Carlos not tell you the name of the person he had this business deal with? Was it anyone in the band? That's what you told me earlier.'

'No. It was woman.'

Too much to hope for, I supposed. I'd try again. 'There might have been a customer in the May Tree the night of the trouble called Ambrose Fairbourne. Did Carlos mention that name? You might have known him during your visits there too. He was an archaeologist, dug up historical sites.'

A blank expression, then light came to her at last. 'He was in pub sometimes when he played.'

'Who played? Carlos's father?'

An impatient shake of the head. 'No, no. When the Charros played.'

'So you *did* know Carlos all the years we were married.'

A reminiscent smile now. 'Only last year. Carlos very

jealous, even then,' she said lovingly, and for a moment I was whisked back to our own sex life. It had been good.

I forced myself back to the present. 'Was Carlos friendly with Fairbourne then? Do you remember that?'

'Carlos friendly with everyone, so yes, he friendly with Ambrose. He was a rich man, Carlos said, so maybe Carlos ask him for money when we run away.'

This was so unexpected I thought I'd misheard. *Ask him for money?* 'Are you sure about that, Eva?' I held my breath. '*Did* Carlos get money from him to go to South America with you?'

'Yes, he get money.' Another flicker of a smile.

'From Ambrose Fairbourne?'

'Neil tell me his father give it to him.'

I reeled, then thought this through. 'But Frank Watson wasn't there in the 1980s. It can't have been him.' Or was he there? Eva, Eva, I silently pleaded. *Tell* me.

'Who this Frank man? I tell you *Carlos's* father give him money.' More impatience. 'Sometimes you stupid, Jack.'

This was going round in circles and so was my head. Carlos, Ambrose, Neil and Frank . . . Belinda had said Frank wasn't around in her time at the pub. If he had kept a low profile, however, how could she have known who he was? Perhaps he did nip in to listen to his son's band. Only Neil would have known who he was – and perhaps Betty, although she had only seen Frank once and that was ten years earlier. It sounded to me as if Carlos had put Neil up to telling Eva that his cash injection was from his father, or maybe he had led all the Charros to believe that story. That would avoid the truth coming out if in fact it was Frank supplying the cash when Carlos tried a little blackmail on him. I tried that theory for size and it fitted nicely.

Which left Ambrose.

I wouldn't get any further with Eva on that question, so I went back to basics. 'Eva, you told the police that Carlos was dead when you arrived.'

'Yes,' she said piteously, 'I see him. I run away.'

'How did you know it was Carlos?'

'His coat.'

That rang true, as it implied she knew his face had been shot away. 'You're sure, Eva?' I double-checked.

'Yes. Sometimes I tell truth, Jack.' She managed a smile, and I felt an affection for her that had somehow surmounted the years. This time I believed her story.

TWELVE

The problem with spare wheels is that they have no one to share their burdens with, whether positive or negative. After I returned on Thursday I'd rung Cara to tell her the results of my talk with Eva, but apart from being glad to hear that I now believed Eva's story – as Cara did herself – she either wasn't interested in hearing how my investigation was going or hadn't got the time to listen. Neither explanation quite fitted but I had too much on my mind to take it further.

Brandon was ruled out as a sharer of burdens because he had not been convinced by the Frank Watson angle. Len and Zoe were always a possibility but they needed sympathy themselves at present. The Frazer-Nash was defying their best efforts – the spark advance was not yet advancing. I had to face the fact – alone – that I had blithely entered a blind alley where Frank Watson was concerned, now that I had realized Jonathan must have lied to me. His whole story about Watson becoming a clergyman had been a fictional red herring.

Finally, even Zoe noticed my mood despite the attractions of the Pits. 'Snap out of it, Jack. What's eating you?'

Zoe for once sympathized and even Len paused briefly while I related the continuing saga of Frank Watson.

Len began the response with a grunt. 'Who did you say started this story about Frank Watson taking the cloth?'

'Jonathan Lamb.'

'Thought he was in that band Mendez ran. What's he know about Frank Watson?'

'His son was his partner.'

'Why should he know what Frank did after his son's death though?' Zoe asked patiently.

I stared at her. 'Good point, Zoe. They must have kept in touch.' Then the clouds parted and the blessed truth shone out. 'Frank *must* attend those parties. If he was dead, there would be no need for Jonathan Lamb to concoct fairy stories about Dorset. So . . . he's alive and not too far away.'

I grabbed hold of Zoe and danced her wildly round what little space there was in the Pits.

Len looked on with mild astonishment. 'Want Vic's address now?'

I did. I also wanted to ring Tony Wilson, who listened to my thesis reasonably patiently, although I could hear him breathing heavily at the other end of the line, as though he was already on the trail.

'I'm right with you, Jack,' he said. 'Frank dead? No way. We're like old soldiers, we villains. We never die. We just fade away. That's what Frank's doing if you ask me. Like a blinking chameleon he is. I've been after him ever since Her Majesty's Prison Service kicked me out. Hear the odd whisper now and then, and then he's gone again. Never no hard facts.'

'Do any of these whispers place him in Kent?'

'Not so far. If they do, I'll get to him first, Jack. Trust me.'

I went a vital step further. 'You should be the first to hear any whispers, as Betty goes to that anniversary lunch for Frank's son Neil.'

'I would,' he agreed. 'Which is exactly why old Frank doesn't go to them, whatever name he might be using.'

That figured, I thought. I'd been wrong about the lunches. Jonathan must be in touch with Frank, but Frank didn't dare risk attending the lunches because Betty might recognize him or put two and two together. If he was still alive, however, at least I now had some kind of line on him – whatever name he might be using. It was high time I put Vic Trent into my picture. Undoubtedly, Tony Wilson would have been on the blower to him immediately I hung up, but it was going to be interesting to see what would come next.

Vic Trent lived above the shop – which was one of those invaluable convenience stores that sell everything seemingly every hour of every day of every week – although I gathered that his son now ran it. As I had driven through the congested roads to reach it I had half regretted coming, as it felt like a detour from the main path of the case. I reminded myself that

the anniversary lunch was only two weeks away now, and
I wasn't going to get an invitation without some hard work. I
needed more facts at my disposal before I could demand an
invitation that the Charros couldn't refuse. No Poirots would
be welcome at their party, but if there was any chance of picking
up a clue to Watson's whereabouts I needed to be present. This
detour could therefore be valuable. For all Tony knew, Vic
could have been in contact with Frank or even sheltering him.

I found the shop, albeit with some difficulty. It was indeed
a corner shop and buried in the heart of an estate in an area
of Greater London that in the past had been notorious for its
highwaymen, but none have been arrested recently. Not on
horses with cloaks and masks, anyway. The estate looked as
if it dated from the 1960s with rambling, neat identical houses.
The shop was somewhat in need of paint, but it was very
clearly part of the local way of life. It boasted a small post
office within, and there was a wine department too, but even
so it failed to enchant. The vegetables looked tired and so was
the greeting from – presumably – Vic's son.

'Could I have a word with Vic if he's about?' I asked, buying
a bottle of wine as an offering for Vic.

'Who wants him?'

That wasn't a good start. 'Jack Colby. Len Vickers
suggested I look him up.'

He disappeared into the storeroom behind the shop and
reappeared so quickly with the man himself that I guessed
Len as well as Wilson had already called Vic.

Central casting could not have provided a better stereotype
for a semi-retired shop owner. Vic was a big man, almost as
tall as me, and with a much fatter beer belly. He looked placid
though, as if he had come to terms with his past life. He sized
me up equally quickly, and I must have passed muster by
whatever standards he was applying because he ushered me
into the storeroom and then upstairs to his flat. I could hear
a Mrs Trent (presumably) moving about but the living room
remained our private domain. Slow and direct was Vic Trent,
rather like John Wayne in his later film career; he was the sort
that eyed his opponents carefully before drawing a gun.
Metaphorically, I hoped, in Vic's case.

'Len said you wanted my take on Frank Watson.' Vic's face did not move a muscle. 'Good sort, Len.'

'Don't I know it,' I agreed. We chatted a bit about Frogs Hill while we took each other's measure, then I plunged in. 'I've been told Watson became a clergyman in Dorset.'

Vic appeared to think this over even though Tony would have passed this snippet on. 'Pull the other one,' was his verdict. 'Who told you that load of cobblers?'

'Jonathan Lamb, who was the partner of Watson's son Neil, who died in the nineties.'

'Heard about Neil. Never met him, even as a kid.' A pause. 'You know I was inside for a while over that job?' And when I nodded, he continued, 'Came out in 1984, started this place thanks to my wife and never looked back.'

'Nor has Tony,' I remarked. 'Except with wistfulness at the missing cash from the Crowshaw Collection.'

Vic chuckled. 'We'd all like to win the lottery. Me too. Doesn't mean I can't live without it. I'm with Tony though. If that skunk Frank is living back here, I'd like to ask him what happened to my share. Mind you, if he is here, he's got another identity now but no dog collar.'

'People do sometimes want a different direction in life.'

'Not Frank. He'd have turned his life around with the help of the cash. Tony told me that if he'd been a free man when Frank's son was mucking around with that band of his, he'd have had a few words with him. I'd have done so myself, but I wouldn't go nowhere near the May Tree when I got out. Spilt milk, I tell Tony, but of course there's the Joannie issue for him too. If Frank is back here, what happened to her? Is she still with him?'

'Tony seems very happily married to Betty now.'

'Sure he is, but he would still want to know what happened to Joannie. He wouldn't forget her. He worshipped the ground she trod on, did Tony, and no wonder, she was a stunner. So he'll be as keen as you are to find Frank.'

'Did you like her?'

He shrugged. 'Sharp eye for main chance, I always thought. I reckon it was her who planned the scam to scoop the lot, not Frank. She had an eye for men all right though, and Frank was one of them.'

'Brian Thompson's death wasn't planned though.'

He looked uncomfortable. 'Shouldn't have said what I did. It's a long time ago now. Still, now it's out. I always thought that's how Frank scarpered, and Tony worked it out too. The stuff was in Joannie's car, so she just kept to the original plan for the four of us – five plus her. She'd go over to Calais and we'd all meet up there – only, the last bit didn't work. She used her car when events hotted up, Frank followed in his – and they both went off in his car when they met at Dover, having loaded it with the swag. They must have had a different plan originally or we'd have been after Madam Joannie and Frank like a flash when we realized what was happening.'

'That seems to add up.'

'I'd plenty of time to think about it in the Scrubs. Well, it's a long time ago and I've a new life now.'

'Do you mind this talk about the old one?'

'Why should I? It's over thirty years ago, and I served my time. We're happy enough here, with or without Frank Watson's cash. That's how Tony and I think of it, because you can bet your bottom dollar that the Crowshaw Collection has been smelted down or sold to some billionaire, so there's no reason for anyone to go murdering folk over thirty years after the event. That's what you're here for, ain't it? Carlos Mendez. What's your angle on all this, anyway?'

'Mendez ran off with my wife in 1991, but I've discovered he was at the May Tree on the night of the shoot-out.'

He didn't look surprised. 'Yeah, Tony told me that. So what? I didn't *know* him just because he was in the pub. Joannie was in her element that night – I did notice that. Some cheeky young bugger was chatting her up – was that this Carlos? – and that archaeologist bloke was too.' He paused. 'The one who's just copped it along with Mendez. That anything to do with you?'

'It is. You're sure it was Ambrose Fairbourne? Can you tell me more about him and Carlos that night?' I waited interminable seconds until he replied.

'No problem, Jack. I've gone over it enough times already.

I was only ever at the May Tree the one night, so I know what I saw and when I saw it. Brian's plan was that we steered clear of the May Tree before the actual day so that it wouldn't be the first place that the rozzers would raid. We all came back to the pub in our own cars, but slipped in at the back entrance so as not to draw attention to ourselves. About six thirty that was. The band had just arrived, but wasn't yet set up. The others were all busy piling the stuff into Joannie's car, so I strolled into the bar to see what was what. This young chap was at the bar, and Joannie was giggling with him. Then this Fairbourne bloke turned up, went straight to the far end of the bar and made a dead set at her. Joannie played them off against each other. Favourite game of hers, didn't mean nothing.

'I went back later and Frank was with them. We took it in turns to see all was OK out in the bar and buy a drink or two. Joannie was quieter by the time I got out there and the conversation changed smartish as I arrived. Then it all speeded up – in my memory, at least. The band got going, customers rolled in, and Brian was making his pitch in the back room with us three about how he was going to take more. Brian was a good chap, but we'd already agreed who was having what so it wasn't going to be changed. Tony started yelling at him, and I could see what was going to happen.

'I was standing back, so was Frank,' Vic continued, 'then Frank moved forward, quick like, and Brian drew, thinking Frank was coming for him. He never did, but Tony made this lunge. Brian didn't like that, the gun was trembling in his hand, and as Tony saw it he drew too – well, I rushed to stop him like a fool and caught Brian's bullet in me leg, and the next thing I knew I was on the floor in agony and Brian beside me, blood everywhere.'

Vic grimaced. 'All hell broke loose then. Tony was gobsmacked, couldn't move, nor could I, and people were rushing in, calling the rozzers, women screaming. No sign of Frank. Tony rushed out and came back yelling that Joannie had gone and there was no sign of Frank. I told him Joannie would have gone to France like we arranged, but he wouldn't have it. He was right. No word of Joannie, Frank or the loot since. When the police arrived, half of the customers had gone too.'

'Including Ambrose Fairbourne?'

'Must have done. I never saw him when I was carted off, though that doesn't mean much owing to the fact I was on a stretcher. Last I saw of Carlos, the band – and of the blooming Crowshaw Collection too.'

When I returned from my visit to Vic, the current lady in my life arrived, and like Daisy she was a welcome one. It was Cara, and she was not happy. Cara is usually so sanguine about life, and so clear about her own path through it, that I was even more concerned to see her looking so down.

'Can I stay a few days?' she asked.

'Of course.'

'No lady friends I'd be embarrassing?'

'I wish.'

That made her laugh. 'We're a fine pair, aren't we?'

'Are we?' This sounded bad. I took her inside, settled her with a cup of tea and then asked: 'Not going well on the Harry front?'

'No.'

'Harry *is* the problem then,' I ventured when she said no more.

'Only whether I'm really cut out for a life with nature. *And* Harry.'

'Explain.'

'I love him and he loves me, but his nose, eyes and mind are all focused on the land in front of him. I know that's important but . . .'

'You feel there's more to life?'

'Yes. People, for instance.'

'Such as you?'

She giggled. 'Yes. So a little time away could do us both good. I've got time off until after the weekend. OK by you?'

'Very OK. Just don't expect me to cook breakfast.' A vision of the tray I once prepared for Louise came to me and had to be thrust back into the archive. 'Is that what's brought you here?'

'Plus Eva.'

'What news?' I asked cautiously.

'There's a date for her trial. Fifteenth of January.'

'That's quick.' It was almost July now, and those months were going to race by.

'She's not doing well, Dad.'

'Her story's changed again?'

'No, but she has. I've never known her so quiet. Almost as if she was giving up.'

This didn't sound good and tallied with my impression. 'Do you think that's because of the case, or because she's lost Carlos?'

'Mainly the former. The warmth had gone from their relationship, as they say. I don't think it was all fantasy that she and Carlos were splitting up. Eva was banging on about some cousin in Spain whom she fancied years ago.'

'Here we go,' I groaned.

'But she's not even talking about him any more. Give me some good news, Jack. How's your side of things going?'

'It's not good – not in the short term, anyway. They're just bits and pieces.'

'Can I help glue them together?'

'Not unless you can find a man who's been missing for over thirty years, plus get me an invitation to a party in just under two weeks' time.'

'Neither. Is it any particular party you have in mind and is it important?'

'Yes.'

Cara listened as I explained the situation on both counts, then she fastened on to one point. 'This Belinda, who'll be at the party, does she come into the Carlos story?'

'She's Daisy's grandmother.'

'Who?' Cara asked patiently.

'She's Melody's owner.'

She gazed at me, and I grinned. 'Melody's a car, Daisy's a client, Belinda's her grandmother.'

Cara honed in. 'Does this Daisy owe you?'

'Yes and no. She depends on me.'

'Make it yes and ask her to order her old granny to get you an invitation.'

'She won't,' I said gloomily. 'I'd be the cuckoo in the nest.'

'Push it, Pa, push it.'

*   *   *

Daisy was the simpler part of the mission. She didn't know what was involved, so she gaily replied, 'Easy,' when I put my request to her the next day. I had bent the truth and told her it might help find Melody, and she therefore saw no reason that Gran Fever would veto my presence.

I received my prompt comeuppance that evening in the form of an imperious phone call. 'What the hell do you think you're playing at, Jack?'

'Playing at nothing, Belinda. It's a murder case. It's my job. I need to be there.'

'For Melody?'

'She's part of it.'

'You know full well you have no right to be at the lunch and that it could ruin it for those who still mourn Neil.'

'I still need to be there.'

A long pause. 'Any *real* reason I should talk Jonathan and Clive into it?'

More stretching of the truth. 'I'm told that the case against Eva is collapsing. The people at that lunch are highly relevant to what happens next.'

'So?' she replied impatiently. 'The guilty party could be tracked down. Why ruin the lunch?'

'Because Frank Watson could either be there or someone have information about him.'

A pause. 'And if he's not present? Will you give up the hunt for him?'

'No. But you could tell your friends that the police will have them in their sights for shielding Watson.' I didn't care how far I stretched truth now. The link between Melody and murder must surely be getting shorter, and it was time to shorten it even further. I had to be at that lunch.

'You told me Frank was a clergyman in Dorset and might be dead by now.'

'I did, but let's assume he's alive, shall we, Belinda? And that he is not a clergyman in Dorset.'

She didn't laugh. She merely said, 'I'll see what I can do.'

I should have guessed that Melody's story was not yet over. It couldn't have ended as peacefully as it appeared. I still had a way to go before the party, and I was returning from a depressing visit to Eva – depressing for both of us, as I still had nothing to tell her. I could almost smell trouble ahead. As I turned into the gates of Frogs Hill I could see it. To my horror the old Volvo was once again parked there, and once again Daisy was haunting my premises. She saw me coming, jumped off the wall, ran over to me as I opened the door of the Alfa – and burst into tears.

'Justin?' I asked, almost hopefully.

She shook her golden curls. 'No.'

'Then it's Melody. Crashed her?'

'No. She's *gone*.'

'*Again*?' I couldn't get to grips with this calamity. The story was not making sense. Then the pieces clicked into place. 'Someone's playing a joke on you, Daisy,' I told her soothingly.

'If so, it isn't funny.'

I made a supreme effort not to laugh. 'When did she vanish?'

'During the night.'

'How come you didn't hear anything?'

'We were still keeping her in the drive,' she moaned. 'No one would steal her *again*, we thought. But Mum and Dad woke up and saw her being driven off down the street. They started yelling and half the street woke up, but they never caught her. She's *gone*.'

'Doesn't she have a car alarm?'

'No.'

'Locked?'

'Yes. It's *not* a joke, Jack.'

I was beginning to think she was right. A pro could easily have unlocked Melody and started her up. Even so I could see what Dave was going to think. Merely a joker at work.

And then came the dreaded words: 'What are you going to do about it, Jack?'

My duty, of course. 'Try to find her,' I said wearily.

'Good. And this time,' she told me severely, 'I don't want her stolen *ever* again. See?'

THIRTEEN

On the ninth of July I drove the Gordon-Keeble to Conygarthe Manor, the hotel where the lunch was to be held, determined that I would turn the day into a watershed for the Carlos case. The manor is on the far side of Canterbury, and although I had heard of it I had never visited it before. Nor was it likely to be home territory for any of the Charros, as it seemed a fair distance from any of their abodes. I had been impressed by what I had seen of it on its website. It looked my sort of place (when I can afford my sort of place). An old Georgian house of mellow yellowing stone, wisteria on its walls and the remains of a monastery in its grounds, which the website informed me stemmed back to Saxon times. That brought back King Egbert to mind and Ambrose's vain quest to discover his burial mound and goods. Eastry was not that far away from Conygarthe Manor, but today I had to concentrate on Carlos, so a memorial visit to Eastry in Ambrose's honour had to be put on the back burner.

When I reached the manor gates, I could see that the house lived up to its website. I was surprised to see a board posted outside, however, announcing that the restaurant was closed today owing to a private function. By my reckoning we would only be a party of ten at the most, or a few more with partners, although it was true I had had no such information from Belinda, who had reluctantly sent me an official invitation. I parked in the designated area to the left of the building and walked back to the entrance.

The door was open, and its guardian receptionist ushered me through the house to the gardens. My first shock. From my first sight of the group it seemed more like a large wedding party than a memorial lunch, both in size and attire. No funereal pomp for this anniversary. The women were dressed in all colours of the rainbow, and amongst the smart casual male attire I saw several white charro suits. One of which clad Jonathan Lamb, who came immediately to greet me.

'Good of you to join us, Jack.' There was no trace of sarcasm in his voice.

'Thanks for inviting me.' No trace of sarcasm from me, either – albeit with some difficulty.

'Not at all,' he murmured. 'Let me get you a drink and introduce you. You won't know everyone here.'

I doubted if he did either, although perhaps I did him an injustice. Were all these people – eighty or so at a rough guess – his customers, perhaps? They surely could not all be Neil's relations and friends. Those I talked to over the next half hour while drinks circulated had varied connections, but they all shared one thing. They had all not only heard of Carlos and the Charros, but also seemed to know the band's music extraordinarily well. Call me cynical, but I wondered whether Jonathan had provided all guests with a CD beforehand. If so, I had not been included in this freebie distribution.

This was a party organized in style. The white suits of Jonathan, Matt and Clive made a stunning picture, and Josie, in a gorgeous slinky white silk dress, was almost unrecognizable. The years fell away, and I could see what an impact she must have made twenty years ago. She was with her mother, but there was no sign of Tony, so either the guest list did not include partners or – I felt a rising excitement – Frank Watson might indeed be here. Tony would have recognized him, but even with the passage of time I had to acknowledge that Betty might not. Vic had only been to the May Tree that one night and so had Frank, according to Brian's plan. I had not thought of that angle and my hopes rose slightly from rock bottom that Frank was indeed here.

'Are you performing today?' I asked Josie.

'Any problem with that?'

I was taken aback by her return to belligerence. 'None. I'll look forward to it.'

I had been about to soothe her, but Jonathan came once again to join us – almost as if he wanted to keep an eye on me. 'Do all these people come every year?' I asked innocently.

A speedy answer to this. 'No. It's a special year.'

'To commemorate the Charros because of Carlos's death?'

'To remember Neil *and* Carlos.'

What better way to hide Frank Watson than in a crowd this size, I thought. Most of them were strangers to me and possibly to each other. '*All* these people?' I asked sweetly.

A smile was Jonathan's only answer before he melted away in the crowd – taking Josie with him.

Nice one, Jonathan, I thought. I sipped my glass of wine and looked around at the group. The Sancerre was good, just right for the summer sun. But then Jonathan was in the business of getting things right. Today, I was too. I worked my way through to Belinda, who looked stunning in a primrose coloured outfit.

'In search of someone, Jack?' she cooed.

'Pity the guests don't have name badges,' I rejoined merrily. 'Why are there so many people here, Belinda?'

'All of them remember Neil. Schoolmates, college friends, work experience friends . . .'

'And his family too? His father, for instance?'

'I wouldn't recognize him even if he was,' she countered offhandedly.

'He's central to two murders, Belinda. Three if you count 1978. Do try to keep an eye open for him.'

'You're still on the wrong side of the road, Jack,' she warned me. 'You'll meet an awful lot of traffic coming right at you if you keep going. Get back on course.'

'Very cryptic. Thanks, but I'll choose my own route.'

'Take care you don't miss the countryside around you. Gorgeous here, isn't it? Have you seen the monastery ruins?' Belinda slithered smoothly out of the danger zone. 'They're over there, disguising themselves as rockeries.'

'Not yet. I thought I should talk to *everyone* here.'

I did my best. By the time we were summoned to lunch half an hour later I had worked my way round half the guests at least. My small talk had been the smallest possible in the circumstances and it had got me nowhere. Several men fitted the criteria for Frank, but the fuzzy photograph I had copied from the police files proved useless, and unless they were lying as to their connections with Neil and their current

employment and status, Frank Watson was not amongst them.
How could I know for sure though? Any one of them could
have been him. For a few minutes I felt lost as to what to do
next – but that, I realized, was exactly what Jonathan wanted.

And that meant Frank *must* be present.

I still had the other half of the guests to work my way
through, and as the party began to move indoors, I reasoned
I might stand a better chance here. The stars were with me.
It was a seated lunch, with a place arranged for each guest.
Unfortunately, unless Jonathan had a sense of humour, I
guessed I would not be placed next to Frank Watson.

I wasn't, nor was his name on the table plan. On my right
was Neil's Aunt Lizzie and on my left Betty Wilson. Why?
I wondered. So that she could report my doings to Tony and
Vic or because she was a safe bet not to know what Jonathan's
plans were as regards Watson? I chatted amiably to Betty
about how good Josie looked and to Aunt Lizzie about her
memories of Neil. I did venture a question about Neil's father,
but it turned out that Aunt Lizzie was actually his landlady
when he first came to university in Kent and *all* the students
called her Auntie Lizzie. No, she had never met Neil's father.
I sensed Betty listening with interest but she must have been
as disappointed as I was because she began to talk avidly to
her other neighbour.

Looking around the table, I picked out five more contenders
who might be worth investigating, and I decided I would give
them a polite grilling before the party broke up. I would also
talk to *everyone* here, male or female. After all, Joannie herself
might be here, although Betty would hardly pass that news
on to Tony.

The lunch was so good that I almost – but not quite – forgot
my mission. At its conclusion, I expected Jonathan would
make some kind of a memorial speech about Neil, but he
didn't – or at least only a very short one to announce that as
everyone was here because of Neil, the company should move
into the garden for the best memorial of all to him. The Charros
would play.

And play they did. I was impressed, particularly by Josie.
That shimmering silk dress, the hair and the songs had me

captivated. They were performing on a platform erected in the gardens, with the audience gathered around, and even the staff came out to listen to 'The Bamba', 'Beloved Mexico' and 'You Belong to my Heart'. Was Josie thinking of Neil or Carlos, I wondered. She certainly put her heart and soul into song, and if, as she had claimed, she had lost her voice over the years, it had miraculously been restored with only the odd glitch. It was, as Jonathan had said, indeed the best way of remembering Neil.

'How are you faring, Jack?' Belinda unexpectedly materialized at my side as I applauded.

'On the trail,' I said lightly. In fact I had by now no great hopes of the afternoon achieving anything, even from those last five prospects on my list. One of them was Neil's uncle, a benevolent sixty-year-old plus who regarded me with mild curiosity, as did his companion, surely his wife – they had the same benign smiles as I introduced myself as a friend of Jonathan's.

'You're Frank Watson's brother?' I asked with interest.

'Brother-in-law Mike,' he told me. 'This is my wife, Neil's Aunt Lizzie.'

'I've already met one Aunt Lizzie.'

'Right.' A merry laugh. 'Neil's landlady. He used to joke about it.'

'His father isn't here, is he?' I asked carelessly, as a friend of Jonathan's might do.

'Frank? Crossed out of the family Bible years ago,' Lizzie informed me cheerfully.

'Sorry to hear that.'

'We're not.' She giggled nervously. 'Blot on the family escutcheon. That's what he was.'

'Jonathan told me he was a clergyman in Dorset now.'

'That's right. Or was. Clergyman, anyway,' Mike said defensively. 'Don't know where or even if he's still in the land of the living.'

The answer had come back quickly – too quickly? – and somewhat threw me. Had I made a mistake over this clergyman business or was this whole gathering in on some kind of conspiracy to hide the existence of Frank Watson? 'Are there more siblings, or are you the only one, Lizzie?'

'Just me and Frank,' she replied. 'His getting mixed up with that hijacking at the May Tree was the last straw. Then he vanished, and good riddance.'

'You'd have thought he would have come on a day such as this though, especially as he was a clergyman.'

'Expect he would have if he was alive,' Mike said firmly.

'You really don't know?'

'No,' they both told me in unison.

They were both watching me very carefully, I thought, but perhaps that was my imagination. 'I'd assumed your brother was still living in South America with Joannie Wilson until Jonathan told me otherwise.'

Mike looked uncomfortable. 'Well, he's not.'

There was an air of finality in this that suggested I could now get lost. I did just as poorly with the other four candidates, with the result that as the afternoon ended I found myself caught up in a mass of people heading for the car park and kicking myself for having failed. Frank himself was not here, and no one was going to give me any clues on his whereabouts. I had duly paid my respects to Jonathan and resigned myself to joining the traffic jam.

Unexpectedly, the jam cleared, both the one in the car park and the fuzziness in my mind. At last! I reminded myself that *I was a car detective.* To be certain that Frank Watson was not here, I had only to hang around, take some photos, see which of my candidates took off in which car, note the number plates – then get the details of the owners from the Swansea licensing agency.

It's always interesting to see who owns which car, and in this car park it was more than interesting. It was essential. Lizzie and Mike climbed into a Renault Megane hardtop; another candidate, who told me he was Frank's brother (interesting, since his sister didn't seem to know she had another brother), climbed into a BMW M3; one who said he had been Neil's college tutor roared off in a Porsche Boxster, and another candidate in a Vauxhall Astra. One by one they all left, but despite the assurance of their car registrations being in my possession I remained a worried man. Why? Because Belinda, Betty, Jonathan, Clive, Matt and Josie all seemed remarkably *un*worried by my presence. Clive even gave me a friendly hello.

Jonathan must have been watching my every move because as I waited – I thought unobtrusively – until most cars had gone, he came over to me. 'I used to collect train numbers as a kid,' he remarked, looking pointedly at my iPhone and notebook.

I put them away, with a bland: 'Car numbers aren't nearly so much fun.'

'So what do you hope to discover?'

'Frank Watson,' I told him.

He merely grinned and strolled off back towards the hotel. I watched him go. I was dispirited to say the least, since I had no great hopes of the Swansea venture turning up trumps. There was something about the cocky way he was walking away that riled me. I was missing something, and I was damn well going to find it.

In desperation, I walked over to have a look at the smaller car park marked, Staff Only, behind the main parking area, since as well as the staff cars I could also see Belinda's Thunderbird and Jonathan's Bristol. Just for luck, I took some photos of them too. At least they were great cars, even if I now had to admit I wasn't going to find that missing X factor. Not today, anyway.

I set the Swansea plan in motion as soon as I reached Frogs Hill. I didn't get any results for twenty-four hours, and unsurprisingly none of them made Frank Wilson a possible candidate for ownership. Even gloomier now this avenue was closed, and frustrated that nothing seemed to be happening about pinning down this mysterious boat one way or another, I roped Cara in for a recce of Allington Lock. The fact that the boat (if it existed) had gone by the time Brandon's men tackled the question was not proof there had *not* been one. Anyway, the trip was something to do, and perhaps the fresh air might even clear my addled brain. It would also provide an opportunity to be with Cara. I had seen little of her, despite the fact that she was living in the farmhouse. On the rare occasions she was at home in the evenings she seemed to be perpetually on the phone. To Harry, I presumed. I didn't dare ask.

Cara wasn't convinced the mission was worthwhile, but I could see she shared my feeling that doing something was better than doing nothing, with Eva's plight so much on our minds. Cara said she would come along as a 'sounding board'. I could bounce my ideas off her, and she could tell me when I was going off the rails. This appeared an excellent plan. The only flaw in it was that I had run out of ideas to bounce. In vain did she and I march up and down the towpath, gazing at endless boats that told us nothing except that some of them were permanently moored, some temporarily and some passing through. Cara had no other ideas either. What she did have was determination, so we duly inspected all the many boats and talked to the many owners. To no avail. Even Cara was forced to abandon this quest in favour of lunch at the Malta Inn.

'Where now?' she asked, that enjoyable respite over.

'I'll leave you here for five minutes while I take a walk.'

She fixed me with a glare. 'Along the towpath? Are you trying to spare my feelings?'

'He was your stepfather.'

'Which is why I'm coming.'

There was no answer to that, so we set off, with the noise of the weir deafening us as we passed the bridge. What on earth had brought Carlos along here in the semi-dark? Cara didn't flinch when we reached the point where his body had been found. 'Here?' she asked, when I stopped. And when I nodded, she said in bewilderment, 'But there's nothing here.'

'That's the reason.' I explained the theory that his murderer could have been looking across the river to point out the boat to him, and she was dubious, as I feared.

'Carlos wasn't stupid. He was pretty careful over his own skin. He wouldn't walk along here without good reason. He wouldn't know where he was going, for a start, even if he was with this so-called business colleague Frank – or a floozie, of course. All he'd see was a lot of boats over the far side of the river and expect to go over there. Though there are quite a few moored this side too,' Cara added. 'And Carlos would have expected to be walking in the Maidstone direction.'

'But in front of us—' I broke off and gazed in amazement at this prodigy I had sired. 'Daughter mine, that is *it*. Carlos wouldn't know that his chum's boat *didn't exist* and that it wasn't *ahead* of them round the bend in the river and moored to the towpath.'

Cara laughed, as delighted as I was. 'Easy when you think of it. What else can you solve, Dad?'

'Where else to look for Frank Watson.'

'A very elusive man,' she commented. 'A Scarlet Pimpernel of sorts. Anything remarkable about him?'

'Tried that one. I was told that the only remarkable thing about Frank Watson was that he is or was unremarkable.'

'In what way?'

'Not noticeable, I suppose, just an accepted part of the landscape, like Chesterton's postman.'

'Did you notice any postmen at Conygarthe Manor?' she asked.

'Very funny. No—' I did a double take. '*Again.* Cara, you are brilliant. You are the most remarkable daughter I ever had. Forget Harry. Join my team.'

'Cars aren't my thing. What have I solved now, Dad?'

'Postmen, Cara. Postmen.'

'Explain.'

'The staff,' I told her. 'I saw them, but I never looked *at* them.' They had been there in their penguin suits, listening to what was going on. 'And, jubilation, one of them must have been Frank Watson. He was there all the time, and the numbers at the lunch had been swelled to make him even less conspicuous.'

Jonathan's cockiness as the last car left the main car park had been for that reason. That it was all over. He had seen me put my iPhone away and known I had swallowed the bait. Frank had been one of the staff – most probably a waiter, so that he could mingle. He was either a permanent employee or a casual through an agency, in which case he could have covered his tracks and would be untraceable. What Jonathan did not know, however, was that I had looked

at the cars in the staff car park, even if I had not written
down the registration numbers.

My photographic memory for number plates can't cope
with a large number of them at one time, but there hadn't
been many cars there apart from the two I already knew. I
had, I remembered with relief, taken the photos of the Bristol
and the Thunderbird, and in them the other cars appeared in
the background. They would be too distant to read the plates,
but it would help me to remember them, so with good fortune
and a fair wind behind me I could bring the numbers to the
forefront of my mind.

When we reached Frogs Hill, Cara went off for a walk to
the village and I repaired to the Glory Boot to look at the
photos and *concentrate*. There had been five staff cars left,
none of them straight off the production line. They were a
VW Golf, a Honda Jazz, a Toyota Yaris, a Ford Ka and an
elderly Audi A3. Which one would Frank Watson choose?

I came down to the Golf or the Audi. So I concentrated on
those, willing the numbers to return. Maybe Dad saw me and
took pity, maybe it was my lucky day, but one at least returned
in full instantly. The other was only missing one letter.
Eventually, it came to me and in two days' time I had my
answer. The Golf was registered to a Mrs Barbara Heywood,
and the Audi to a Mr Stephen Frank, who lived in Folkestone.
No contest as to which I would be following up.

By rights I should have alerted Brandon, but pig-headed as
I can be on occasion, I decided to have a scouting expedition
to see if I could catch a glimpse of this Mr Frank. I didn't
want to be fretting, wondering what was happening if I had
reported it right away. Stupid? Perhaps, but I'd had enough of
false avenues. As I prepared to set off for Folkestone on
Saturday I was once more full of hope that I was on my way
with this case. Frank Watson, wanted for theft and involvement
in murder, living on the profits of the theft and being black-
mailed by Carlos for a second time. Now murderer of Carlos
and Ambrose, for reasons yet to be determined but which
should not be hard to discover.

It being a weekend, I might spot Stephen Frank in his
garden. Even if he was employed full time at the manor, he

had to have some days off, and Joannie might be around. On balance I thought that he was probably employed there, rather than a casual, as that would explain why the lunch had been held there. It had been for his benefit.

Once more my plans were stymied, however. There, once again sitting on my wall, was Daisy. Guilt returned in full force.

'Off to find Melody, Jack?' she called.

'Another case, I'm afraid.'

'I'll come with you.'

I was about to say no, but changed my mind. 'Why not?' I replied. On a scouting trip it might help to have a female companion. I would look more innocently 'normal'. Moreover, having a Daisy on any trip isn't exactly a penance, although I didn't want to listen to too much talk about Melody while I needed to think about Stephen Frank.

'Lagonda?' she asked hopefully, jumping off the wall.

'Not today. My aim is to escape notice.'

The Alfa it was, despite her disappointment. Both my beloved Gordon-Keeble and the Lagonda would be far too conspicuous for my purpose. Luckily, Daisy was happy enough. 'Where are we going?' she asked.

'Folkestone area.'

'Oh good, I like the seaside.'

'So do I, but this trip is inland.'

Folkestone is a large sprawling town and spreads quite a way back from the sea, so I humoured Daisy by taking the Hythe coastal road to approach Folkestone in order that she had her taste of the sea. Then I branched off into the town's back streets to find Elmore Close where Mr Stephen Frank lived blissfully unaware that Nemesis was about to descend on him. As we turned into the close and I was busy looking for number eight, there was a shriek from Daisy.

'*Melody*!'

Fortunately, I had been driving slowly, but even so shock made me slam on the brakes. When I'd recovered my breath from the jerk I enquired: 'What, may I ask, was that all about?'

She was already jumping out of the car, even though we were still in the middle of the road. 'Whoopee! *Melody*. It really is her.' She was shouting this back even as she raced back to the car.

I turned round to have a look. The car was indeed pinky-grey, and indeed it was a Morris Minor 1000. I parked as speedily as I could and ran to join her. It was only as I reached her and the car that I realized that we were more or less outside number eight. I was dizzy with shock. What kind of conjuring trick was this? Stephen Frank's home, Frank Watson – and Melody?

Daisy was by now shrieking and dancing with joy. 'It's Melody, Melody . . .' she cried, attracting curious looks from the one or two people who passed us. 'Look, Jack, it *is* her. Look at the number plate.'

I did, and she was right. It *was* Melody.

Daisy busily examined the car from top to bottom, end to end. 'She's only got a scratch on it, and look, that's where Justie tied the number plate on again. I can drive her home,' she crowed.

'No way, Daisy,' I yelped, wondering what had happened to my planned unobtrusive visit to spy out the land. 'There are procedures to follow.' I felt as ancient as Methuselah delivering this line, but it had to be said. There were indeed procedures and, more importantly, this car could still be part of a murder case and would need checking over yet again.

'What *procedures*?' Her face darkened.

'I have to call the Car Crime Unit. I'll ring now, plus,' I added, 'she could still be involved in something more serious.'

Daisy was furious, even when I pointed out that there was no key in the ignition, so that unless she had brought the spare set with her Melody would be going nowhere without a low loader.

She ignored that fact. 'Are you telling me I won't be able to have her even *after* the police have been here?'

'They'll probably take her with them.'

Disbelief all over her face. 'You're joking.'

'Afraid not. I wish I were. I'll ring now while you guard the car.'

'You bet I will.' Gone were the sunny smiles. I got the message. If I'd had a commission from her I was sacked.

At that moment, however, I had more on my mind than Melody. Mr Frank. I rang Dave, whose remit covered all Kent – which might apply to Brandon too. I didn't care. If I rang Brandon to announce that I thought I had found Watson, the complications would be endless. He'd want to know a lot more before he'd act.

Should I hold my horses until Dave arrived? No way. I just could not resist temptation. Watson would vanish as soon as he saw anything resembling a police car.

So what did I do? I took a deep breath, walked up the drive of number eight and rang the doorbell.

FOURTEEN

'Stephen Frank' did not blink an eyelid when I told him who I was and why I was here – now that *was* remarkable.

'They said you were good,' he remarked.

'You're not so bad yourself. I imagine you've been living here quite some time.' I saw what Tony had meant by his being unremarkable though. Stephen Frank must be about seventy, thinning nondescript brown hair, middle build, middle height, and a 'middling face'. Not too lined, not too alert, not too dull, regular features and a look halfway between content and resignation.

'Twenty years or so. I take it the Old Bill's on its way?' He grinned when I nodded. 'They don't waste time. It was thirty years ago. Why don't they spend their time cleaning up today's crimes?'

'This one *is* today's crime. Car theft,' I told him blandly.

'Eh?' His face registered complete astonishment.

'One Morris Minor.' I turned round to point it out.

'That old heap? What makes you think I nicked it?' He was still doing a good job of looking amazed rather than defensive.

'Because it's here.'

'So what? I don't own the road, so why pick on me?'

He was defensive now, perhaps realizing he'd gone too far in his over hasty acceptance of my appearance on his doorstep. All to the good. Except that I was none too sure where to go from here. There was no sign yet – naturally enough – of Dave's team, let alone any sign that he'd been in touch with the local police or Brandon.

Should I go or stay? Go! 'Look after Melody for half an hour or so, Daisy,' I called out to her. I turned back to Frank Watson (as I thought of him). 'Here or inside?' I enquired.

He said nothing, but ushered me inside to his living room, which helpfully overlooked the street. 'You can keep an eye out for the rozzers from here.' Deadpan. No glimmer of a grin now. 'It's only about this car,' he continued. 'Don't know nothing about the other stuff, so you can forget it.'

'Difficult.'

'They'll never prove it now. You know that. Wanted for questioning, that's all it will be.'

'So why bother to change your name?'

'New life, Mr Colby. That's why. When Neil died, I didn't fancy South America no more. I'm a Man of Kent, through and through. I married again, and stayed here. You'd be surprised how easy it is to disappear.'

Not for this guy, I thought. He was a chameleon. How far should I go in pushing him? If I went much further, tempting though it was, Brandon would have me on toast for breakfast. And yet the question of Joannie Wilson hovered so temptingly. Was she the bride that matched the 'married again' and was Number Two the current wife? Or was the current wife Number Three? I resisted asking him – as I did its companion questions, such as: 'What about the money?'; 'You do know your old mates are eager to know what happened to it?'; 'How does a rose taupe Morris Minor fit in?'; and 'Do you attend all the anniversary parties?'

The words trembled on my lips, but they stayed there, which was probably just as well. Instead I asked him to talk about Neil, interrupted by his wife, who popped her head round the door to ask if I wanted coffee, which I politely declined with thanks. Not Joannie Wilson, I thought. She looked a pleasant woman of about the same age as her husband, but this lady could never have been the firecracker that Joannie apparently was. I wondered what she knew about Frank's previous history.

After Frank had chatted about Neil and his university course to the point where I was silently screaming in frustration, I was at last able to steer the conversation to the Charros. I thought he would baulk at the subject, but after a moment's hesitation, he said, 'My boy's death was down to that louse Carlos Mendez. Neil gave up a real good chance of getting somewhere with a biology degree, but he'd always wanted to make music number one, so he threw the course up. Daft, I told him, but he wouldn't have it. So when Carlos walked out on them he reckoned he was finished.'

'He seems to have had a good relationship with Jonathan,' I ventured.

'He did. That was half the trouble. Jonathan had great plans for himself – but Neil wouldn't fit into that arty crafty stuff. That made him feel worse, a complete washout.'

'Did Jonathan feel guilty because his own plans couldn't include Neil?'

'Maybe.' His tone said subject closed. Perhaps he had seen what I had – a police car drawing up outside. 'That car – you're not serious about it, are you? It's been parked there for days.'

'It's a special car.'

'But . . .' Frank put two and two together and made an uncomfortable four, and his eyes bulged, as they say. 'You mean they'll nab me on *car theft*? Typical!'

We went to the door together as two young PCs, directed by Daisy, marched up the path. Frank turned to me as he opened the door. 'You want my advice, Colby?' He didn't stop for an answer. 'Don't open up no boxes until you're bloody sure what's inside.'

And then the PCs' inquisition began: 'Is that car yours, sir?'

'No. Come in.' Then an aside to me: 'Not you, Mr Colby.'

I wasn't surprised. He wasn't going to risk my input in case the name Frank Watson came up.

Daisy was hopping up and down in frustration when I joined her. 'What's going on, Jack? Just like you said, I can't take Melody home. Can't you tell them all this evidence and stuff is bunk? She's already been done and dusted.'

'No.' I tried to explain. 'This is officially a new crime.'

Daisy fixed me with a beady eye. 'So then they'll bring her back and she'll be nicked again.'

I skirted round this. 'Is there any damage this time?'

'No, and she's *mine*. Look at that lump of mud in the back seat! That man in there who pinched her is a vandal. I'm having that mud out for a start.'

Before I could stop her, she'd wrenched the passenger door open, knelt on the seat and made a dive at the rear seat, seizing the largest lump – not that it was very large.

I grabbed it from her. 'It's not just mud, it's chalky,' I told her. 'It could be important.'

That made Daisy shake with laughter. 'You mean it's a *clue*?' she asked in sepulchral tones. 'You're having me on.'

I probably was, but the unexpected thought occurred to me that it might indeed be a *clue*. It wasn't a large lump, just a clod of earth that might have fallen off something such as stone or garden produce or boots.

One of the constables emerged from the house, no doubt to see what was going on with Melody. Not entirely to my surprise he told me that their briefing from Dave was to stick to the car and nothing else until further orders. Frank was unlikely to do another runner now – especially as Melody had been found. What plans had he had that involved her? I wondered. Had he stolen her or had a third party done so at his request? And why? That little question asked it all.

'This might be relevant, when Dave gets here,' I told the PC, handing him the mud lump. 'It was on the rear seat.' He looked at it (and then at me) in bewilderment. 'Only a lump of mud,' he said, carefully replacing it inside the car.

Daisy let out a peal of laughter. 'No crown jewels stuck in the middle?' she mocked. 'Officer, you disappoint me.'

He went red, poor chap, and muttered something I couldn't catch to her.

'Daisy,' I said threateningly.

'Sorry.' She grinned. 'When do I get my car back *this* time, please, officer?'

The constable knew where he was now. 'We'll be in touch,' he said grandly, and noted Daisy's details yet again.

It took time for her to recover her spirits on the way home. 'Kids' stuff,' she remarked to me finally.

'What is?'

'This police work. Examining lumps of mud. Why don't they just arrest that guy? Then I can have Melody back.'

As we turned into Frogs Hill Lane, my initial jubilation over finding Frank Watson subsided rapidly. The case would be in Brandon's hands now. Fortunately, Daisy was so set on regaining Melody that she hadn't asked me a single question about the 'guy' who'd pinched it. If he had, of course. Innocent until proved guilty. But there was not a thing I could do to further the case now – and that was a position I did not like.

Cara came out to meet me, and shock was written all over her face as she saw Daisy. The Volvo was still in the forecourt, of course, but now Cara had seen its driver a whole different complexion was apparently put on the situation. For me to be with Daisy on a Saturday afternoon, seemingly enjoying a carefree trip out, implied that this golden girl was more than the client I'd assured Cara she was.

With great delight, Daisy greeted her as an old friend. 'Hi, Cara.'

Cara was clearly not delighted, something that Daisy cottoned on to right away and decided to play up. 'We had a great time, didn't we, Jackie boy?' she continued. 'Won't forget our clubbing last night. Good thing we got out before the cops arrived. Hear about that, did you? Hi Zoe, hi Len.' Daisy waved at the Pits where Len and Zoe were still slaving away on Frazer-Nash. Daisy, was bent on mischief however.

'Nice place Jack's got here, hasn't he, Cara? Len and Zoe think the world of him. Seen his Lagonda, have you? Jackie boy and I have had some great times in it.' She then proceeded to rush over to hug and kiss Len and Zoe. Zoe objected strongly, Len looked rather pleased.

'Cara,' I squeaked, in the hope of putting matters right.

'Don't bother, Dad,' Cara said stiffly. 'I quite understand I'll be in the way. I can find somewhere else to stay while *I'm* looking after Eva.'

Daisy had started back to us by then and was all innocence. 'Hey, I'm not chucking you out, am I? Jackie wouldn't like that at all.' She fluttered her eyelashes at me so provocatively that I thought even Cara wouldn't be taken in. I opened my mouth to demolish Daisy but once again I was too late.

'I'll leave, Jack. I don't like playing gooseberry,' Cara informed me in clipped tones.

'Enough,' I barked. 'Cara, you're not an unwanted third. Daisy, it's time to quit. *Go.*'

'Oh, Jackie.' The corners of her mouth turned down so charmingly I could almost believe she was serious.

'*Go.*'

I took her over to the old crock with a firm hand clamped on her arm. 'Just what do you think you're playing at, Daisy?'

'You deserved it,' she said mutinously, 'for letting them take Melody away again.'

I sighed. 'She'll be back. She's not been nabbed by a bunch of gangsters, she's with the police.'

'And what if one of them pinches her? It's been known.'

'Daisy, just *go.*'

'So much,' Cara said as Daisy did indeed drive off, 'for the Jack who was so heartbroken over Louise.'

I groaned. 'Do I *look* like a middle-aged git to you?'

'Yes.'

'Do you *really* think I'd fall for a twenty year old?'

'Seems you have.'

'She was stringing you along and getting back at me. She's a client and far from amused at the way I'm handling her case.'

'You seem to me to be handling it all too well.'

I looked at my daughter, appalled. For an awful second, I thought Eva was back with me again, storming through my life with her green jealous eyes.

Luckily, she wasn't. Cara crumpled and burst into tears. 'I'm sorry,' she wept. 'I thought I'd lost my dad again.'

I felt choked. I tried to speak and failed. Tried again. Finally, I managed something inadequate. 'Never that, Cara. *Never.*'

That would have to do, and she must have understood because she pulled herself together. 'It's all this stuff over Eva. It goes on and on.'

'There's cautious good news. My lead might be working out.'

'Really? Is there evidence backing this lead?'

'Too soon to say. I don't know what the forensic position is, only that motive sticks out like a mile and the even better news is that the whole story is beginning to dovetail.'

'Then why didn't you look full of the joys of spring when you returned – just like your little Daisy?'

'Because—' I stopped.

'Don't tell me. It's because you don't like the ending.' While I considered this, she added, 'That's the only thing I remember from the time before Eva took me away.'

'You were only three.'

'That's why I don't remember more. But this part I do. The nursery rhyme. Humpty Dumpty who fell off a wall. It frightened me, and you said you didn't like the ending either.'

'All the King's horses and all the king's men,' I began.

'Couldn't put Humpty together again,' she finished for me.

I gave some thought to this. 'Cara, you're a clever lady. I've been trying to put Humpty together again, and today I thought I had all the pieces to nail Carlos's death down, but I haven't.'

'What's missing?'

'That's the trouble. I don't know.'

'Probably,' Cara said brightly, 'Humpty's like a *boiled* egg. You have to smash a bit off the top before you can get to the goodies inside.'

'I'll consider that solution,' I told her gravely. 'Meanwhile, you're a smashing daughter.'

'So now be a smashing dad and make us a cup of tea.'

I mused about Humpty-Dumpty for a while as Cara went off to the supermarket. Smash the top off – but of what? The case against Frank Watson or the Carlos case, plus Ambrose? The first would be all too easy. Frank hated Carlos for taking Neil away from him, but how did Ambrose, and, worse, Melody, fit in? Did Ambrose know Frank had killed Carlos? No, that didn't fit the egg. Ambrose had been in no state to bear witness against Frank or anybody. Frank, just like Tony Wilson and Vic Trent, seemed to have a modest lifestyle, which didn't suggest that any of them were living off the fat of the land. But then Frank or either of the other two, I reasoned, could have squandered the takings of that robbery in the meantime. Or perhaps Joannie had run off with the lot. None of the gold had shown up on the market, but that might simply be because the valuable objects had been smelted down if they were gold or sold direct to unknown buyers. And of course there were the Charros to consider. Carlos unexpectedly returned to their midst and old scores, including Frank Watson's, could have been resurrected. OK, Humpty – but where did Ambrose fit in?

To my horror I could see Len and Zoe still in the Pits, although it was nearly seven o'clock, so I went over to urge them to return to their homes for what remained of the weekend. I knew this well-intentioned errand was doomed, however, when I saw them both still poring over the Frazer-Nash. Whatever the problem was there, I was sure that Len would be on to it much quicker than I could sort out a solution to my conundrum.

Maybe I should take my cue from them, I thought, watching them at work on the ignition system. The engine was the focal point. So what, I wondered, was the central point of the case I was trying to solve, assuming that Carlos, Ambrose and Frank Watson were all involved. It had to be the shoot-out in 1978. No doubt about that. They had all vanished by the time the police arrived, although granted many others had too.

The next seemingly unassailable fact was that the Crowshaw Collection was in Joannie's car and she had scooted off with the lot. The presumption was that she'd scooted with Frank, and so could I really be sure that the present Mrs Frank was not Joannie? Personalities can change with age. I kicked myself for not paying closer attention to her. Frank had seemed eager to give me the impression that his second marriage had been after Neil's death in the early nineties – and so he would if in fact that bride had been Joannie. After all, what else could have happened to her? She went off alone? Possible, but she would be stuck with a lot of very valuable objects for disposal. There were flaws in this thesis though. Betty Wilson might conceivably not recognize Frank at those parties, but she would certainly not overlook Joannie. Easy enough for her to stay at home, of course, but even so I felt this piece of Humpty was not fitting easily.

So, consider Carlos, I thought. He had disappeared from the May Tree by the time the police reached it – but he was only twenty or so, rather young to take on a lady like Joannie, even if she had been flirting with him. Ambrose had been chatting her up at the bar, and both he and Carlos could have arranged to meet Joannie after she had left with the Crowshaw Collection – or at least *thought* they were going to meet her, according to plan. Joannie might have had different ideas.

Nevertheless, I toyed with the idea that it was not Frank but Ambrose whom Carlos had expected to meet at Allington Lock. Would that work? I had been told that he had rung *Josie*, but suppose he had in fact rung Wychwood to speak to Ambrose – not knowing that he was in the state he was or that Josie was in residence? Could Ambrose have been the person from whom Carlos was hopeful of getting money, regardless of the fact that Ambrose hardly looked flush with it – certainly not enough to keep Carlos in the style to which he thought he should be accustomed? Take it a step further: why should he have expected Ambrose to help him unless he had something to hide? I was back to blackmail. But who was Carlos blackmailing or had done so in the past – Frank or Ambrose?

I tried not to go too quickly so that I could take it step by step but it was hard not to rev up with such a straight road ahead: could Carlos have seen or discovered that it was Ambrose not Frank who had taken the Crowshaw Collection and run off with Joannie?

That balloon burst. All very neat but the engine didn't start. Why on earth would Ambrose steal the collection – or Joannie? He had a good reputation and he was an archaeologist given to digging hoards out of the ground not helping himself to the spoils of a robbery. And as for Joannie – Ambrose had adored his wife, and Joannie sounded an unlikely replacement for Muriel.

Moreover, Joannie had clearly not settled down with Ambrose. He had continued living at Wychwood and patronizing the May Tree. It was theoretically possible he had helped Joannie dispose of the gold in consideration for cash, but that just did not tie in with his reputation as an archaeologist.

Back to the problem's engine again. Why wouldn't it fire? Should I look again at Carlos himself? Was he capable of running off with Joannie *and* pinching the loot? Yes, yes, yes. Capable at any rate, I still wasn't so sure about his being Joannie's chosen soulmate number two though. Ambrose or Frank were much better candidates for that. Should I run this by Betty Wilson again?

It was then I realized what was worrying me. I'd been staring at the engine too long and failed to see the missing nut.

Correction: I *had* seen it but not this angle. Back to the anniversary lunches and Betty Wilson. Betty had been seen with Frank Watson during the 1978 shoot-out. Both she and Belinda had denied meeting him during the Charros era, but suppose one or both had lied? If Frank Watson had been present at all those lunches as Neil's father, something would have clicked. Someone – which in effect meant everyone – would have known exactly who Stephen Frank was.

So why had no one denounced him? There was the Crowshaw Collection to think of. Not *everyone* would have overlooked that element for the sake of Neil's memory. *Did* Frank take the collection along with Joannie or had he been the convenient fall-guy? Again, it didn't fit. Either Frank had left Joannie with or without the money raised from the collection, or Ambrose must have done so – and Carlos discovered that. Then I began to despair. Ambrose was in no position to tackle Carlos at the lock, so once again I was back to Frank Watson.

I clutched my head, haunted by an image of Eva still in gaol. What could I do now? If Watson was guilty of killing him I'd get no further and it would be over to Brandon. He was no doubt working on it, but what could I do? Answer: pursue the Ambrose front.

Josie was still living at Wychwood, and I arranged to visit her after the weekend. She had sounded so welcoming that I guessed the loneliness was getting to her, grateful though she was for the job and the roof over her head. The house seemed more like a tomb than ever and as I arrived I wondered who would buy such a place. Without Ambrose, Josie seemed lost and the house larger than ever. She took me through to the living room, and I could see through the windows that the grass was neatly cut and the flower beds immaculate, so it seemed that Matt Wright was a frequent visitor. I offered to make some coffee for us both, and Josie was pathetically grateful for this small gesture.

'That Thursday, the first time I came to Wychwood,' I began, 'Ambrose said he had been to Eastry recently.'

'He was always saying that. Meant nothing. How could he have got there?'

'You didn't take him?'

She stared at me as though I were mad. 'No way. It was his imagination. It was my day off, anyway. He only told me about it later when I mentioned my next day off – it was his way of getting at me when I went out on my own.'

'He wasn't expecting any visitors?'

She shook her head.

'Was there anything odd about that day? Anything at all?' I asked her.

'Nothing. He'd spent the day in the garden – I suppose that was unusual.'

'How do you know he did? Because he told you?'

'His shoes were muddy.'

A hopeful sign. 'Suppose he actually had been to Eastry? There would be mud on his shoes then.'

She sighed. 'He wouldn't know how to drive that Renault even if he'd remembered it was in the garage.'

'Could someone have taken him there in his or her own car? His son perhaps.'

'I suppose. No one came though, and if it was Dr Fairbourne he'd have warned me or left me a note.'

'Someone else could have come with that Morris Minor and taken him.'

'The one in the barn? Could have, I suppose.'

'Did you check the barn when you got back?'

'No. I never go there. Why should I?'

Why indeed. Josie, I had to remind myself, was in the best position of all to take Ambrose anywhere or to influence him. Strangling an old man as weak as he was would not be beyond her strength. So far as I could gather through Dave, there had been no prints or DNA that the lab could identify on Ambrose's body. Josie could also have lured Carlos to the towpath. But with what motive? Revenge was the answer to that. But how about evidence? I asked myself. None – to my relief. I'd come to like her, so I hoped that theory remained just that.

'One last thing.' I could see that Josie was already anxious to get rid of me. 'When did Ambrose's Alzheimer's begin?'

She thought about this for a moment. 'I came in 2004 and

he'd been losing it for a little while before that. He had a housekeeper before me, but she didn't live in.'

'And did he always talk about Eastry right from the beginning?'

'Far as I can remember, yes.'

The beginnings of an idea were springing up, so I rang Keith Fairbourne when I'd left Wychwood and arranged to meet him at a pub the next day, Tuesday.

We settled on one at Chartham Hatch, which was handy for the Canterbury Road and therefore suited both of us as a halfway point. At the top of the Downs, it had such wonderful views that we chatted for some time before I had to get down to brass tacks.

'Would it be true to say that your father still associated Morris Minors with Eastry?' I asked him.

He grinned. 'I see you're still mulling over that car in the barn. Yes, the answer is quite probably. As I told you, he shared the Morris Minor mania with my mother – first the one they owned together and then the later model until he switched.'

'You told me that was in the late seventies. Which year? Can you remember?'

'You're a tough questioner. We're going back a while. 'Seventy-eight or 'seventy-nine, I think. I know I pestered him to give me the Moggy, but I was still a couple of years off seventeen then, so he refused.'

If he was right, then Ambrose probably had a Morris Minor at the time of the shoot-out and there was a chance it was involved in the disappearance of the Crowshaw Collection. If someone other than Josie had taken him to Eastry to revive old memories, what would those memories have been? His theories about King Egbert, perhaps, and where the king's grave and grave goods might be, but they were nothing to do with Carlos and the shoot-out. Ambrose would hardly have taken the collection to Eastry unless he was bonkers at the time. Which he wasn't. He would have returned it to the Martinford family.

'Do you see any possible connection between the hunt for King Egbert's grave and your father's death?' I asked Keith.

'I don't see how. He was deeply involved in the earlier digs, but, as I told you, in 2006 when *Time Team* arrived in Eastry he was too far gone even to take it in. He did get very excited over watching it on TV, presumably because he was thinking of his own failed dig.'

'Can you tell me anything more about that?'

'As much as I can, but I wasn't closely involved. At the time of his first dig on Woodlea Hill I was only four or five years old. I do have vague memories of sitting in the sun and my mother allowing me to dig a trowelful of earth out, but nothing more. If they'd expected to dig up the golden statue of Woden, then no such luck. Dad told me later they'd had great hopes of it and there could have been a burial there, but there had been nothing to indicate it was a king's grave. So he and my mother went home to lick their wounds and eventually came up with another possible site on the hillside. This one really convinced them, but then my mother died.'

'But he didn't give up the hunt, did he?'

'Far from it. For my mother's sake, Dad saw it as his mission to see the quest through. Like the previous site, this new one was on the hillside but a little distance from where he calculated the track used to run. This time Dad laid on a proper dig. All the drums and whistles. This was going to beat the Suffolk hoard, he hoped, but again it produced nothing. I was about ten by then, so I went along on one of the three days' digging. Once again a lot of hopes raised, but nothing firm found, even though Dad was sure he'd nailed it this time. Dad never talked about Eastry after that, not until his mind began to go. He concentrated on other sites, both in Suffolk and Kent, and by the time the nineties arrived he had money worries so he turned to writing and TV work and left Eastry behind him.'

'Did he ever write about Eastry?' I wondered what had made Egbert's grave prey on his subconscious mind to such an extent that his illness brought it to life so many years later.

'Never. Odd, really, because he wrote about every other site, but not that one. I think he couldn't bear to think he might have failed my mother. Sorry, Jack, but I think this Eastry line is a storm in a teacup.'

I clung to the last vestiges of hope that it might lead somewhere, though for the life of me I couldn't see how. 'Even so, could you take me to the place where he believed the grave was?'

No hesitation from Keith. 'Sure, if you think it's worth it. Can't guarantee any results though. Want to go now? There's a footpath nearby, so we don't need permission to look at it – not unless you want to take a trowel in the hope of finding Woden's statue.'

He was a man after my own heart. I did want to go now. If this was another false avenue I wanted to know sooner rather than later, even if it meant all I could do would be stare at the ground that was so important to Ambrose Fairbourne – once upon a time.

The fates were with us. Even the sun emerged to wish us well. We had made a brief stop for Keith to show me Highborough Hill where *Time Team* had dug in 2006 and then parked in the centre of Eastry village itself. The village lay slumbering peacefully, and it seemed almost sacrilege to park so casually on ground underneath which could be Anglo-Saxon, even Roman, burial grounds, royal palaces, and homesteads. Keith took me on a brief tour to show me the sites of some of the other digs – the one in the grounds of Eastry House, and the others off the main street in a secluded corner where the church and Eastry Court lay. A cat ambled up towards us took one look and passed on; a villager or two looked at us curiously and did the same.

The pub was still open when we rejoined the main street, so we went in for a quick drink while we studied the map. Our route lay further along the street we were on, which was the old Roman road to Dover. We would be walking south along it out towards the original boundary of the village. Woodlea Hill, our destination, would be on our left before we reached it. The hill was part of Woodlea Farm, the owner of which, we were told, was Ken Parker, who lived at Northbourne, a mile or two away. However, our informant told us helpfully that 'old Silas', Ken's father and the former owner, was sitting 'right there' at the bar.

Silas, once fortified with another beer, and having summed us up, told us all in one breath that he'd no objection to our going for a walk over his son's land and what's more he'd come with us, and if there were any caches of gold coins they were his, not Ken's, and all dropped by chance so no need of this treasure trove rubbish.

'Agreed,' Keith told him cordially.

A footpath led from the road up to the high ridge along which Ambrose's track line ran. It took us across gently rising fields, and on a day such as this it was easy to think that the Iron Age wasn't that long ago, and that the Anglo-Saxon era was yesterday. I didn't expect to see golden cups lined up to greet us when we reached the higher ground, but the reality was certainly starkly different. Grass, trees and fields with scant signs of habitation made my quest look doomed from the start, even if I'd been sure exactly what it was! Keith must have understood, because he advised, 'Look down, Jack, not out at the big wide world.' Maybe he thought that was my problem – don't keep trying for an overall answer; study the case detail by detail – and perhaps he was right.

When we were close to the highest point, though not quite at it, Keith stopped to look around, then branched off to the right, with Silas and myself in his wake. We were in rough meadowland with trees and bushes close by. Keith stopped again to study the map. Silas, however, was more interested in studying the ground.

'Someone's been digging round here,' he said severely.

'My father,' Keith explained. 'Years ago, in the seventies.'

Silas chuckled 'That chap? I remembers him. Thought he'd go off his rocker when he found nothing. This is recent digging though.'

I joined them, but could see nothing strange. Keith could though. 'This is near enough the spot, Jack, so far as I can work out. And Silas is right. The turf's loosened.'

'Sheep?' I said, but this earned the scorn it deserved. The experts were both working their way with their hands round the clumps of grass.

'About four or five feet by three,' Keith said eventually.

'No one asked me or Ken,' Silas grunted. 'They've blooming

well dug and filled it in again. Metal detectors, most like. Come here, and dig away for England. Think they own the place, some of them.'

'Not all,' Keith said mildly.

Now was not the time to mention the metal detector I'd glimpsed in his car boot when he extracted his walking shoes. 'Any hope of our digging here – with your permission, of course, Silas?' I asked hopefully. Hopeful of what, I wasn't sure.

'Not today,' Keith said firmly. 'Forgot to bring my bucket and spade. How would you feel about it, Silas? I'll bribe a few of my students and we could do the thing by the book, if you and your son have no objection.'

'What you aiming to find?' Silas asked cautiously. 'One of them gold cups, like Ringlemere?'

'Can't say,' Keith told him. 'That's the fun of being an archaeologist.'

'The fun of being a farmer is you get to clear up afterwards,' he grunted.

'No mess, we're fully house-trained,' Keith told him cheerfully. 'And if it's gold we dig up, your son gets rich very quickly.'

'What do I get out of it?' Silas asked practically.

'Fame and a day out. You can play with my metal detector.'

Silas shot a look at him. 'Suits me. I'll talk to Ken. He likes these newfangled things.'

It suited me too, only not from the fame angle. 'It's good of you to set all this up,' I told Keith on the way back to the car park. 'I don't know what I'm after though, so is there anything in it for you? If that's the site where your father dug, then you already know he didn't find anything in it.'

Keith considered this. 'Call it bloody-mindedness. Dad had a mission to see this Egbert's grave quest through to the end because he owed it to my mother; I feel the same about owing it to him now that there seems to be a question mark over it.'

I was silent. There was indeed a question mark. Did I go fully into what it consisted of? Keith must suspect from our previous conversations that it might concern his father's involvement in something murky.

He picked up my reaction immediately. 'Look,' he added,

'you think Dad was mixed up with the Crowshaw Collection robbery, don't you?'

'I don't *know* – that's the problem. And even if he was, why would it be connected with King Egbert?'

'Let's find out, Jack,' Keith told me. 'I'm willing – because I know that my father was a responsible archaeologist and a highly moral man. The honesty of his academic mind wouldn't let him run off with something like the Crowshaw gold unless he was going to return it to its original owners which—'

He broke off as the same thought must have struck us both, and we stood in Eastry High Street staring at each other.

I spoke first. 'But who are the original owners? The Martinfords at the manor?'

'Or King Egbert of Eastry.'

'His grave goods. You said –' my words were tumbling out now, although I hoped not so incoherently as my thoughts – 'your father believed that grave goods belonged in the ground, not in museums.'

I could see Keith gulp. 'Dad took them back to Egbert's grave? Is it possible?'

'You tell me,' I said. 'How and when did the Martinfords get the Crowshaw Collection in the first place?'

Keith was very pale. 'I don't know. Not even the British Museum knows much about it, except that the manor has owned it for hundreds of years.'

'How many hundreds? Wasn't there –' I scrabbled in my mind for the results of the reading I'd done about Eastry – 'a collector who lived here, in Brook Street, who discovered one of the graveyards to great acclaim in the late eighteenth century?'

Keith gazed at me, and I saw him swallow, his academic training clearly fighting archaeological excitement. 'That was the fashion then. Everyone who had time and money started digging into the past, physically and mentally, and whether in Italy or here. Sir John Martinford – I think that was the manor's owner then – could well have come here and paid the farmer a pittance to let him dig, or not even bothered. Just dug.'

'And Ambrose realized what had happened.'

'I'll do some research.' Keith paused. 'But who's been digging recently, Jack?'

I parted from Keith on a high, convinced that we now had the missing link: Morris Minors, Eastry – and the Crowshaw Collection. Keith would set up the dig within days, and somehow, soon, surely Eva would be freed of all charges. Then I could relax just a little.

All seemed set fair when Keith rang me to say his father had been called in to give an expert opinion on the manor collection before it was sold. And then Dave rang me and the barometer sank rapidly. I was back in the real world.

'Thought you should know,' Dave said blithely, 'that Brandon is dropping the Frank Watson line. We can't pin the Morris Minor theft on him, and Brandon won't move on the Carlos front. Alibi like a brick wall without any loose mortar. The most Brandon can do is refer Watson as a 1978 cold case. Meanwhile, he's a free agent.'

'Oh great.'

'There's no evidence against him at all. Yet,' Dave added encouragingly.

FIFTEEN

Woodlea Hill seemed an entirely different place than the site I had visited with Keith eight days earlier. This time I was an outsider and I walked along that footpath and up the hillside alone. Keith and his 'gang' were already gathered there, judging by the cars parked by the roadside, and as I looked up to the crest of the hill I could see their outlined figures moving along like a shot from a John Ford film.

'Glad we chose a Wednesday,' was Keith's welcoming remark as he came to meet me. 'It's Wodensday, the Vikings' divine boss.'

'Found his golden statue yet?'

'Only an ancient beer can so far.' He paused. 'I take it we're looking for buried treasure of a more substantial nature?'

'Egbert's grave, and whatever your father or his companion was looking for recently when that ground was disturbed.' What if there were nothing though? That was highly possible, as it had been recently dug. I fought back panic and doubt. I had to go on.

'I've marked out a grid with stints covering a wider area than the one we looked at the other day,' Keith told me. 'It's good practice for measuring resistivity.'

Keith's contribution to the day consisted of about a dozen young students, plus Silas and someone who was probably his son Ken, an army of tools that would make an iron-age worker jump for joy, some businesslike machines and a dump of flasks and picnic stuff to keep the troupers going.

'That's Kelly.' Keith pointed out a blonde girl about Daisy's age who looked too slight to hold a trowel let alone the unwieldy machine she was moving around with the help of a young toughie exerting himself by holding the cable. 'She's in charge of the machine that checks the resistance in the ground, such as walls or other blockages, or indicates the contrary in the form of ditches and cavities.'

'That sounds good for a burial mound search.'

'Not if the land's been ploughed or dug a lot over the years. Can't always tell. Silas says that, apart from the bit we first looked at, it's hardly been disturbed in his time, though, because the ground's too sloped, too uneven and too near what was probably always woodland.'

I could see another two of his party going round with metal detectors, with Silas enthusiastically in charge of a third. All reservations as to their use had clearly been forgotten. 'Any luck with them?' I asked Keith.

'Not much so far, only one soft buzz. No gold brooches, no coins, no Ringlemere cups yet. But don't despair. There can always be reasons why things don't register.' He glanced at me. 'Come and have a look at the rez machine.'

I duly peered over Kelly's shoulder as she reached the area we'd first looked at, on which I was still pinning my hopes despite someone having been there before us. I admitted there didn't seem much logic to that because anything of value would undoubtedly have been removed, and if there hadn't been anything in it, it wasn't worth the effort of re-digging. Nevertheless, Keith was still adamant that this was the spot his father had picked on, and the fact that it had been disturbed reinforced that conviction. That was why he wanted to check it again. Why did I? Call it sheer obstinacy.

Keith peered at the rez machine over Kelly's other shoulder. 'These aren't too good on metal, but it likes this patch at least. Good reading for cavities. That could be the result of the loosened soil, of course. Let's have another go with the metal detector.'

He picked up his own detector as I watched, hardly daring to hope. That was wise because even I could tell that the one faint buzz it emitted was hardly likely to indicate that the Crowshaw Collection was beneath our feet. Nevertheless, Keith didn't seem perturbed and continued to supervise the rez readings round the rest of the area marked out by the stints. It was a painfully slow operation, one of which I felt Len would have approved, but eventually the digging itself began.

Keith had extended the original area to cut an oblong trench of about ten feet by four. I didn't query why; he knew what he was doing and wouldn't want an impatient amateur breathing down his neck. Even so when the chalky topsoil was eventually out and they were down to a depth of two feet, the digging was clearly getting harder, and I found it difficult not to keep peering down in the hope of spotting the odd buckle or golden cup. There's a child inside all of us, and mine was wreaking havoc with my patience. Every so often something would be extracted from the shovelfuls and then trowelfuls of earth, examined and put on one side. I hadn't a clue what for, but none of the finds looked like the Crowshaw Collection.

Keith worked on keeping the trench level throughout and they were down to about three feet when he yelled an urgent: '*Stop*,' and climbed out of the trench together with the helpers.

'Found something?' I croaked. A cliché, I know, but we all speak in clichés when we're too choked with emotions to sort out something better.

'This is as far as the initial area was dug, and the detector's still giving that gentle buzz at one spot. We'll go easy now.'

The words Crowshaw and King Egbert were on the tip of my tongue but I held them back. Hope sprang inside me, though, like the firing of an engine on the fifth crank. Keith's call had brought all the students gathering round. Up here the birds were chirping and the whole world seemed to be still and waiting. With our little army of students I could almost imagine that any moment Saxon or Viking hordes might come storming up to take the ridge. What was I hoping for? I couldn't even focus on that. King Egbert's grave? His grave goods?

'Here's what I found,' Keith told me, showing me what was in his hand.

It was only a piece of heavy cloth, but Keith was not happy about it. Then, only then, did he get back into the trench, where he set to work with his trowel while the rest of us watched. I could hear my heart beating as I watched him reveal more pieces of cloth. Could this be a blanket put by Ambrose round the Crowshaw Collection to protect it? No, the metal detector would surely have picked up such a hoard. I was sick with tension as my imagination ran riot.

And then imagination stopped. It wasn't needed now. Something was poking through the cloth. A bone.

'A sheep, Chris?' one of the students asked uncertainly in the dead silence as Keith worked further, gradually pulling the pieces of cloth away.

'It could be a sheep,' he agreed.

I knew he thought it wasn't. Not with that cloth around it. Cloth that could not have dated back to the seventh century and King Egbert's death. I wasn't going to let him bear this alone, so against orders I climbed down to the far end of the area some three or four feet away from him and, on my knees, reached out to pull away a few pieces of the cloth myself. He didn't object, until suddenly he shouted: '*Out!*'

I obeyed instantly and grabbed his hand to pull him out after me. The rest of the cloth had come away in one piece and now we saw what it had covered.

It was a skeleton, more or less intact, and it was human.

My turn to take control, though I'd never felt less like doing so. 'I'll ring the police,' I said. My mouth was very dry. The skeleton could well be within the seventy-years limit when the coroner has to be called in. No prehistoric burial this, given the circumstances.

Keith did not comment as I did so, but we must both have been thinking the same thing – Ambrose's question: 'Are you going to take me to Eastry?'

We all had to wait now. I wondered what the metal detector had picked up and peered in, trying not to think of that skeleton as a human being. I didn't have far to look. There was a wedding ring still hanging from that skeletal finger. Silas had noticed that the site had been disturbed not long ago, but no way could these sad remains be as recently interred as that.

At last Keith began to speak. 'This may not have anything to do with my father.'

'No,' I said.

'But you think it has?' he said furiously. 'Is that why you started this charade?'

'I had no idea that this would be the result.' So much for buried treasure. So much for the Crowshaw Collection.

'It's not my mother,' Keith said aggressively. 'She died in hospital.'

'I hadn't thought it was.'

'Who then?'

I had to force myself to put it into words. 'I think it could be the late Mrs Joan Wilson.' Poor Joannie. Where was her flirting, her love of life now?

Ambrose. Everything centred on him. Right from the beginning when Carlos had made that first call and spoken to Josie, not Ambrose as he had intended. Whatever answers were to be found started with him. The rest of that long day at Eastry was a nightmare, with neither Keith nor I able to talk freely: Keith because of his undoubted realization that his father must have been involved; I because of unjustified (I hoped) guilt that the dig had turned out so disastrously. We had parted silently, both perhaps wanting to talk but unable to find common ground.

Only Brandon's brief words to me had helped: 'Thanks, Jack. This might lead somewhere.'

A step forward in our relationship, I felt. Only two things seemed certain to me: Ambrose's involvement, and that there had been a third party present at that recent dig. In the world I chiefly move in, cars, all the pieces fit. I only wished this case was the same. Here I was the assembly line, and the engine had been Ambrose. And still there were missing pieces.

It took two weeks to identify the skeleton as Joannie's, even though Tony had identified the wedding ring. All I had to do was to juggle the missing Crowshaw Collection with three murders. Eva was still in prison, and the weeks were marching on towards autumn and the fifteenth of January.

'What's niggling you?' Cara asked, no doubt tired of my gloomy face as she was just off to drive back to the farm. 'Still the case?'

'Ambrose Fairbourne.'

'You should go after that son of his,' she declared in dictatorial mood. 'Something odd there.'

'Keith would hardly dig up a site in order to reveal his father's involvement with a murder.'

'Why not, if he wanted you to find it?'

I glared at her, and she hastily added, 'This Josie then. Carlos spoke to *her* on the phone, and she spread the word to the Charros.'

'Who spread it to Frank Watson,' I finished crossly. 'Been there, done that . . .'

'I'm trying to *help*,' she shouted at me. 'Start again.'

'With Frank Watson?' I yelled back.

'No. Go to Wychwood.' And she marched out.

Wychwood House seemed to be contemplating me with its evil eye as I drove up. I'd taken the Gordon-Keeble for luck, as I was beginning seriously to hate this place. Even in the sun it looked eerie and on a day such as this, which was definitely not sunny, it looked downright sinister. By referring to Wychwood, Cara had perhaps been thinking still of Ambrose, but seeing it before me I realized it had a wider scope. Could it be housing the Crowshaw Collection somewhere, whatever Keith claimed? I faced the fact that he could have been lying when he said he'd searched. I couldn't take that theory seriously though. Had it been hidden by Ambrose so carefully that Keith had missed it? No again. Whether this was in the house or at Eastry, had he confided the hiding place to somebody else, such as Keith or Josie or—

Matt Wright?

The Charro whose life had been ruined by Carlos, the man in the background who did odd jobs in Wychwood House itself as well as the garden. The man whom no one noticed very much – Chesterton's postman again. The man who was interested in Ambrose's archaeological collections.

My assembly line did a ninety degree turn so quickly I felt almost physically sick – and even sicker as the Gordon-Keeble purred gently to a halt outside Wychwood House. I parked it right next to Matt Wright's van, and there was no sign of Josie's Polo.

The murders were linked, and Matt was the murderer. It was glaringly obvious now that Frank Watson was out of the picture. Matt had good reason to kill Carlos when he heard he was back. He would know when Josie's day off was and, having concocted a plan to steal a Morris Minor to take Ambrose to Eastry, he had dug at the place to which Ambrose took him, King Egbert's grave. But when he found no golden goblets, no ornate belt-mounts, no golden buckles or state helmets, what then? Or *had* he found them?

The evil eye of Wychwood seemed almost to wink at me. Its message seemed to me: what now, Jack?

I had three options: find Matt Wright, possibly hunting in the house for the collection, having got Josie out of the way; call Brandon; go home. Option three was out, and so was option two. Brandon wouldn't believe me, so I had to be on surer ground. Which left option one.

I was only armed with an iPhone, so all I had was bravado with which to burst cheerily in upon a double murderer. Easy – in theory, at least. I pressed the bell and heard it ring in the dark corridors of Wychwood House. I rang again when no one answered, and again no one came. The house had that empty look about it. Next, the garden. Matt might be looking for Ambrose's hoard there, buried in the earth or under a shed. I walked round the side of the house and saw windows open but no sign of movement inside the house. Nor in the garden either. The flowers waved merrily at me in the breeze, but no human being stirred.

The garage? I thought. Or, better still, that old barn. If Matt Wright had used it for Melody, perhaps he had for the Crowshaw Collection too. If he returned with it from his expedition in Melody with Ambrose, he might have buried it there. I walked up the track, thinking of my last trip along it, and the memory was not pleasant.

The barn door was not padlocked, and I opened the door half fearing what I might find. There was nothing here, however. No dead body, no Matt, no trunk marked 'King Egbert's Property', no sign of where anything could conceivably be hidden. Relieved, I walked into the barn to double-check.

And then I turned and saw the gun in Tony Wilson's hand.

'You would come, wouldn't you?' he said as I stared at it in disbelief. 'You should have left well alone, Jack. I'm too old to go back inside now. They've taken DNA from Joannie's family. No use my saying it wasn't her ring. It was. I brought this shooter to dump here, and so now I'll have to dump you with it. You're in the way. You know about Carlos and Joannie.'

'Do I? Blind panic was all I knew until I took command of myself. I had to. I would be dead otherwise. Not Matt Wright at all. Tony Wilson – with as much access to Wychwood as Matt, and he was going to kill me. At least I now knew why none of the Charros gang had betrayed Frank Watson. It hadn't been Frank whom Tony had been hunting, much as he had tried to direct us otherwise. It had been Carlos.

'You thought Carlos had run off with Joannie and the Crowshaw Collection,' I said matter-of-factly.

'Yeah, but he told me down at the lock I was wrong about the stuff. Said Ambrose had taken it. He saw him taking it out of Joannie's car and loading it into his bloody little Morris Minor. I believed him.'

'So why did you kill Carlos?' Daft as it sounded in my situation, I really wanted to know why Eva had had to go through this nightmare.

'He went off with her and wouldn't tell me where she was. Kept saying he didn't know. I loved that woman, I did. Killed him for Joannie's sake. I told him this story about a boat being moored round the bend in the river just a bit along the towpath, and I went prepared to give him the frights if he didn't come clean. He smirked all over his greasy face, telling me he'd done well out of the May Tree, what with the woman he'd run off with and screwed and then blackmailing Ambrose. Then when I found that skeleton in that hole and knew Ambrose had done it, not bloody Carlos, I went spare. The stuff wasn't in the hole, only my Joannie – so I brought him back here to at least get the gold from him. No joy there either. I came here today to turn the place over, but there's no sign of it. He got his comeuppance all right.'

I felt very cold 'That was *my* wife Carlos said he'd run off with. In 1991, not after the shoot-out.'

For a moment Tony faltered and the gun shook slightly, but

it didn't drop. 'When I saw her skeleton . . . Well, I loved her, Jack. Still do. That creep Fairbourne. It was me took him out to bloody Eastry expecting he'd at least remember where he buried the stuff. He went straight to that hole, and I dug it like crazy for him. Until I got to the skeleton and saw that ring. I choked. Knew it was Joannie's right away. So he had to go. No choice. He must have killed her right after the shoot-out. Why?'

'It was the Crowshaw Collection,' I said. 'Joannie must have argued with him, so he killed her. He thought the collection should be returned to King Egbert's grave.'

'There was no stuff there,' Tony said savagely. 'It was only Joannie's grave. But the old fool's gone now, and so's the gold. You too, Jack. You should have known Joannie, then you'd understand.'

There were tears in his eyes, but whenever I made a move his grip on the gun tightened.

'You really think killing me is the way out?'

'You know the whole story. There's no way out for any of us now, except Betty. She's a survivor. Didn't know anything about this deal. Believes any rubbish I tell her. But I'm not going back inside. Not at my age. Not without Joannie. Or you, mate.'

He raised the gun, turned it on himself and pulled the trigger.

The sound cannoned through me as though I were the victim not him. As I looked at the bloody mess on the ground, as I saw his blood spattered on my clothes, I seemed to be standing apart looking at myself, a lifeless lump of flesh. Then I felt my lips trembling and gradually my body and knew I was alive. I got my phone out and dialled 999.

I walked to the tree trunk where Josie and I had sat not so very long ago and hoped that she and Matt – if they were together – would not return until the police had arrived. The barn was once again a crime scene, and this time I was not just a witness, I was part of it. Prints, DNA, the machine would go into action and it had to be endured.

Death spreads ripples in its wake and they depart only slowly. During the next few weeks, the police unearthed sufficient forensic evidence in Tony's car (parked well out of view of the house) and home, which, coupled with the gun and my statements, gave the CPS enough to drop all charges against Eva.

There was only one downside to that. The last ripple. Eva herself.

Cara had returned to Suffolk, but now she came back to take charge of Eva when she was released – although thank heavens they weren't staying at Frogs Hill. But one benighted morning I was in the Pits as Cara's car drew up. It contained not only Cara but Eva too.

'Sorry, Jack. I had no warning,' Cara called over to me.

'Jack, thank you, my darling.' A thud as Eva hit my body with her own, arms flung round my neck so tightly that I fought for breath. She smelled of her favourite French scent – at least, it had been her favourite during our marriage. It seemed out of place in a Kentish farmyard, especially one that usually smells of petrol with that indefinable whiff in the air that announces classic cars are around. And so was Eva. I took them into the farmhouse, glad I had Cara as back-up. I took advantage of Eva's absence in the bathroom to ask Cara what her plans were.

'I'm taking a few more weeks off,' she told me. 'Harry's OK with it.'

'Why?' I asked with foreboding as Eva swept back into the room earlier than I had hoped.

'Darling, don't be too sad,' Eva said grandly. 'I came here because Cara said I should and because I love you.'

Instant panic. I gave Cara a furious glare, and she looked innocently back at me.

'I must care for you,' Eva kindly explained.

My life was in crisis. 'Darling,' I spluttered, 'you can't sacrifice yourself for me. We'll sort something out for you.' A desperate glance at Cara, but she merely looked amused.

'My dear one, I know I belong here,' Eva began.

'But it would not be possible, Eva, much as I—'

'It would, beloved, but—'

'You'd hate it in the country,' I babbled. 'You always did.'

She wasn't listening. 'Without my Carlos,' she continued, 'how can I live at all? You look after me—'

'No,' I howled, and even Eva looked surprised.

'Darling.' Her hand went to her brow. 'I know how hard this is for you. But you must be brave.'

'No,' I moaned.

'You must,' she said firmly. 'I go now with Cara.'

I heard only the magic word 'go'.

'To fetch your luggage?' I asked cautiously.

'Is in Cara's car. She drive me to Southampton and then on boat—'

'You're not staying here?' There was hope yet. Cara was looking demure.

'We go to Cartagena,' Eva explained.

'*What*?'

'Where my darling Sandro lives. He love me. He worship me. He say go live with him. Cara will take me, so, darling, I must leave you.' Another heavy thud as she hurled herself at me again. 'Try to be brave, my darling.'

'I will,' I managed to gurgle. 'I will—' A little more fervently.

'I will come to see you often, my darling.'

'It is better not.' I was getting into the swing of the drama now and could see how this might run. 'I could not bear to think of you in another's arms if you came here to visit me. It would be cruel of you. The torture.'

'Darling.' Eva looked pleased. 'Perhaps—' She cast a glance at Cara, who came to my rescue as I panicked all over again.

'No, Eva,' Cara said firmly. 'Sandro deserves your love now.'

'So he do. He do.' She beamed. 'And I shall reward him.'

'And what of you, Cara?' I asked her quietly as Eva mopped her eyes – not too hard, I noticed, in case she removed her make-up.

'A few more weeks won't hurt Harry while I do my own thing. The magazine's closing down so it's a perfect opportunity. I'll see how things stand after that. You never know, I might fall in love with a Spaniard. Not,' she added, 'anywhere near Eva and Sandro.'

To my relief, Keith had agreed we would pay a last visit to Eastry together, now it was no longer a crime scene. We climbed the hill together in companionable silence. If he still blamed me for the discovery of Joannie's remains, with its inevitable conclusion that his father had killed her, he did not say so. My view of that tragedy was that Ambrose had taken not all, but part of the collection with him when he left the May Tree – Joannie sounded too canny a lady to let him take the lot. Whether she thought they were running away together, or that he was going to help her sell the collection, or whether it was a genuine misunderstanding as to what should become of the collection, I had no way of knowing. I suspected the third, and that they had agreed to meet at Eastry, Joannie thinking they would be joining forces there for the Channel crossing. Perhaps she thought he was arranging a secure temporary hiding place for the collection, as all the ports would be too closely watched for a while. Whatever the reason, they must have quarrelled after he discovered their plans for the collection differed, and he'd killed her, whether by accident or design, and buried her. He'd have had to have driven her car to Dover, but it wouldn't have been an impossible task, if he'd driven it halfway, returned to his own on foot, then repeated the procedure for the second half of the journey. Dover was not that far away.

It was all a long time ago, and yet in some ways it seemed only yesterday, now that as much of the truth as possible was known. Or was it?

'Are you coping?' I asked Keith at last.

'Not quite. And you?'

'Much easier for me. Can we talk about it?'

'Yes, I need to.'

We walked on until we reached the new returfed site of King Egbert's grave. 'There's a problem,' I said. 'I understand why your father wanted to bring the collection back to its rightful home, as he saw it, but if he did want to rebury it here in Egbert's grave, why put Joannie's body in it too? Wouldn't that seem like defiling it?'

'Yes. And where,' Keith added drily, '*is* the collection?'

I grinned. 'Didn't like to mention that.'

He laughed, and all was well between us again. 'I'm an archaeologist, Jack. It's not a question that's escaped my mind.'

'Are you sure it's not here? Perhaps just a few yards away?'

'Ninety-nine per cent certain. This is on the ley line he worked out, and nothing comes up on the metal detectors or the rez machines or any other gadget that suggests buried metal in quantity.'

'So as your father – we're presuming – did bury Joannie here, what does that tell us? And what would he have done with the collection?'

Keith frowned. 'I know this sounds weird, considering my father was almost certainly a murderer, but he was a man of the highest principles. He wouldn't have lugged it back home – he'd have put it in Egbert's grave and nowhere else. *Here*.'

We both stared at the ground which had nothing to show now but earth, grass and the odd clump of wild flowers of mud. Here in 673 a grave had been built for a Saxon king and his grave goods interred there, whether his earthly body was laid there in its entirety or just a token part of it.

I thought back over everything Keith had told me, and then something struck me. There seemed one last chance. 'What about the earlier site he found when you were a child?' I asked him.

He looked blank at first, but then saw my point. 'He ruled that one out. He dug there with my mother, found nothing and realized they had made a mistake.'

I almost felt King Egbert was with me as I produced my nugget of gold. 'Of course he wouldn't have found anything, even if it *was* the right site.'

'Explain?' Keith looked at me as if my mind had gone AWOL. If it had, it was right back here now.

'It was the early nineteen seventies when he dug there. The hoard was still at Crowshaw Manor, where it had lived ever since the grave goods were dug up by Sir John Martinford and carted back home.'

A short astounded silence, and then Keith let out a delighted whoop and punched the air. 'It's *there*, Jack. That's what he said to me. Not "it's there" meaning a general it's somewhere around. But, "It's *there*!" I can still remember his saying it. He meant he was still convinced the grave was there. He found this other site hoping he was wrong, but it wasn't the right one, and when he realized that the Crowshaw Collection must have been Egbert's grave goods he knew he was right. After the quarrel, when he found he had a dead body on his hands, he wouldn't have left her remains in the *real* site, so he opened up this one. Then he buried the grave goods in the original site.'

'And where,' I asked Keith quietly, 'was that?'

He stared at me aghast. 'I don't know,' he wailed. 'I was only six years old.'

I had a horrible feeling I could see where this was going. 'Did your father deliberately lead Tony Wilson to the wrong site?'

'No,' he said sadly, 'he must just have forgotten where the original site was.'

There was nothing to be done. The Crowshaw Collection was somewhere unknown with King Egbert. As for Keith and myself, we downed several glasses in Eastry's Five Bells pub and swore to remain chums for life.

Which left Daisy, Justin, Belinda and Melody. After the dust had settled, I invited them all (including Melody) to the May Tree Inn, which seemed a good fit. There were loose ends to consider. Melody looked wonderfully curvy as we waited for Belinda, who roared up in her wonderful Thunderbird. I took the Lagonda, to be equally sporty, and the three cars sat side by side by the green, where we could admire them as we lunched at one of the tables in front of the pub.

'What are your plans now, Daisy?' I asked.

'I've given in my notice,' she told me proudly. 'It's too dangerous working at the bakery.'

'Afraid of being hit by a flying loaf?'

A scathing look. 'Too dangerous for Melody. I don't want her disappearing again, eh, Justie?'

He blushed. 'It wasn't my fault.'

'It was,' I pointed out. 'You decided to pinch her in the first place. How did Tony Wilson find her?'

'Tony must have spotted her in the pub car park,' Belinda replied. 'He took her to jog Ambrose's memory, but it didn't work, so then he left her in that barn.'

I knew how it went from there. 'Then I came along so it

was time to lose her again, in case he'd left any fingerprints on her. He left her at Wormslea, because he didn't want to keep incriminating evidence around; he knew it was Daisy's car, but he didn't know where she lived. My guess is that he decided to pinch her again after Ambrose's death in the hope of pointing the finger of suspicion even more at Frank Watson. He even planted a lump of chalky mud in the car before dumping it outside Frank's home. He'd already convinced Vic that Frank took the collection with him, and thought it would be a payback for Frank's getting away scot free all that time.'

'If he does,' Belinda commented.

'Not much evidence left against him now.'

Belinda looked puzzled. 'But Tony thought that Carlos had run off with Joannie and the collection.'

'He wouldn't tell Vic that if he wanted to keep the lot, would he?' Justin said brightly.

'Hey, Justie,' Daisy said admiringly, 'that's really cool. Fancy joining me for a trip in Melody?'

'When? Now?' Justin looked nervous.

'I'm going on a long trip.'

'Where?' he asked.

'Well, how about we start off and see where Melody wants to go?'

The look of dawning joy on Justin's face was a pleasure to behold.

'Better get a passport,' Daisy added.

'Got one.'

'Then let's go.'

'Now?' he asked again.

'Now, baby. We'll stop by home if you like and pick up a few things.'

Belinda and I watched with amusement. 'Better get Len to tune Melody up first,' I advised Daisy.

'Oh.' Her face fell.

'Do it, Daisy. Melody needs it,' Justin said firmly. 'Then we'll go. Tomorrow, maybe.'

She gave a beatific smile. 'All right, Justie. If you say so. I'll take her down now. OK by you, Jack?'

'OK by me.' I was going to say 'tell Len I sent you' but

there was no point. He would do more for Daisy than me. He might even do it speedily.

The wink Daisy gave me as she obediently followed Justin was not altogether indicative of an entirely peaceful future, however.

With Melody's welfare settled, I had Gran Fever all to myself.

'And now, Belinda, we come to you,' I said.

'I rather thought we would.'

'Who starts?'

'I will. I did tell Josie that Melody was lost, so Tony might have kept his eyes open for her.'

'And you began this whole farrago about Melody in the first place, didn't you?'

She actually blushed. 'I like Justin,' she said defensively. 'He's right for Daisy but they'd never have got together if I hadn't given things a push. So I might just have suggested he do something to show how bright he really is.'

'Such as pretending to steal Melody. Very bright.'

'I didn't know it was going to end up in a crime scene! And I'd no idea Tony Wilson was looking out for a car like that. Betty had nothing to do with all this terrible business. She's taken it very hard. Josie told me she'd taken that call from Carlos and that he'd wanted to speak to Ambrose. I did wonder what was going on, but I knew Ambrose couldn't have killed Carlos and certainly *Josie* couldn't have done so. She told her mother as well as the Charros about the call quite innocently, and Betty must have passed it on. Tony Wilson was a self-contained bastard. Maybe that's what a fifteen-year-stretch does to you, or maybe he was like that all along. I reckon he rang Carlos, realizing that he was after Ambrose for cash but not knowing why. Betty didn't know. She's truly an innocent. She couldn't believe her luck when her ex-boss came out of prison and married her, even though she knew she was wife number two and that Joannie still came first.'

'Will she pull through?'

'We'll all help.'

'We?'

'The Charros, Jack. I'm sorry I had to keep mum about

Frank Watson. I knew he hadn't taken the collection – we none of us thought he had, even Betty, so we all kept quiet. She didn't dare tell Tony he was still around because he kept his beliefs about Carlos to himself and nothing she could say would convince him that Frank didn't have the collection or Joannie.'

'So who did she think did take it?'

'Joannie,' Belinda said simply. 'Betty thought she was a first-class bitch and had fooled everyone and gone off alone with the spoils. But Frank is a good man, Jack. He was divorced at the time of the raid and devoted to Neil.'

At last. 'And how do you know that, Belinda?'

She could have wriggled out of it, but she didn't. She looked me squarely in the face. 'You win, Jack. Frank was my first husband. Neil was my son.'

I purred through the lanes in the Lagonda, relieved that the case was over. Eva was free, I had a wonderful daughter, and friends for life in Daisy, Keith – and, I hoped, Belinda. I had Len and Zoe and the Pits. This month I even had just enough money to pay the mortgage. And I had the Lagonda and the Gordon-Keeble. Who could ask for anything more? Except Louise, of course. I put her gently aside as I shifted to first gear and turned into Frogs Hill Lane.

ACKNOWLEDGEMENTS

The Jack Colby series was the result of a conversation during a long car journey with my car buff husband Jim, and his input then and in all Jack Colby's cases since that time has been indispensable. For *Classic Mistake*, I also want to acknowledge the help of Dr Michael Snarey and his wife Zsuzsanna, who when Jim and I walked as complete strangers into St Mary's Church in Eastry not only immediately welcomed us and answered questions, but gave me invaluable information on the village both then and subsequently. The fictional spin on its Anglo-Saxon history that I have built around this, including Egbert's grave and the ley line, is my own, however. I have also to thank Lesley Feakes of the Lenham Archaeological Society, and Derek Palmer at TNL Engineering at Elstow, Bedford, who explained the intricacies of the Jowett Jupiter. I'm immensely grateful to all the above, and any mistakes would most certainly be down to me, not to the expert help I was given.

Among the written sources I have consulted are Martin Wainwright's delightful *Morris Minor*, *William Thorne's Chronicle of St Augustine's Abbey Canterbury*, *Anglo Saxon Studies in Archaeology and History, 1979*, and the *Archaeology of Kent to AD800*, edited by John H. Williams.

Severn House, my publishers, have as always been a pleasure to work with, and my agent Dorothy Lumley of the Dorian Literary Agency, to whom I owe so much, has once again been the rock that never fails me. Thank you both.

THE CAR'S THE STAR

James Myers

Jack Colby's daily driver: Alfa Romeo 156 Sportwagon
The 156 Sportwagon is a 'lifestyle estate', which means that
it's trendy, respectable to have on the drive, although it lacks
the interior space of a traditional load-lugger. For those who
value individuality, its subtle and pure styling gives it the edge
over rivals such as the BMW 3-Series. It gives a lot of driving
pleasure even with the smaller engines.

Jack Colby's 1965 Gordon-Keeble
One hundred of these fabulous supercars were built between
1963 and 1966 with over ninety units surviving around the
globe, mostly in the UK. Designed by John Gordon and Jim
Keeble using current racing car principles, with the bodyshell
designed by twenty-one-year-old Giorgetto Giugiaro at
Bertone, the cars were an instant success but the company
was ruined by supply-side industrial action with ultimately
only ninety-nine units completed even after the company
was relaunched in May 1965, as Keeble Cars Ltd. Final
closure came in February 1966 when the factory at Sholing
closed and Jim Keeble moved to Keewest. The hundredth
car was completed in 1971 with leftover components. The
Gordon-Keeble's emblem is a yellow and green tortoise.

Jack Colby's 1938 Lagonda V-12 Drophead
The Lagonda company won its attractive name from a creek
near the home of the American-born founder Wilbur Gunn in
Springfield, Ohio. The name given to it by the American
Indians was Ough Ohonda. The V-12 drophead was a car to
compete with the very best in the world, with a sporting

twelve-cylinder engine which would power the two 1939 Le
Mans cars. Its designer was the famous W.O. Bentley. Sadly
many fine pre-war saloons have been cut down to look like
Le Mans replicas. The V12 cars are very similar externally to
the earlier six-cylinder versions; both types were available
with open or closed bodywork in a number of different styles.
The V-12 Drophead also featured in Jack's earlier case, *Classic
in the Barn.*

Morris Minor 1000 post 1956

Like the VW Beetle was known in Mexico, the 'Minor' might
have been nicknamed the 'belly button' because for quite a
few years in Britain it seemed that 'everyone had one'. The
Minor (or 'Moggie' as it was affectionately known) was
designed by a small team led by Alex Issigonis in the late
forties. It was introduced in 1948 and soldiered on until 1971,
by which time some 1.3 million had been built. Minors were
available as two-door or four-door saloons, convertibles
(tourers), a Traveller (wood panelled estate), and panel vans
(a favourite with the GPO) as well as pick-up variants. Today,
Minors are very sought after classics and are well catered
for as to spare parts, restoration and even some specialist
garages and dealers. The Morris Minor club is thriving, see
www.mmoc.org.uk

1958 Ford Thunderbird

For the 1955 model year Ford (US) introduced a beautiful
new two-seater 'sports car' to rival its arch competitor,
Chevrolet (with its 'Corvette'). These two models were
America's answer to the British and European two-seater
roadsters which were selling well in the US in the fifties.
Ford's version was called the 'Thunderbird' and continued
in two-seater form through the 1956 and '57 model years.
Then Detroit's evolutionary tendencies to 'bigger, fatter'
struck yet again and, for 1958, the 'T-Bird' gained much
weight and girth as a four-seater (but still two-door) model.
Much as the earlier model was lamented, in fact the new

version was attractive in its own right and has continued through various incarnations to this very day – the latest model being somewhat of a throwback to the original '55–'57 two-seater models.